ALL I'M ASKING

ALSO BY J. MARIE RUNDQUIST

As Though You Were Mine

ALL I'M ASKING

J. MARIE RUNDQUIST

Book, Ink

ISBN: 978-1737928713 (eBook)

ISBN: 978-1737928706 (Paperback)

Library of Congress Control Number: 2021924419

For my mom, who always believes in me—unconditionally—and supports me in everything.

AUGUST

Sent August 19
To: Jessamine Lewis <steamyenergy@gmail.com>
From: Naomi Wellington <myownperson02@gmail.com>
Subject: How To End Summer Badly

Jessamine,

You know how when you try to get ice out of a dispenser and at first, only a couple of cubes fall into your cup, then you try again and fifty thousand crash down, and you're thinking, "I wanted more ice, but now I have way too much," and you dump some out, but they're crammed in so tightly, way too many fall out of the cup and you have too little again?

That.

Except, the ice cubes are students. Or classes. Last year I had one course, but a bazillion students and the directors said, "Yeah, but you only have one curriculum to follow, so that leaves you more time to handle more students." This year, I asked for a mix-up of things because I want to explore more of our courses to be ready for our department's new curriculum cycle. "Oh, you want a little variety? HERE'S EVERYTHING." I mean, seriously. It might be pre-created curriculum since it's online, but it's not pre-created in my BRAIN. So once again, I'm starting my school year early.

Of course, Leyanna did not appreciate this plan (as though we hadn't just spent a whole week together up north for vacation) and said her dad might as well pick her up a day early since obviously I was "done" with her already. (Almost) twelve years old is such a joy. (Total side note: I know he's your brother, and you know I love him, but I can't believe Jax just posted a Vaguebook post. "Just not sure where it's all going." What IS that? Since Leyanna's "done" with me, maybe she can go fix her dad during her week with him.)

Oh, and my mom called, and in case you weren't aware, I am selfish, unappreciative, self-absorbed, a poor role model, and greedy. To think I went almost three months forgetting about all these things about me. Some days, I almost wish she were back to petty theft and defrauding other people instead of drunk-dialing me.

Except, obviously, not really.

BTW, I know you're totally not reading fanfic anymore, but seriously, HotForCrime just posted a new story, and it is SO. GOOD. I mean, it's got Detective Rialto all up in a mafioso's business, a hot, jealous Kates, and their inevitable hook-up. What's not to love? You know you want to read it.

Cheers,

Naomi

@@@@@@@@

[5:03 Aug 19]

LEYANNA

Dad, mom's doing it again.

DAD

Doing what again?

LEYANNA

Going cuckoo overboard

DAD

Baby girl, you know I don't know what that means

LEYANNA

With work! School! With me!

DAD

Yeah, I know how she gets with work. But how's it a bad thing she's getting you all ready for school? This is a big year for you!

LEYANNNA

OMG. It's middle school not a trip to the moon. She's driving me

DAD

She's excited. Aren't you?

LEYANNA

I guess. Can I come a couple days early to stay with you and Whitney?

DAD

Nope. Spend these last days of summer with your mom before things get really busy.

LEYANNA

One day early?

DAD

How about I stop by on my way back on Saturday from a certain candy store you like with some sweets for my sugar girl? Will that help?

LEYANNA

YES PLEASE Lemon drops

LEYANNA

And pop rocks

DAD

Obviously!

LEYANNA

And those cherry jellies mom likes so much

DAD

That's my girl

@@@@@@@@@

Sent August 19
To: Naomi Wellington <myownperson02@gmail.com>
From: Jessamine Lewis <steamyenergy@gmail.com>
Subject: Re: How To End Summer Badly

N,

I already took a screenshot of Jackson's post and PM'd him with a "why are you like this?" message because ain't nobody got time for that guessing game nonsense.

Also, if you've got the malfunctioning ice machine, mine is plain empty. Classes start up again at the university and making a schedule for all these full-time students is pure hell. Plus, a bunch of them will quit on me after two weeks to say they "simply can't handle" the job AND their class load. I really need my floor manager to take her vacation earlier in the summer so I'm not stuck with this mess every year.

Chin up with Leyanna. I'm pretty sure I was "done" with my momma at the start of sixth grade, too. I thought I was grown, and she kept trying to baby me and I didn't want any of it. And you and I both know middle school is a hot mess.

I have mixed feelings about those years. On the one hand, coming out was not exactly great. OTOH, Momma was great about supporting me through everything, plus I met you. And then in eighth grade, I met the first love of my life. Thank God you and I have never shared the same taste in girls.

I guess I'm saying don't let your mom get into your head. Needing to do extra work at certain times of the year doesn't make you self-absorbed or a poor role model for Leyanna. In all of her professorial wisdom, my lovely and brainy wife assures me our work ethics are POSITIVE influences on our kiddos (praise all for that, since mine go practically a whole month without seeing me between Thanksgiving and Christmas).

Take all those ice cubes and make a smoothie, babe.

-Jess

P.S. Girl, *Prime Crime* ended, like, seven years ago. Who in the world is still writing fanfic for it?

@@@@@@@@@

Sent August 19
To: Naomi Wellington <myownperson02@gmail.com>
From: Jessamine Lewis <steamyenergy@gmail.com>
Subject: Re: How To End Summer Badly

Fine. Send me a link. You know how much I love an in-your-face-badassery Rialto. She's my kryptonite.

@@@@@@@@@

Sent August 20
TO: JESSAMINE LEWIS <STEAMYENERGY@GMAIL.COM>
FROM: NAOMI WELLINGTON <MYOWNPERSON02@GMAIL.COM>
SUBJECT: MIDDLE SCHOOL MAGIC

Jess,

Okay, yeah, my subject line is ridiculous because middle school is a lot like walking on a lawn full of tree roots, EXCEPT when you meet a friend like Jessamine Lewis, and she and her family basically save your life. Leyanna was asking about doing online school, and IDK, it seems like an "I'm too scared to try something new" kind of question, you know? And Leyanna has me instead of my mom (which is what you keep telling me, right?). And Jax instead of a dad who disappeared to God-Knows-Where. And a thousand times better support than I ever had. It'll be a good experience for her.

When in doubt, though, I look to books. We've started reading *The Best At It* by Maulik Pancholy, even though it's a little young for her reading level. It's all about exploring and finding your "thing," which is 100% middle school, isn't it? Also, bonus: gay!

BTW, did I tell you I joined a new, online book club earlier this month? Someone from the Minnesotans for Candy Comebacks FB group invited me after we rambled into a *The Count of Monte Cristo* tangent from a post about sour gummy worms (don't ask). I guess they're reading books from one of those prolific "one hundred books everyone should read" lists.

Our current read is Romeo and Juliet. I'm totally digging it more than I ever did in high school, although it's kind of scary to think these characters were barely older than Leyanna is now. What was Shakespeare thinking?

Rest you merry, dear Jessamine,

N

@@@@@@@@

ForumsForAll-ForumsForAll-ForumsForAll

Minnesotans For Comeback Candy Book Club

BOARD: ROMEO AND JULIET by William Shakespeare

▽ **TOPIC**: Discussion Question 1: What makes this work by Shakespeare so iconic? Does it still hold relevance today?

Tyrell: Can this be even counted as a book? I mean, it's a play. Isn't that different?

Grant: I found an old paperback copy in book form of this play.

Susette: We read this in high school, and it was in one of those hard-bound literature books. So, maybe not really a book if it's in one of those anthology things?

Maxine: I just downloaded an ebook of it. EBOOK. Therefore, BOOK.

Naomi: But it's not meant to be read—it's meant to be performed and watched/listened to on stage. Therefore, maybe not a book? (By the way, YAY! Thank you for inviting me to this little book club! Who knew my sugar addiction would also lead me to finally having people to talk books with again? I have MISSED this in my life!)

Chester: What about audiobooks? Or movies made from books? Does that mean those are no longer books, either? (Also, thanks for inviting me, too. Downing Pop Rocks while reading is like popcorn and movies. A perfect pairing.)

Lisa: Seriously? Look, I'm halfway through the thing already, so I don't care if you think it's a book or not. Just answer the fucking question.

Naomi: Cheers, Lisa. If we're looking at "relevance" today, I think we're sort of discussing one angle of the question, but we'll jump in again with more thoughts when we've caught up to you. *Tosses back half a "can" of Soda Can Fizzy Candy*

Tyrell: Soda Can Fizzy Candy is nature's energy drink.

Naomi: "Nature's?" No. But also, YES.

Lisa: btw, you guys are getting "book" mixed up with "novel." This is not a novel, it's a play, and it's all bound together in a book, and if you want to get technical, then Maxine's copy of the play is a file.

Chester: So, you DO care about whether or not it's a book.

Lisa: No.

Maxine: Maybe we could discuss the book itself. I mean the play.

Susette: We could start by answering the actual question.

Lisa: That's all I'm asking.

@@@@@@@@@

Sent August 24
To: Jessamine Lewis <steamyenergy@gmail.com>
From: Naomi Wellington <myownperson02@gmail.com>
Subject: Lovely, Lucky Lists

Jess,

Today was all about lists. Clothes shopping list for Leyanna. School supply shopping for Leyanna and me—I love getting new notebooks and pens and miss getting all the other fun stuff for when I was in the physical classroom instead of the online one. The über-long online class set-up list for me.

On the way back from school supply shopping, Leyanna asked me if I'd ever thought of homeschooling with her. I said, sure, for a little while after her asthma started up I did because she caught every virus in existence and spent more time at home sick and with her nebulizer, but Jackson and I had agreed it was better to roll with it instead of making it The Only Thing about her. We didn't want to impose restrictions or make her feel like she was fragile.

"But you guys never asked me if I would have been okay with it," she said.

"What would you have told us if we did?" Kinda obvious at this point in the conversation her answer.

"I would have liked it."

"Why?"

"Probably easier for everyone."

Ha! It's like she thinks the lessons and practice would have magically appeared and "POOF," no complaints, ever, about doing it all!

"Easier doesn't necessarily mean better, though," I told her. "Besides, it probably would have been kind of hard to do that with you *and* teach full time with my online job."

What an understatement. Do you remember our conversations a couple of years ago? The academy was just starting up. And while exciting to be a part of something from the ground up, it was a ton of work. Worth it, but I wouldn't have had the energy to give Leyanna's education justice.

Then she brought up again wanting to try out online learning.

Why?

"Easier," she said.

Ugh. No, not easier. I reminded her how much she liked classes like orchestra, art, and consumer science. Those classes weren't all possible online. She proceeded to argue how I could drive her to school every day for those classes—and then pick her up again, obvs—and whoa, no way. It sure felt like a lot of "privilege" for her plan to "try out" online learning. I reminded her how my students weren't "trying it out." It was the only option in some cases and in others, truly the best method because things weren't working for them in the traditional environment.

And then I reminded myself it was the fear talking. Since she mentioned a couple of her classmates deciding to go to the arts programs on the other side of the city, I figured this was part of her thing, too. Being someone who does something "different." I couldn't really fault her for that.

I asked if she wished she were going to the arts school instead. She loves her cello and drawing.

"No, that's not the point."

"What is the point, then?"

"I told you. Easier."

And there we were, back where we started.

Did you and Faith ever talk about homeschooling Olivia? She loved kindergarten and sounds super excited to start a "number" year. Would she feel the same way for her first day of school—at home? Sometimes I think how homeschooling could have been a fun choice, but as a public school teacher, I'm naturally pro-public schools, too.

I've promised Leyanna a box braid weave before school starts, and like magic, she forgot all about online learning!

Do you think you could help a girl out and pick an ultra-cool outfit from your store and give me some sort of friends and family discount? xoxoxo

-N

@@@@@@@@

Sent August 30
To: Jessamine Lewis <steamyenergy@gmail.com>
From: Naomi Wellington <myownperson02@gmail.com>
Subject: Cheers

Have you ever watched that show? I think it still airs on some cable station late at night or something. All I remember about it is everyone calling out some guy's name when he'd walk in the bar. "SAM!" they'd all say. This is how I felt walking into my coffee shop this morning. (You know the one: The Polar Cafe, opened last year, located around the corner from my house, which is the most awesome, better than any chain, and especially better than its northern climate counterpart.) Well, I guess it was only Sayeed who called out my name, and yet, it was perfect. Tracy tossed a pack of Now and Later candy on the counter, so it was kind of like she yelled out my name, too.

(Also why The Polar Cafe is awesome—where else am I going to find Now and Later candy?)

I hadn't been going there as often over the summer since my schedule was a little more wonky with Leyanna home and me trying to teach some whirlwind summer school sessions. I'm starting up my new routine this week since I still have a bazillion hours to put into prepping for all my new courses.

I tried to encourage Leyanna to use this week to practice getting up earlier. She's with Jackson this week, though, and I know he's your brother, but he was all "Nah, Nay" to me (ugh) and said why punish her during the last week of summer? He's not wrong (except for "Nah, Nay"ing me, *obviously*).

And without Leyanna around, I'm in heaven with my daily Breve, and I'm super-caffeinated right now and ready to crank out these class set-ups (with way too many added requirements this year, but whatev. Did I tell you, yet, I've had caffeine and sugar?).

:D

-N

@@@@@@@@@

Sent August 30
TO: NAOMI WELLINGTON <MYOWNPERSON02@GMAIL.COM>
FROM: JESSAMINE LEWIS <STEAMYENERGY@GMAIL.COM>
SUBJECT: RE: CHEERS

Mimi,

First of all, *Sam* isn't the one who everyone calls by name when he walks in the bar; it's NORM. Sam's the dumb jock, and look, let's not ever talk about this again how I know this better than you do, got it?

Second, not gonna lie. I kinda smile every time I imagine Jax calling out, "Nah, Nay" to you. It's a little too funny to see you irritated because then you mix up all your words and girl, the face you make? The best. Almost as entertaining as the fit you put on when he then says "Watch me" and puts on those nae nae moves. I honest to God don't understand how things between you two work. I mean, you were together to make that beautiful girl of yours, but never actually *together*. I'd almost call it a business arrangement if y'all didn't get along so well. He and

Whitney are good together, though, and Jax is mad excited about the baby. Family looks all kinds of ways.

Thank you for the photo of Leyanna previewing the outfit I sent. One of my girls at the store is pre-med, but she's got hella skills in styling our customers. I usually make a couple of my department managers share her to put her in charge of our mannequins in both our men's and women's departments. I think she's pre-med because her parents want her to be. She's only a sophomore—maybe I can convince her to shift to fashion and design, although I should check in with Faith on if the university here supports that major.

I know you love what you do, but I also remember how you get when you have a mission. You get tunnel vision. You told me to remind you about balance. This is my reminder.

Isaac drew a picture for you while I typed this email. I'm attaching a photo of it. I think it's him hugging you? Or maybe it's a tree. Hard to say.

-Jess

Attachment <IMG_365.jpg>

@@@@@@@@

BOARD: ROMEO AND JULIET by William Shakespeare

▽ **TOPIC:** Discussion Question 2: Candy most likely to be eaten by Nurse (Juliet's attendant).

Maxine: I see her eating Chuckles jelly candies. She likes the layer of sugar, best.

Grant: And her favorite ones are the green ones. She opens all five packages she got at the market and eats all the green ones first.

Susette: Juliet is totally cool with that because you know she only eats red candies.

Tyrell: For real, tho.

Naomi: I agree with the Chuckles and any sort of gummy candy. Worms, bears, all of them.

Lisa: Chuckles and the occasional Clove Gum because she's got a little bit of a bawdy side to her.

Tyrell: yassss

Chester: Like you, Lisa?

Lisa: Fuck off, Chester

Lisa: You might not be wrong, though.

Susette: I love you, Lisa.

SEPTEMBER

Sent September 16
To: Jessamine Lewis <steamyenergy@gmail.com>
From: Naomi Wellington <myownperson02@gmail.com>
Subject: Sickity-sick-sick

Not me, Leyanna. We're not yet two weeks into the school year, and she's already sick. *Sigh*

I don't think she's all that upset about it. This transition to middle school has been a little rocky. The "making new friends" thing is not happening super fast, plus crappy adolescence. She brought up homeschooling yet *again*, even though we've had the debate for what seems like a billion times in the past month. It's only been two weeks, I told her.

"Two weeks of drudgery," she said. "We're still only doing 'this is how you turn in an assignment' stuff instead of, you know, *learning* things and actually *having* assignments to turn in."

"Routine is huge," I replied. "You'll appreciate how well your classes will go when everyone has been trained in how to do these things."

Naturally, she only rolled her eyes at me. Because, (almost) twelve.

Anyway, right now she is vegging happily in front of the TV, exploiting all Hulu has to offer. I'm kind of jealous because I already have a thousand papers to grade, a department blog post to write, two different online sessions to run, and I really would love to snuggle up with her and binge-watch *Brooklyn* 99 right along with her.

I have a love-hate relationship with September. I love how students are all like, "Oh yeah, school is a piece of cake. I totally got this," and they are active and submitting stuff and asking questions and making us all forget *why* they are doing an online alternative program. (Don't get me wrong, a bunch of students thrive in this program because traditional didn't do it for them, but bunches more will drop out before the year is out because we still can't figure out how to make it work for those kids.)

What I don't love is how it is So Much All At Once. And you know what? It's because even online we're trying to set up routine and good habits. I'm emailing and calling students non-stop, desperately hoping this will make a difference to those who might drop out. That I really *can* make it work for all of them.

Six weeks. That's how long it takes until teachers get back into the groove. Only four more to go!

Smooches to you,

-N

@@@@@@@@@

Sent September 17
TO: JESSAMINE LEWIS <STEAMYENERGY@GMAIL.COM>
FROM: NAOMI WELLINGTON <MYOWNPERSON02@GMAIL.COM>
SUBJECT: RE: 1000 HOURS OF SLEEP

Poor Livvy!

All-day school for little ones is exhausting. When Leyanna was in kindergarten, she'd conk out during the car ride home from the after-school daycare. Then, when we got home, we'd both be so snippy with each other until your mom told me to have protein snacks ready for both of us. String cheese, peanut butter and celery (or crackers), yogurt. What a lifesaver! So yeah, it's not surprising Olivia is sleeping her first days away, even now in first grade. She'll adjust! You'll be back to her non-stop chatter in no time.

I don't have a lot of conversation coming out of Leyanna right now, either. I can't tell if she is tired, too, or is buckling down as she finally has homework now that the whole "learning routines crap" she complained about earlier is done. Actually, I think she is also reading a lot. That's my girl! She binge-reads authors like your momma binge-watches reality TV. She finished all things L.M. Montgomery and is currently gorging on Jason Reynolds. What should I nudge her with next? Do you think she is ready for Toni Morrison?

Her current hair color is electric blue, which looks fabulous, especially with the braids, and her latest jewelry creations are chunky neon globs that look a bit odd, but I guess they match her hair? IDK. Whitney works with someone at the dealership who brings in odds-n-ends beads and other weird items for Whitney to bring home. The whole jewelry-making thing bonded her and Leyanna back when Jackson started getting serious with Whitney, and I don't want to mess with that. Besides, it's pretty unique, and I love when Leyanna strikes out to do her own thing.

We have a new department chair, and I couldn't tell you where he came from, but it certainly wasn't our department. I guess he used to work for some other big education vendor and probably demanded to be chair as a condition for hire. Anyway, I'm trying hard to like him, but he's coming in like A) he understands anything at all about how we've run things in the past and B) a pretentious know-it-all. I'm not sure I would have wanted the chair position if given the opportunity, but I don't quite understand why they didn't consider someone else who has been with our program.

Give my Livvy a hug and throw in some smooches for Isaac.

-N

@@@@@@@@@

Sent September 18
To: SOHIGHSOLOW@MAIL.COM
FROM: NAOMI.WELLINGTON@AESAMN.EDU
SUBJECT: RE: TEST

Hi sohighsolow, (< — note the greeting)

I will be happy to let you re-take a quiz (according to the syllabus guidelines). Can you please (< — note the courtesy word for the request) let me know which class you are in and the name of the quiz? Also, unfortunately, I don't have everyone's email addresses memorized, so if you can tell me your full name, too, that would be great!

Thanks, (< — note the courtesy closing)

Ms. Wellington (<— note the sign-off with my actual name so you know who I am)

On September 17, sohighsolow <sohighsolow@mail.com> wrote:

Subject: test

<< i want to redo my quiz >>

@@@@@@@@@

EARLY WORLD HISTORY - DISCUSSION

<u>Discussion Participation Rubric</u>

<u>Discussion Forum Guidelines and Expectations</u>

UNIT ONE: DAWN OF MAN

>**Question One**: Which skill—toolmaking, fire, or language—gave hominids the most control over their environment? Why?

>**Question Two**: How were Neanderthals similar to people of today?

▽ **Question Three**: **MS. W's CHOICE** - What might archeologists 1,000 years from now learn—and make conclusions from—regarding our current culture? What artifacts and remains would lead them to those conclusions? How accurate would they be?

Luis: i don't really get how archeologists figured out when ppl started talking (like, why wouldn't they always been talking?) but my mom never understands half the stuff i say so i idk slang or something might be something to guess about us

Sh'rae: 🙂 < 🔧🔧 4 🗣💯

Cassie: 👆👆👆 This.

Ms. W: And what would those 1,000 years from now think about the emojis? The abbreviations? Would they think it was like going back to hieroglyphics or cuneiform? And if so, would they think we developed, or did we take a step "backward"?

Luis: well it's not like we have to draw those altho i guess some ppl r still doing the old-style keyboard art, so maybe a step backward

Kenneth:

(\ (\

(-,-)

o_(")(")

Luis: ⌐(¬ ¬¬)╒

Tabitha:

```
.............(¯``•.
.............(¯`•.(¯`•.............._/)/)
.............(¯`•.(¯`•..........((.....((
.............(¯`•.(¯`•..((.)..(.`/)
.............(¯``•.(¯`((.)....|\_/
........,,,~”¯``¯`(_,´(_.)......|
....(((./.............................)__
..((((.\....),,...........(...../__`\
..))))..\. .//... ¯¯¯¯¯¯`\.--/...//
.(((...../ .// .............. | ./.....\/
.)))).....| ||................| |.........♥♥♥
((........) \\................) \...........\|/
.^^^^.""""".^^^^^^^^.."""".^^^^."""""
```

Luis: whoa, yeah, like nvm. step forward not backward 4 sure

@@@@@@@@@

Sent September 18
To: Jessamine Lewis <steamyenergy@gmail.com>
From: Naomi Wellington <myownperson02@gmail.com>
Subject: the Why

In this generation of sharing everything on social media, no matter how inappropriate, I'm almost supportive of it since it results in my students being super open about why they're doing online classes with us, what they're worried about, and what they're looking forward to. This is all in our first month of school homeroom discussion board.

Some of my kids have major anxiety. A couple got kicked out of school for missing too many days because they had to take care of their siblings while their mom or dad worked. Another said she got into too many fights in school, and another had a baby over the summer and is doing online so she can take care of her kid and still get her diploma.

I want to give each and every one of them a hug, which is definitely one disadvantage to online education. Today I start another round of phone calls, and I can kind of give hugs through the phone, can't I? Seriously, some of these kids will do totally fine with this online alternative, but the others? This might be a little easier, but they're still struggling with so much at home. One kid said it was his last chance with his parents. If he doesn't pass his classes, he'll be kicked out of his house.

And now my heart hurts again. For sure, there might be more going on with him than he's sharing; maybe he's doing drugs or is violent at home, IDK, but I can only go with what I know so far, and I wish I could guarantee it will all work out okay.

It worked out for me, but I got lucky. You found me. And let your family be my family.

I'm so grateful.

<3

-N

@@@@@@@@@

Sent September 19

To: Jessamine Lewis <steamyenergy@gmail.com>
From: Naomi Wellington <myownperson02@gmail.com>
Subject: Polar Cafe

You might be all Starbucks Is Stellar because you now live out west, and obviously I used to be that way, too, but can I just expound a bit about the Polar Cafe? First, as an aside, how perfect is the name for a Minnesota coffee house? Right? Anyway, I love everyone there. Tracy is my conscience. She'll let me get whipped cream with my latte, but pushes back on me when I ask for extra.

"Medium latte, extra whip," I say, confidence trumpeting out of me. I know what I want, and I don't care what anyone else thinks!

Tracy then hovers her finger over whatever button on the screen would enact my request and then tilts her head *just so* to blink at me.

"I need it today," I whine. "Fifty kids submitted their essays all at once on the differences between the federal and state government structure. The extra whip is energy!"

Tracy shrugs her shoulders and, as she presses the button, I say, "WAIT. No, you're right. Just a regular amount of whipped cream. Or no, none. I will have a medium-sized, no-nonsense latte. And a blueberry scone. And another pack of Now and Laters."

Of course, then Sayeed is the one who fills the orders, and he gives me an absurd amount of whipped cream and says to me as I pick it up from him, "Don't let Tracy intimidate you. If you want half a can of whipped cream, you shall have it."

And then the guy who orders after me—or sometimes before me, either way, it's right around the same time every day—grins at me as he grabs his large whatever which obviously has no whipped cream and his banana or orange or some other stupidly healthy choice and I suddenly feel enormous and rush out of the shop with my breakfast pick-me-up loaded with mixed feelings calories.

Some days I stick around, craving the "real world" stimulation. I don't regret leaving the F2F classroom for the virtual one, especially because of Leyanna, but you can't replicate visible behaviors. Like how Hot, Healthy Guy gets everything set up *just so* before he eats his banana or orange or whatever and reads his book. Or how Pencil Skirt Woman smiles shyly at the other customers waiting for their coffee orders. It's such a pretty smile, and I'm so glad she doesn't hide it away in spite of the uncomfortable awkwardness of milling about the pickup area.

Then there's Sloppy Jock and Super Suit who I think might be brothers. They look a lot alike and stand with the same slight lean backward while stroking the edge of their chins with their thumb. I think it's fascinating how they almost never sit and have their coffee together. It's like a daily check-in, and I love how close they are if this is how they connect. Daily!

Of course, when you have *our* relationship, we don't always need to "see" one another because we know each other so well that if right now you were to say, "that's just wrong," I could see your lips pucker and the tilt of your head as you shook it from side to side. Or when you say, "#ThatIsAll," how you've got your air quotes going and your White Voice over-enunciating each word. (One of my favorite things, btw.)

That's not to say when I sit at my little corner table and take everyone in that I don't miss you desperately. Or miss trying to convince you this ramshackle coffee spot is not too hipster for us to hang out in (even if it is—but don't knock it because it's close to my apartment and is my oasis from the start of A Year—shut up, I am NOT using hipster language already. Shut up.)

Hugs to Faith and the little people.

Send me candy!

-N

Sent September 19
To: Naomi Wellington <myownperson02@gmail.com>
From: Jessamine Lewis <steamyenergy@gmail.com>
Subject: Re: Polar Cafe

Okay, Little Miss, you go on and take your little corner of preciousness and fence yourself in because you're acting like your cutesy teddy bear shop is unique. I got my coffee connections, too. And the coffee itself? Definitely better than panda-poo's. They draw pictures in my coffee because yes, yes it IS a Starbucks. Homegrown out here in Washington, so it's koala kute, too.

This one is literally ten feet away from my store, and not all Starbucks are chain-store sellouts. My Starbucks has Mina (and she is *fine*, but don't go bringing that up around Faith, thankyouverymuch), and she has kids (and a husband, so don't you go letting your mind go weird places like it does). It's nice to have someone to share stories with who gets it. I know you get it, but Leyanna is (almost) twelve now. Mina's kids are seven and four, and she gets it right away in the here and now. So, like, you telling me about Leyanna's transition to kindergarten is hella helpful, no doubt. But Mina brings it home by commiserating each morning. Plus, she's a manager, and we can share stories. You love all my crazy stories. Mina appreciates those AND all the nitty-gritty things involved with running a business.

No lie, though—she's the only solid, regular person there. The others are college kids with crazy inconsistent shifts. The same kind I keep hiring because Faith wants me to. Yet, I can't rely on many of them. I swear it's not the same as when we had jobs when we were younger. These students ghost all the time. Some of them show up a week later thinking they can clock in and work their old shift like I haven't already taken them out of the system and moved on. What are they thinking? They aren't, Faith says. "They're a different generation, Jessie-Mine (you can be sure she's launching into something to butter me up when she says my name like that), and we have to adapt to them rather than the other way around."

I'm not sure I like that answer, and while I still hire some of the university students (especially in November-December and also because I have a higher chance of getting someone who isn't a precious white snowflake because by then they've discovered they need the money), I prefer the permanent residents. I have more patience working with people who live here and need the regular work. It almost feels more—honest, I guess.

Look, some of my employees have never worked with a Black person before, let alone have a Black person as their boss, and sometimes the shit they say to me without even thinking is just so wrong. Still, they also don't talk all "I am using a microaggression as a defense mechanism for my lack of broader world experiences" like all of Faith's colleagues do (did you like my Faith professor-speak, there?). Like they are so above it all. They're not wrong, but when one of my sales clerks says, "we don't have people stealing stuff as much as you're probably used to," I don't give a little smile and ignore it. I go full-on BOSS and "well, actually" them before they can try it on me. I tell it like it is, and because they don't have anything to prove, they usually say, "Oh! Okay." And then we're good.

Anyway, have you read that Mira Jacobs graphic novel memoir yet? It's kind of killing me because Olivia is asking me questions now, like Jacobs' kid is. Her latest: "Does the president hate me? Antonio says the president hates all the kids from Mexico, and I asked if he thought the president hated me, too, and he said, probably, but maybe not as much." First grade is already going to be way harder than kindergarten, isn't it?

-J

@@@@@@@@@

Sent September 20
To: HISTORYSTUDIES_GROUP@AESAMN.EDU
From: NICK.JONES@AESAMN.EDU
Subject: CURRICULUM ALTERATIONS

Hello colleagues,

This message is a gentle reminder that we are not to alter the curriculum in our courses in any way. The courses and their objectives are set, and changes are confusing and disruptive for students.

This includes "bonus questions", "extra resources", and "add-on" discussion forum topics.

Please let me know of any questions.

Best,

Nick Jones
Department Chair
Society and History Studies
Alternative Education Solutions Academy
"There are no secrets to success. It is the result of preparation, hard work, and learning from failure."-- Colin Powell

@@@@@@@@@

Sent September 20
To: AESAALLSTAFF@AESAMN.EDU
From: MARY.SLAUSON@AESAMN.EDU
Subject: LEAVE OF ABSENCE

My esteemed colleagues,

Effective immediately, I am taking a leave of absence. My mother's health is rapidly deteriorating, and I am choosing to step back temporarily from the Academy to care for her in what are likely to be her final days.

Our assistant director, Mark Sumner, will take the helm as Interim Director with Karen Amberson-Nass covering some of the primary assistant director duties and the department chairs taking up the other responsibilities.

Thank you for your support, and I hope for you and our students a great year!

Warm regards,

Mary
Mary Slauson
Director
Alternative Education Solutions Academy

Alternative Education Solutions Academy seeks to provide a safe learning environment where all students can meet success on their own terms.

@@@@@@@@@

Sent September 20
To: Jessamine Lewis <steamyenergy@gmail.com>
From: Naomi Wellington <myownperson02@gmail.com>
Subject: more leadership change

As if Nick from Nowhere wasn't bad enough, now our assistant director is acting interim director because Mary is taking up to a year's leave of absence. Her mom's health is deteriorating, and Mary is taking time to care for her. It's the right decision for Mary, but you know how I feel about Mark the Shark.

Mark's the one who assigned me all of those different course sections this year and who says, "Oh, I guess those last ten student enrollments slid into that course at the last minute before we could close it. So sorry!" And then he does nothing to fix it. And he's the one who nitpicks over every single penny on our monthly expense reports. Like, I'm sorry if my ISP charges by the precise number of days in a month instead of a generic, static monthly amount. I've sent you a copy of the bill. What more do you want?

I can only imagine how he'll be in the top chair. Fortunately, one of the other department chairs, Karen, will be filling in as assistant, and I've heard she's pretty organized, but also laid-back. No micromanaging.

You don't micromanage, do you, Jess? Or do you have to in a department store because everything needs to look "just so" for people to like shopping there? I love seeing all the polo shirts and shorts lined up neatly on the displays and seeing a definite difference between the regular clothing lines and the clearance racks. If shelves aren't looking great, I guess focusing on those seemingly little things is necessary for the bigger picture? Am I comparing apples to oranges with our two jobs? (BTW, those are both fruits, so why do we think that comparison is super contradictory? Shouldn't we say "comparing apples to hot dogs"?)

I've got forty-seven "this week in the news" summaries to read, and that isn't even half of what should already be turned in. Also, they're all just going to Google, aren't they? I think I'll change it up and make sure they include at least one local story, too. These kids are from all over the state, so a small town "we got a new stop sign" bit might be kind of fun to see interspersed with all the depressing "president said something racist" stuff.

-N

Sent September 21
To: Naomi Wellington <MYOWNPERSON02@GMAIL.COM>
From: Jessamine Lewis <STEAMYENERGY@GMAIL.COM>
Subject: Re: more leadership change

Which of our jobs is the apple and which is the hot dog? Hm? HMM?

You know what? I'm owning the hot dog. Managing all kinds of different people with all areas of this store is definitely like a mish-mash of meat-like ingredients. I have no idea where some of my employees have come from, that's for sure.

Also, surely you *must* be well-aware my job is way more than making sure all those sweaters are folded in perfect alignment, right? But, let's take your example. I *could* inspect each rack myself and note exactly who took care of which one. This would be micromanaging. And hell no, I don't do that. Instead, I rely on my floor managers to look after the racks and do what they need to do to ensure the store looks good.

Have you ever thought about putting your name in the draw for department chair? (It seems kind of weird, btw, based upon all you've told me about how schools work, to have some sort of outsider come in like the one guy. Completely normal for business, but maybe an online program works differently.) You have all kinds of ideas, and babe, you are super passionate about your job. You'd probably kill in that position.

-Jess

@@@@@@@@@

Sent September 22
To: Jessamine Lewis <steamyenergy@gmail.com>
From: Naomi Wellington <myownperson02@gmail.com>
Subject: Whitney

I just got off the phone with Jax. My heart broke when I heard his voice crack. He was so excited about that baby.

Your mom stopped by with veggies from the garden and told me about the miscarriage. She was pretty gutted, too. "Jackson had that twinkle in his eye like he did when you were carrying Leyanna," she told me. "He looked young again, like he's supposed to. Lately, he's been walking around like he's carrying the weight of the world until he found out about this new baby. And now?"

I hadn't really thought about it, but I think Momma Junie is right. Jax *has* been a little off. Do you think he and Whitney had been trying for a while to get pregnant? I mean, they haven't been together super long, but Jackson's been wanting more kids for forever. The whole trying thing is stressful when it's not happening as quickly as you think it should (especially when the last time it happened was an accident and only took one try 🙄), and I feel like he hasn't mentioned any other things going on. I mean, obviously he doesn't tell me everything going on in his life... IDK. What has he told you?

Leyanna will be so sad. She was really looking forward to having a little brother or sister. I hope I don't say or do something super awful and insensitive at Sunday dinner, because I feel like Whitney and I were finally hitting it off, you know? I need you to come home for a visit to run interference. Why did you and Faith have to move so far away?

-N

@@@@@@@@

Sent September 25
To: Naomi Wellington <myownperson02@gmail.com>
From: Jessamine Lewis <steamyenergy@gmail.com>
Subject: YOU ARE THE BEST

Mimi!

I squealed when I opened your package today and saw Angie Thomas' SIGNED copy of *On the Come Up* and have already started reading it. I love it! Don't get me wrong; I loved her first book. This one, though? It's gonna crawl right up into my heart. I've got the lines in me bustin' to come out! Thank you for standing in line with all those teens for me. I don't get why Faith has a thing against YA books, so I super appreciate you buying them for me every once in a while. She reluctantly read Thomas' first one and agreed it was better than she thought it would be. Maybe I'll convince her to try this one, too. I'm all for some of the literary stuff she has me read (I do love Toni Morrison and even some Edgar Allan Poe), but other kinds of fiction are no less important, you know?

I mean, yeah, of course you know. It was a good day to get your package, is all. Faith's colleagues at the university get on my nerves sometimes with their academic superiority like my MBA ain't nothing and my position as a store manager isn't as impressive as... what? What should I be instead? This is what I don't understand. Faith has some snobbery with reading material, but she gets it, usually. She grew up in private schools, but still on scholarship. On the other hand, I love how smart she is because I've overheard her do some pretty awesome verbal takedowns with some of those same colleagues. At least once was about me, and it reminded me all over again of why I fell in love with her.

She says you should apply for a leadership position at your school, too, btw. She's got some good contacts she can tap into in the education department if you want some ideas for current research trends.

Muah.

-Jess

Sent September 25
To: Jessamine Lewis <steamyenergy@gmail.com>
From: Naomi Wellington <myownperson02@gmail.com>
Subject: Re: YOU ARE THE BEST

Jess,

Lines busting to come out? Please tell me they are better than the ones you came up with in undergrad. "I got meat you can greet when you show up to compete," anyone?

I could pull up a few others if you need reminding. A whole notebook full of 'em.

-N

Sent September 25
To: Naomi Wellington <myownperson02@gmail.com>
From: Jessamine Lewis <steamyenergy@gmail.com>
Subject: Re: YOU ARE THE BEST

Oh, we doing this, now?

How about your wax museum of Egyptian pharaohs using melted crayon wax?

Sent September 25
TO: JESSAMINE LEWIS <STEAMYENERGY@GMAIL.COM>
FROM: NAOMI WELLINGTON <MYOWNPERSON02@GMAIL.COM>
SUBJECT: RE: YOU ARE THE BEST

Barbie dolls wearing marker-colored tissue gowns?

Sent September 25
TO: NAOMI WELLINGTON <MYOWNPERSON02@GMAIL.COM>
FROM: JESSAMINE LEWIS <STEAMYENERGY@GMAIL.COM>
SUBJECT: RE: YOU ARE THE BEST

Fanfiction about presidents?

Sent September 25
TO: JESSAMINE LEWIS <STEAMYENERGY@GMAIL.COM>
FROM: NAOMI WELLINGTON <MYOWNPERSON02@GMAIL.COM>
SUBJECT: RE: YOU ARE THE BEST

UNCLE

(P.S. YES, to Faith's offer. TY!)

@@@@@@@@

BOARD: LORD OF THE FLIES by William Golding

▽ **TOPIC:** Discussion Question 1: Who would you follow—Ralph or Jack?

Tyrell: Neither. I'm going with Jack White on this and his song, "Entitlement." These guys crash land, and instead of "holy shit, what just happened?" they're all, "yo, let's party."

Lisa: I'll add on to that... boys. I mean, right off the bat, they were dismissing the smartest kid there, Piggy.

Naomi: IDK, Ralph and Jack are twelve and/or thirteen, right? Girls at that age? Not sure they'd be much better.

Lisa: Yeah, you have a point there.

Chester: I'm just going to say it. Jack, because c'mon —BACON.

Naomi: *snort*

Lisa: That is so idiotic, but also, word. Bacon is the world's most perfect food.

Chester: Huh. I would have pegged you for a vegetarian. Vegan, even.

Lisa: I'm not even going to ask.

Maxine: I like how Jack overcame his fear of hunting, but then he got all... wild. Ralph seemed more rational, and despite how he kind of betrayed Piggy at the beginning, he was smart about consulting him later. That's what good leaders do.

Susette: But what were the real chances of them getting rescued? It's not like today, where we have all this great technology to find people. Back then, Jack might have been their best hope for survival.

Tyrell: Except technology never found that one plane a few years ago that was going to China, did it? Maybe Susette's right.

Naomi: Why is it always one or the other? Why couldn't Jack and Ralph find a way to work together towards both goals? What does it mean when it's one way or the highway?

Lisa: Because MEN.

Grant: You're not wrong. It sure seems like men, in general, are all about who's the top dog.

Tyrell: Not all men.

Lisa: OH NO YOU DID NOT.

Tyrell: Sometimes it's just too easy with you, Lisa.

Naomi: Maybe we should all try experimenting with hormones. Balance us all out.

Susette: OMG, this is the best idea to come from this discussion group yet.

Naomi: Right? I've got a colleague or two who could use something. They are on a total power trip.

Chester: So, you push back, right?

Naomi: Hell yes, but I don't do it waving a spear.

Lisa: Preach.

Maxine: I'm a push-over. I wish I had been more like you, Naomi and Lisa, when I was younger.

Lisa: It's not too late, Maxine! If you want something, we can help you get it/get it done!

Maxine: Well...

Naomi: There IS something. Tell us! Take the conch!

Maxine: It's kind of silly.

Lisa: A perfect situation to start, then.

Maxine: Okay. Well, here goes: I subscribe to the daily newspaper, and it's always delivered at the end of my driveway, except it's supposed to be delivered to my doorstep. I called customer service and asked if they could deliver it to my door, and the delivery person called me later to assure me she had been most definitely bringing the paper to my door every day. I told her I didn't understand how it would end up at the end of my driveway instead, if that were true. A few days later (the newspaper was still showing up at the end of my driveway), she called me and said in the past few days, she'd been delivering my paper and then doubling back with her lights off to see if she could find out what was happening. It turns out my next-door neighbor has been picking up the paper and then tossing it to the end of the driveway.

You see, I don't... I don't like to leave my house. I know it's not normal. I know I'm a weirdo. I can't change at this point. I don't know how.

I still get the paper because the mail carrier usually picks up the paper for me and knocks on my door to give it to me personally, bless his dear, sweet heart. I suppose the neighbor is trying to help me, but I wish he'd stop. Each time I think about it, I feel sick.

I should be able to walk to the end of my driveway to get my paper, but I can't. I know it's silly.

Lisa: Maxine, first of all, THIS IS NOT SILLY. This is a TERRIBLE thing. It's harassment at the least and terrorizing behavior, if we're honest. You need to report him. Call the police.

Naomi: Maxine, I'm so sorry! Your neighbor is an asshole. Lisa's right. He's harassing you, and that's a crime.

Maxine: The police won't help me. They think I'm a freak. They talk to me like I'm eighty years old and I'm not even sixty yet. I feel stupid and foolish around them.

Naomi: I hear you, Maxine. How are you about opening the door? It sounds like you're able to do that much with the mail carrier, yes?

Maxine: Not comfortably, but yes, if I'm a few steps back, I can handle the open door.

Lisa: I'm guessing Naomi's saying you could try talking to this neighbor of yours. Before you do, make sure it's who you think it is. Wake up early, don't turn on any lights, and look out your window or peephole if you have one, okay? You want to be safe.

Naomi: You can do this, Maxine! He probably only needs to realize you're aware of what's going on and he'll stop. What he's doing is cowardly, and he won't have the guts to keep doing it once he knows you've found him out.

Susette: I've had someone bother me like this at work once, and I finally got so annoyed and told them off. It turned into a big thing, and I wished I had confronted the person way earlier instead of waiting until my explosion point. Hopefully, confronting your neighbor now will prevent worse things later.

Maxine: Okay. Well. I'll try.

OCTOBER

Sent October 1
To: Jessamine Lewis <steamyenergy@gmail.com>
From: Naomi Wellington <myownperson02@gmail.com>
Subject: Idiot school systems

Today I graded an essay test by a student who wrote "I don't know" and then gave me three more paragraphs about how much she hated taking these online courses. She was only doing it because her school didn't think it "appropriate" for an obviously pregnant teenager—setting a bad example, you know. "*I'm not stupid. I can do the work, and shouldn't they be happy I'm still trying to finish high school?*"

I don't even know how a school can be this stupid and short-sighted. And then they just throw her into this whole online thing with zero support. When she first started, I had a bazillion emails from both her and her mother because they were so confused. When I called the school contact—who was neither a counselor nor even a teacher—and asked about whether they did some sort of orientation and how they determined the courses, she said—and I kid you not—"No, that's up to you to figure out. She made the choice to switch over to online school."

What IS that?

And now I find out she *didn't* make that choice. Unless you call getting pregnant and being told "online or drop out" a choice.

I almost wanted to give her partial credit on the essay response, even though it had nothing to do with the question. I didn't, but then I told her I was sorry about her circumstances in the comments. And then I emailed her a much longer message of support.

So many people think online teaching is more impersonal than face-to-face.

It's not. It's really not.

-N

@@@@@@@@

Sent October 2
To: Naomi Wellington <myownperson02@gmail.com>
From: Jessamine Lewis <steamyenergy@gmail.com>
Subject: had to fire someone today

N,

One of the worst parts of my job is when I have to fire someone. Sometimes it's hard because I might have liked the person, but most of the time it's hard because of the huge amount of work it shifts onto the rest of us. Honestly, letting Katie go was a relief. She was so much work. Petty arguments with George and Letitia about display fixtures (I mean, she'd have her associates hide them for their own use. Real mature, right?). She'd mess up schedules, and finally, the thing that tipped her over the edge? She completely forgot to put out stock for a big, chain-wide flash sale we had a couple of days ago. I looked at the daily sales report and about lost my mind when I saw ZERO sales for the Shades of Pumpkin items. Tops, bottoms, scarves, and jewelry. NONE of it made it out to the floor.

Anyway, because she was a department manager, and because I only have four of them, I have to figure out how to distribute her department among the others (and me, because I'll have to pick up all the slack) until I can find someone qualified to take her spot. Even though she's not quite ready to be a department manager, I really want to put my pre-med girl on track for it.

One of the worst parts of managing is managing people, but it's also one of the best parts. I'm good at this job, Mimi, and I'm ready for something bigger, except I'm stuck in this tiny town in the middle of wheat fields with a wife who can't easily re-locate.

Olivia and I are digging a cute new-ish series by Saadia Faruqi. It's about a girl, Yasmin, who's always problem-solving, and usually she doesn't realize she's doing it. Very cute. Olivia can already read so well; we sometimes alternate reading whole pages.

Did you put Toni Morrison in Leyanna's hands yet?

-Jess

@@@@@@@@

Sent October 2
To: Jessamine Lewis <steamyenergy@gmail.com>
From: Naomi Wellington <myownperson02@gmail.com>
Subject: Re: had to fire someone today

Oh man, Jess. I admire you so much for being able to do that. You and Faith tell me I should pursue some kind of leadership position, and then you tell me an actual story about what it entails. And I know you aren't telling me the whole of it, are you? I mean, it's not lost on me how you mentioned she's pulling stunts on George (gay) and Letitia (Black) and not Missy (white) or how probably the other mess-ups are meant to make YOU look bad.

I'm sorry people are so shitty.

-Mimi

@@@@@@@@@

Dear neighbor who keeps moving my newspaper to the end of my driveway,
It has been a bit upsetting to me to discover you are the one who has been displacing my newspaper. I do not understand why you are doing it, but I would like you to please stop.
Thank you, Maxine

@@@@@@@@@

ONLINE LEARNING SYSTEMS MANAGEMENT

Alternative Education Solutions Academy

TEACHER DASHBOARD

03 October

New Submissions: **127**

New Discussion Board Comments: **89**

Student Progress Alerts: **24**

Calendar:

09:00 Help Session/Office Hours

10:30 Department Meeting

13:00 Current Events Seminar

14:00 Help Session/Office Hours

17:00 Academy Staff Meeting

@@@@@@@@@

ONLINE LEARNING SYSTEMS MANAGEMENT

Course [Modern World History] Announcements

Announcement:

This Day in History - October 03

1995

Former football star O. J. Simpson is acquitted for the murder of his wife, Nicole Brown Simpson and her friend, Ronald Goldman.

1992

Singer Sinead O'Connor tears a photo of the pope on live TV (*Saturday Night Live*).

1990

East Germany and West Germany reunify into a single nation.

1989

Art Shell becomes first Black American to coach an NFL team—
the L.A. Raiders.

TODAY

Akeisha R. and Lorelei M. were awarded STAR status for their
collaboration in leading yesterday's Current Events Seminar
discussion. WTG!

Announcement:

Help Session: 2:00pm

Remember today's help session! I'll be talking about how to
approach exam short essay questions. After that, we can cover
any other questions you have. Bring a link to your current music
video to share, too!

@@@@@@@@@

[8:21 Oct 03]

NAOMI

Did Leyanna leave her cello folder at your
place?

JACKSON

Yeah, it's sitting on the music stand. Need me
to run it over?

NAOMI

No, I'll come get it. I'm hyperventilating a little
with my workload right now and a breather
might help.

JACKSON

Damn, Nay. School's barely started.

NAOMI

It's always like this at the beginning of the year.

JACKSON

And the middle and the end.

NAOMI

Like you haven't worked yourself to death with your business?

JACKSON

Not as much anymore. It's doing good now, so I've figured out how to step back.

NAOMI

I know how to step back.

JACKSON

Yeah, sometimes. But I know all you do is work during the weeks Leyanna is with me and Whitney.

NAOMI

I see friends. Besides, my students are special cases. They need extra TLC.

JACKSON

Yeah, I know. You're a good teacher. You just gotta be good to yourself, too, okay?

NAOMI

Okay.

JACKSON

Look, Whitney and I are just kickin' back with some cinnamon bread still warm from the oven. If you hurry, we might have some left by the time you get here.

NAOMI

OMG, leaving right now

@@@@@@@@@

Thank you, Maxine

I don't think I will. You see, it's an experiment. I've heard many stories about you, and this is one way to find out which story is true.

@@@@@@@@@

Sent October 04

To: Jessamine Lewis <steamyenergy@gmail.com>
From: Naomi Wellington <myownperson02@gmail.com>
Subject: customers who need to visit the coffee shop more often

1. Latinx mama who has four kids and has the most amazing control over her children, who are *everywhere*. Seriously, one wanders two steps away from her... behind her back... and she says, "Lucía, grab your sister, please" without missing a beat while ordering tea. Her NBD management is beautiful.

2. White girl who I also call "Gorgeous Hair Babe"—seriously. She has hair that I want to sink my hands into. Preferably while making out, but I wouldn't require it. It's a deep red (natural? dyed? who cares?) with thick curls that rest atop her shoulders. I'm breathing heavily just writing about it.

3. Latinx papa who once in a while comes in after mama and scoops away all the kids with monster smiles, which they follow up with squealy giggles, and mama tries SUPER hard to stifle a smile as she finishes ordering and paying.

4. Dark-haired Indian man who wears a short-sleeved button-down shirt (awesome, brilliant-colored ones—royal blue, deep purple, magenta—I mean seriously, I covet them) with black pants and carries a leather briefcase. He has eyes for Sayeed, and I truly want to find a way to break it to him that even if Sayeed

were bi (which, maybe he is? IDK), Sayeed is mad, mad in love with Tracy.

5. Older Black guy that always has a riddle for Tracy. Sometimes they're easy, sometimes they're funny. Today's: What is the thing you must give before you keep? (Your word.)

I wonder if anyone has me on their list of those they'd like to see more often in the cafe.

There was a message on my voicemail today full of nonsensical yelling from my mother. I miss the days when she used to be your run-of-the-mill criminal thief instead of an addict/sometimes dealer.

-N

@@@@@@@@@

Sent October 04
To: Naomi Wellington <myownperson02@gmail.com>
From: Jessamine Lewis <steamyenergy@gmail.com>
Subject: you need to get laid

Mimi,

I love you, and I hope you simply deleted the VM and poofed it away.

Also, you totally need to get laid. "#Thatisall"

-Jess

@@@@@@@@@

ORDER [161] *07:57 AM*
-Naomi-
[1] 16 oz
Breve
x-tra whip
[1] blbry muffin
[1] bagel - TO GO -
mple fr toast

ORDER [162] *08:09 AM*
-Lanh-
[1] 20 oz
Chai tea
[1] apple chips

@@@@@@@@

Dear mean-spirited neighbor,
This seems unfairly cruel. Why don't you knock on my door instead, and meet me? Then you will discover the real story. Or maybe now I'm not a story, but a real person.
Thank you, Maxine

Except, one of the stories is that you are a serial killer who has the bodies of every victim who has come to your door, and they are piled up in freezers in your basement.

@@@@@@@@

[Submitted by Reese Vaskin on Sunday, October 06 at 11:53 PM]

Essay Response

1. Describe the factors that helped Europeans conquer and colonize the Americas.

Basically, they came over and decided they could do whatever they wanted. Also, disease. Leave it to white people to kill thousands without even having to work at it. Also, all the textbook review questions are about the Europeans coming over to the Americas, and nothing talks about the people already living there. "It was kind of bad what happened. Whatev. Next topic." Same thing going on at home. I get pregnant, and I turn into a footnote. My dad comes home and barely says anything to me. Talks to my mom as though I'm not there. My mom at least asks me about my schoolwork; my dad doesn't let me answer and just keeps talking about his stupid fucking day as if anyone cares about how many new companies they've signed on for their packing materials. Did you know that General Mills uses his company's bags for their generic cereal brands? Who even notices any of that? My mom is a nurse, and do you think my dad might think her job is maybe a million times more important than low-quality bags that don't open without splitting down the middle and spilling little oat circles everywhere? Then again, my mom is like the priests who be saying all the slavery stuff is bad shit (for the Native Americans, not Africans), but I guess that's just how it is. She about fell apart when she found out I was pregnant. Said the Lord was punishing her for something. Now she unloads on me all the damn time for being a sinner, ruining her life by me no longer being a perfect daughter. I guess my sister (she's twenty-two and lives on her own) can hold on to that title all by herself now.

@@@@@@@@@

Sent October 07
To: SOHIGHSOLOW@MAIL.COM
FROM: NAOMI.WELLINGTON@AESAMN.EDU
SUBJECT: RE: ASSIGNMENT

Hi Serena!

Thank you for letting me know which class you are in! I'm still a little unsure of which assignment you might be talking about? Is it the one about changing the course of history? Or the one where you write Cornell notes for the chapter? It looks like both of them might have been confusing to you. Let me know which one we should work on first, and we'll go from there.

--Ms. W.

On October 07, Serena <sohighsolow@mail.com> wrote:

Subject: assignment

<<hi ms w i guess i didnt really understand the assignment. can i redo it? im in the american history class. ty from serena>>

@@@@@@@@@

**Whatz HOT, Whatz NOT Daily Scoop
(whatzhotwhatznot.com)**

Actors Walk Out of Awards Show

Sheena Lewis (staff writer) - *October 8*

More than fifty actors and actresses walked out of Star Framework Theater last night in protest against racist and sexist practices in the industry.

The silent action occurred when actor, director, and producer Dane Hanson took the stage to accept a lifetime achievement award. Applause died away as the mass exodus of actors, actresses, and a handful of directors and producers left in a synchronized exit. Hanson has been accused of "whitewashing" his films created from stories that have characters of color, creating hostile environments on sets with verbal abuse towards people of color serving on the crew, and sexually harassing actresses and female directors.

"The choreographed effort made by these actors was nothing short of beautiful," MC Merrick Curtis commented. "If the Entertainment Guild of America (EGA) thinks their members are going to stand for supporting disgraceful behaviors, then they're right--they will stand right up and walk out."

Not everyone cheered the action. Actress Kimberly Lemon called the walkout "the most selfish spectacle of disrespect" she had ever seen. "You don't just dismiss a person's life work like that."

"He dismissed himself when he refused to change his ways," Ling Carlisle responded.

SHARE >>>

@@@@@@@@@

Sent October 10
To: naomi.wellington@aesamn.edu
From: nick.jones@aesamn.edu
Subject: Current Events Seminar

Hi Naomi,

It's come to my attention that some topics you've covered in the Current Events Seminar have strayed a bit from the traditional "big issues." The purpose behind this course is to address broad issues from front-page headlines and what they mean in our world today. Talking about the latest awards show or the latest "scandal" on Twitter does not meet the criteria.

From here on out, please send the recordings of your live sessions to me for review to ensure the students are participating in the prescribed curricular framework.

Best,

Nick Jones
Department Chair
Society and History Studies
Alternative Education Solutions Academy
"High achievement always takes place in the framework of high expectation." - Charles Kettering

@@@@@@@@@

Sent October 14
To: Jessamine Lewis <steamyenergy@gmail.com>
From: Naomi Wellington <myownperson02@gmail.com>
Subject: annoyingly good looking healthy Polar Café guy

So you know the guy who always orders right before me or after me? The one who always eats stupidly healthy next to my "All The Poor Choices?" I only noticed today that one of his arms is shorter than the other. As in, it stops a little below his elbow. How had I not seen it before? And why is it I originally made the subject line of this email "one-armed guy" as though I'm the most ignorant person on the planet? Fortunately, I changed it, so I'm not the absolute worst anymore, just really close to it. The new subject line is accurate, though. I'm not sure I would call him *hot*, but I don't know... simply really attractive. Charming. A dazzling smile. And if I didn't think he was always laughing at my chub snacks, I might not find his attractiveness annoying. Or maybe it's because he's always eating fruit. And that he looks like he's in good shape.

Okay. Fine. He's not annoyingly good-looking. He's straight-up attractive. And maybe a little sexy. Fine, he's HOT, okay? He's Asian with short dark hair, light brown skin, dark eyes framed by bronze, wire-rimmed glasses, and always has a book tucked under his arm. The shorter arm, which is why it's weird I never noticed that about him before.

Today, though, he dropped his book, and when I squatted (yes, squatted, I do listen to Jax sometimes and want to save my back) to retrieve it, I looked up to see the rolled-up cuff of his sleeve. I have been exchanging smiles and Minnesota weather inanities with him for weeks and never gave a second thought to his dexterity of holding both his huge coffee and an apple or a banana or a whole watermelon in the one hand.

But Jess, I swear I didn't think I was gaping, but the frown on his face when I had the book in my hand? It made me think he suspected I was reacting solely to his arm. But I wasn't, not really. Honestly, I was more intrigued by the book than the arm.

"*Go Set a Watchman*," I said to him. "How far are you? What do you think? About the story? Or about the author and how this came to be? Is it ruining some magical aura you cling to with *To Kill a Mockingbird?*"

And then he laughed. "I thought for sure you were going to throw it at me in horror." He wasn't frowning at me because I noticed his arm. He was worried I'd criticize him about his book.

AS IF. (Also, let's be real. Obviously, he knows I also noticed his arm. Hopefully, I didn't gape.)

He then held his arm out slightly from his side and nodded towards the book, which took me a second to realize he meant for me to slip it back in the grip of his armpit, and I am so relieved I didn't make the whole moment awkward and instead I've put all the freaky reactions here in this email. And thankfully, I can't see your judge face right now, though I'd deserve it.

"I'm not that far in the book," he said. "Scout's only on the train."

And then, fabulous conversationalist that I am, I said, "Oh."

That's it. "Oh." Along with a stupid look on my face. I blurted out a string of questions and then followed it up with a one-word "what-does-that-even-mean" response.

What I *thought* was, "hurry up and read it because I super duper want to talk about it with you because no one I know will read it, and I HAVE THOUGHTS."

Thankfully, he did not run from my blank look and said, instead, "So, we should talk about it when I finish, then?"

At which point I found my voice again, and he said he would let me know when he was done, and maybe we could sit and have our coffee together that day?

Did I mention he's hot? AND he wants to talk books? I may already be in love.

-N

@@@@@@@@

[11:23 14 Oct]

JESSAMINE

So does annoyingly-healthy-one-armed-Asian-hottie have a name?

JESSAMINE

Or did you giggle and rush out with your grande-whip-with-tiny-bit-of-room-for-coffee?

NAOMI

Lahn. aka Hottie Lanh. Mr. Lanh Hottie.

NAOMI

And it wasn't *that* much whip.

NAOMI

Okay, it was mostly whip.

@@@@@@@@

Sent October 15
To: Naomi Wellington <myownperson02@gmail.com>
From: Jessamine Lewis <steamyenergy@gmail.com>
Subject: broken arm

Hey Mimi,

Today has been the longest day, and I'm stupid tired, but can't sleep, and all I want to do is sob in exhaustion, but I already have a headache like a giant pushing my skull into the ground with its foot.

Faith broke her arm today. While on her run, she tripped on a branch and did a pretty good roll, but still landed pretty hard on her forearm. You know her; she was just going to brush it off. She said it wasn't bad and maybe she'd go to the doctor if it still bothered her after her 4:00 class. She hates canceling classes—I can't tell you how many times she's complained about a particular faculty member who is always canceling his Friday classes because he wants to have a long weekend (why doesn't he just teach Tuesday-Thursday classes?). By 9:00 am, she could barely move it without tons of pain, and the department secretary convinced her to see someone and drove her to the E.R. I met up with her there.

It's a pretty straightforward break, and they put a cast on it, saying she should probably only need it on for three weeks.

Sounds like a best-case thing, right?

I have never seen Faith so tense after leaving the hospital. She basically screamed at me when I suggested she still cancel her afternoon class (we finally got out of the hospital at around 2:30), which made me hiss right on back at her. She broke down crying on me. "Babe, it hurts so much. I hate how I'm crying about it. I'm such a baby."

I wanted to turn around, go back to the hospital, and demand something stronger. She wouldn't let me, saying the pain meds would probably kick in soon, and it wouldn't be so bad. She let me text her students about canceling class.

When we got home, I put her to bed, went to pick up the kids and dinner, and by the time we got back and checked in on her, she was still in the worst pain. It scared me, Mimi. Faith is usually so... IDK, stoic. She rolls her eyes at me when I whine about a cold and gives me that "bitch, please" face when I get worked up about stuff. Yet, she was curled up tight in bed with all the lights out and shades drawn. All she could do was nod or shake her head when I asked her questions. Every time I'd check on her, I'd hear these soft moans, and she'd only moan louder and shake her head if I touched her. I think the painkillers finally kicked in because she's been asleep for a couple of hours, and I'm crossing all my fingers and toes that the worst is over.

Jax broke his leg when he was in seventh grade, and I swear I don't remember it being this bad.

I wish I could call you, but I don't want to leave Faith, and I'm scared she'll wake up.

-Jessamine

@@@@@@@@@

Sent October 16
To: Jessamine Lewis <steamyenergy@gmail.com>
From: Naomi Wellington <myownperson02@gmail.com>
Subject: Re: broken arm

So glad we talked this morning. I hope you convince Faith to at least call the doctor, even if she won't go in to see one. I don't know anything about broken bones, but I know you, and I know Faith, and something isn't right.

Anyway, here's something to take your mind off things: You know the online book club I'm in? Our most recent book was *The Hunger Games,* and as usual, one of our threads veered off topic. This time it went to tattoos (don't ask—well, whatever, you can ask—Susette, our moderator, said she got a mocking jay tattoo inspired by the third book) and Grant, the guy who can find something to like about every book we read, even the worst ones (*Catcher in the Rye,* anyone? He said as full of annoying privilege Holden is, it doesn't take away from his apparent depression. Depression can affect anyone. He's right, but UGH) said he has a dragon tattoo because of some dragon books he read once. Plus, a few others not related to books, and I might be a teeny bit in love with him.

But then... pain to my heart... he is married! To someone who has amazing tattoos, I guess. Whatever. DOES SHE READ BOOKS? I bet not; otherwise she'd be in the book club with him, right?

Then Chester jumps in and asks me if I have any tattoos.

Hang on, one of my students is messaging me.

Okay, back. "I didn't know I was supposed to include an annotated bibliography. Can I still submit that?"

Me, out loud to the computer screen, "How could you not know about the bibliography? I've emailed reminders! It's in every step-by-step assignment description! It's in the final checklist! DO YOU NOT READ *ANYTHING*?"

Well, no, of course not.

Me, in my typed message back to her: "Yes, of course you can still submit it. If you need help with it, feel free to message me again!"

Deep breaths.

I have colleagues who dock major points for late stuff, but, I mean, it's like they are completely missing the point of why some of these kids are doing online classes. That traditional crap wasn't working for them, and isn't our "Alternative" solution supposed to help them succeed?

Love you, babe. 🙂

-N

@@@@@@@@@

Sent October 16
To: Naomi Wellington <myownperson02@gmail.com>
From: Jessamine Lewis <steamyenergy@gmail.com>
Subject: Re: broken arm

Oh my god, Mimi, you are a distraction from your own distractions. What did you tell Chester??

-Jess

@@@@@@@@@

Dear gullible Neighbor,
Well, for pity's sake. How ridiculous! I mean, I'd have to own a lot of FREEZERS, for one thing! Have you seen any of them delivered? (No, you wouldn't have, because they'd

bring them to the door, and then you'd have a time of it moving THOSE to the end of the driveway, wouldn't you?)
Sincerely, Maxine

Touché about the delivery bit. I grant it might be true you haven't had multiple deep storage freezers delivered. On the other hand, maybe it's always happened when I've been at work. Okay, well, here's another reason not to knock on your door. I've also heard you always bring a shotgun to the door and threaten to use it on solicitors.

@@@@@@@@@

Sent October 17

To: HISTORYSTUDIES_GROUP@AESAMN.EDU

FROM: NICK.JONES@AESAMN.EDU

SUBJECT: LATE WORK DEDUCTIONS POLICY

Hello team,

This message is a reminder of our late work policy. All assignments (including discussion assignments) and assessments should already have a due date entered into the LMS. All late work will take a 5% deduction for each day it is late. Only our academic counselors may excuse late work.

Best,

Nick Jones
Department Chair
Society and History Studies

Alternative Education Solutions Academy
Great leaders are almost always great simplifiers, who can cut through argument, debate, and doubt to offer a solution everybody can understand. - Colin Powell

Sent October 17
To: HISTORYSTUDIES_GROUP@AESAMN.EDU, NICK.JONES@AESAMN.EDU
FROM: NAOMI.WELLINGTON@AESAMN.EDU
SUBJECT: RE: LATE WORK DEDUCTIONS POLICY

Hi Nick,

I know everyone hates a "reply-all," but I feel like this policy needs some discussion. When was this decided? Why? Isn't this late work policy yet another thing setting these students up for failure in the traditional school setting? I'm very uncomfortable with both taking away the flexibility for these students and becoming yet another teacher to potentially fail them when we are supposed to be helping them succeed.

-Naomi

Naomi Wellington
she/her
Society and History Studies
Alternative Education Solutions Academy
"We realize the importance of our voices only when we are silenced." - Malala Yousafzai

Sent October 18
To: NAOMI.WELLINGTON@AESAMN.EDU, HISTORYSTUDIES_-GROUP@AESAMN.EDU
FROM: NICK.JONES@AESAMN.EDU
SUBJECT: RE: LATE WORK DEDUCTIONS POLICY

Naomi,

We had a full discussion during our last department meeting, to which I believe you arrived late. You are solely responsible for any items covered in your absence. Please direct future questions about this and other policies to me and not the entire group.

Best,

Nick

Sent October 18
To: NAOMI.WELLINGTON@AESAMN.EDU
FROM: LAUREN.HEISLER@AESAMN.EDU
SUBJECT: RE: LATE WORK DEDUCTIONS POLICY

And by "full discussion," he means this is what he decided, and it doesn't matter what we all think. Good luck taking this one on.

-Lauren

Lauren Heisler
Society and History Studies
Alternative Education Solutions Academy

Sent October 18
To: NAOMI.WELLINGTON@AESAMN.EDU
FROM: CORYNN.JEFFERSON@AESAMN.EDU
SUBJECT: RE: LATE WORK DEDUCTIONS POLICY

We tried, Naomi. Losing battle. We threw arguments at him, but he had a rebuttal for each one. Supposedly researched, although I can't imagine it applies to our students. But, you know. RESEARCH.

-Corynn

Corynn Jefferson
they/them
Society and History Studies
Alternative Education Solutions Academy

Sent October 18
TO: NAOMI.WELLINGTON@AESAMN.COM
FROM: ADAN.SALAZAR@AESAMN.COM
SUBJECT: RE: LATE WORK DEDUCTIONS POLICY

Naomi, you don't even know. I wish you had been at that part of the meeting because we needed more voices. This is not the organization it once was.

-Adán

Adan Salazar
he/him/his
Society and History Studies
Alternative Education Solutions Academy

@@@@@@@@@

Partial Transcript of Society and History Studies Department Meeting

October 15

19:00:02

Nick: Welcome, everyone! We're almost six weeks into the school year, and things are going great!

...

...

19:12:45

Nick: Effective immediately, we are implementing due dates for all full-time students. We've already worked out all the dates for you, but you'll need to enter them into the LMS. You can download the zip file from the "Files" tab on the left.

Stacy: I don't see the "Files" tab.

Lance: It's just above the chat box. Next to "Participant List."

Stacy: Got it.

Nick: Please also note that late assignments will lose 5% each school day it is late.

Adán: What? Point deduction?

Nick: Correct.

Adán: Why?

Nick: We want to prepare our students to be ready for life beyond high school. Deadlines are a major life skill.

Lucía: Aren't a lot of these kids already developing that skill with their jobs? Most of them are working and know to be on time for those jobs. Many of them *have* to work, and it's a pretty big accomplishment for them to be working towards their diploma at the same time.

Nick: Precisely why they need to learn the importance of deadlines. We offer a flexible environment for them to work during or outside of regular school hours, but we still need to keep them on track.

Stacy: I still can't find the zip file. I'm looking in the "Files" tab, and I see "Grading Guidelines.docx," "Blog schedule.docx," "schedules.docx." Is it supposed to be the "schedules" one?

Corynn: Why can't the dates simply be guidelines? If they are hard and fast deadlines, we're going to overwhelm a lot of students. Some have enough on their plates with anxiety and other issues, too.

Adán: Aren't we supposed to be a program designed to help students succeed? Taking away points on a late assignment that perfectly demonstrates what they've learned is the opposite of our goal. They've come to us because this kind of traditional assessment failed them already.

Nick: Research supports deadlines. I appreciate everyone's input. Please enter the due dates into the LMS for each of your sections by the end of school hours on Friday.

Carl: Where do we find the zip file?

@@@@@@@@@

Sent October 18
To: NAOMI.WELLINGTON@AESAMN.EDU
FROM: MARK.SUMNER@AESAMN.EDU
SUBJECT: RE: DEPARTMENT VS. SCHOOL POLICY

Dear Naomi,

Thank you for bringing this issue to my attention. We do like our departments to have some autonomy, trusting that academic standards will be met as well as student needs. While this late work policy is a change to what has been in practice before, it reflects broader institutional changes we will be implementing. We will, however, review this departmental policy with Nick to ensure a solid, data-driven rationale.

It is our expectation that you will comply with all policies—school-wide and department-specific—until any changes might be made.

Thank you,

Mark Sumner
Interim Director
Alternative Education Solutions Academy

@@@@@@@@@

Sent October 18
To: NAOMI.WELLINGTON@AESAMN.EDU
FROM: LISETTE.GARCIA@AESAMN.EDU
SUBJECT: EXCUSED LATE WORK

Hi Naomi,

Daniel and I have agreed to review all requests presented to us for exemption from the late work policy and will process them as quickly as we can.

Please forward all requests to us with the subject line changed to "Submission review - StudentInitials."

Thank you for your efforts with our students.

Lisette Garcia
she/her/hers
Academic Counselor
Alternative Education Solutions Academy

@@@@@@@@@

Dear door-to-door encyclopedia salesman neighbor,
Are you a solicitor?
Sincerely, Maxine

I am not a solicitor, no.

@@@@@@@@

Sent October 21
To: Jessamine Lewis <steamyenergy@gmail.com>
From: Naomi Wellington <myownperson02@gmail.com>
Subject: book talk with Lanh

My dearest Jessamine,

I have fallen hard for Hottie Lanh, aka the healthy hot guy at the coffee shop. He finished *Go Set a Watchman* in three days so we could talk about it. In other words, he didn't forget about me wanting to chat it up, took me seriously, and hurried his reading so it would for sure happen.

Hottie Lanh is a financial analyst, which I don't really know what that means, to be perfectly honest, but it sounds smart, doesn't it? He wants to be an English teacher instead. With middle school students! <3 <3 <3

This means him reading *Go Set a Watchman* was perfect because I think it would make an awesome compare/contrast book with *To Kill a Mockingbird*. And then follow it all up with *The Hate U Give* for the more current authenticity for our time. (BTW, he hasn't read that book yet... I'm bringing my copy tomorrow for him to borrow.) It was so much fun debating author intent, original story vs. what was actually published, and how *Watchman* morphed into *Mockingbird*. Do you remember when Jax and I used to argue about books? Those were fun times.

He's got a crazy sexy voice. I also suspect Lanh is trans, although I couldn't pinpoint exactly why to you, at least not without getting all weirdly specific, and you know how I feel about that.

Not that I spent our entire conversation checking him out. Just most of it. Maybe almost all of it. He probably thinks I'm a freak and definitely thinks I spent a lot of time *not* looking at his shorter arm. I mean, obviously I wasn't trying not to look, but I felt so self-conscious about the whole thing, and honestly, I was super interested in his dexterity, which is probably quite annoying, and I just know I'm going to ruin this whole thing tomorrow.

But I hope not. I really like him. He's funny. And because he wants to be an English teacher, we joked a lot about grammar things people get wrong. Loose/lose. Using an apostrophe for a plural word. Firstly. Borrow/lend. It started when I talked about lending him my book, and he gave this big sigh of relief when I didn't say, "I can borrow you my book." I laughed because I totally get it, and OMG, this drives me crazy!

So, yeah, I'm seeing him again tomorrow morning. I mean, I don't know if we're going to sit and have our coffee again, but I reminded him about bringing the book, and I 100% want to sit with him... remind me of how this meet-cute potential dating thing works again?

Jitterly yours,

-N

@@@@@@@@

Sent October 23
To: Jessamine Lewis <steamyenergy@gmail.com>
From: Naomi Wellington <myownperson02@gmail.com>
Subject: Tracy is dead to me

Do you remember Tracy? One of the Polar Cafe baristas? Turns out she doesn't like Percy Jackson.

I mean, what?? Who doesn't like Percy Jackson? Mythology! Action! Heroes who aren't completely clueless and succeed because they know what they're doing instead of by luck or accident!

She said the first book was kind of "cute and all, but got kind of boring," and she *didn't even finish it.*

I may have to find a new coffee shop.

Except, I can't exactly abandon hottie Lanh, so after I pushed my jaw back up and shoved my bulging eyeballs back into my head, I started in on my campaign to fix this travesty. I asked her rapid-fire questions to find out how far she got. Did she know Percy was a demigod? She rolled her eyes. "Duh. Everyone knows that."

"Yeah, but did you get to that part in the book?"

Yes.

"What about...?"

Yes.

"And...?"

"Look," she told me. "I get tired of 'chosen' one stories that depend on parents dying and almighty prophecies and adults who pretend they can't help or tell these supposed chosen ones all they know. It's ridiculous."

Sayeed—who had been rallying right along with me—shrugged and said, "Well, she's not wrong."

But Percy's mother *doesn't* die, and the adults get better, and the prophecies? Well, I guess I couldn't argue about those, but Sayeed interjected to remind me of how many books into the series you have to read in order to see some of that progress.

"I'm not saying I don't want teen characters to have everything handed to them, but to fail at something simply because adults withheld information? Pass."

We debated back and forth, and while I reluctantly gave up the fight, I caught Sayeed with a thoughtful look on his face. I wonder what he's thinking?

One of my students is a super-Percy Jackson fan, and he throws in references all the time with his chapter review questions and essay exam questions. His latest? Comparing all the Stoll brothers' Camp Half-Blood pranks to the Boston Tea Party. He's also great at pulling up super obscure things when he is trying too hard with his cleverness—like saying the reason the Liberty Bell cracked during the Revolutionary War (it didn't, and honestly I think he only read the little "Did You Know?" boxes in the online text) was because when George Washington was on a quest when he was younger, he stole the bell from Hephaestus' junkyard and "you know what happens when you do that!" << Direct quote from his exam response. When it cracked, it supposedly sounded like Zeus' lightning bolt hitting it, at which point I read such a fantastical tale that I almost emailed Rick Riordan to tap my student for his next book idea. (And no, I did not give him credit for the answer, entertaining as it was.)

I've offered to do a daily history fact for our social media accounts. It seemed like something fun and quick, but only a week into it and I'm stressed out trying to come up with something fresh and interesting without being lifted right from some daily thing on a website. Plus, according to Nick, it needs to be unique and with a "why is this relevant today" twist; otherwise he'll ride my ass about it like he's been doing with everything else. (Because as long as we're comparing, Nick the Dick and Mark the Shark may as well be the Titan gods for all of their antagonistic ways.)

I gotta sign off and write a blog post about primary sources.

xoxo

-N

Sent October 24
To: Naomi Wellington <myownperson02@gmail.com>
From: Jessamine Lewis <steamyenergy@gmail.com>
Subject: Re: Tracy is dead to me

N,

Are you serious about not easily coming up with those daily history facts? The ones I heard from you in almost every conversation from high school through our undergrad days? It's because of you I have dumb things like how Paul Revere never even shouted "The British are coming!" during the Revolutionary War. It was all stealth. Or how he was a silversmith. How is any of that information useful to me?

-J

Sent October 24
To: Jessamine Lewis <steamyenergy@gmail.com>
From: Naomi Wellington <myownperson02@gmail.com>
Subject: Re: Tracy is dead to me

What about all the REVERE WARE pots and pans you sell? Hmm??? Where do you think they came up with the name?

Sent October 24
To: Naomi Wellington <myownperson02@gmail.com>
From: Jessamine Lewis <steamyenergy@gmail.com>
Subject: Re: Tracy is dead to me

You are never going to let our one career commonality go, are you?

Sent October 24
To: Jessamine Lewis <steamyenergy@gmail.com>
From: Naomi Wellington <myownperson02@gmail.com>
Subject: Re: Tracy is dead to me

NEVER. Obscure history facts are ALWAYS relevant.

@@@@@@@@@

[4:57 Oct 24]

NAOMI

Leyanna says I can't use Black slang anymore.

JACKSON

Leyanna is right. Whole family has been telling you that forever.

NAOMI

Bet!

JACKSON

What.

No.

NAOMI

That wasn't right?

JACKSON

No

NAOMI

But I was agreeing with you!

JACKSON

No

NAOMI

When Leyanna came home from school today I
told her to wait because I hadn't seen her in a
minute.

JACKSON

No

NAOMI

But it had been all day!

JACKSON

No. Stop.

NAOMI

Fine

@@@@@@@@@

ORDER [133] *07:59 AM*
-Lanh-
[1] 20 oz
Chai tea
[1] seasonal fruit

ORDER [132] *08:03 AM*
-Naomi-
[1] 16 oz
Breve
x-tra Whip
[1] bagel
mple fr toast
[1] scone
cran-orange

@@@@@@@@@

Dear Neighbor who does not sell things,
Then, I hardly think the shotgun would be an issue, would
it?
Sincerely, Maxine

Hmm. I suppose not. Meth lab? Dangerous and mean attack
dog? Someone trapped in your basement?

Dear wildly imaginative Neighbor,
None of those things.
Sincerely, Maxine

Okay, to be completely honest, the rumor I thought most likely
to be true was that you are morbidly obese, and I wanted to
see if you could walk down the driveway without help.

And after writing those words, I realized how terrible they
look and sound. I am ashamed I only realized that after I wrote
it out, and worse, left it on your doorstep. I'm so sorry. I'm an
asshole.
Sincerely,
Asshole Neighbor

Dear Maxine,
I'm sorry for my behavior. It has been rude, mean-spirited, and
I'm a dick, douchebag, jerk, asshat.
Sincerely,
Your neighbor who is a total jerk.

Dear Maxine,
I'm sorry. Please forgive me.
Evan, your neighbor

Dear Maxine,
Here are some personal things about me. I'm 33 and still single,
obviously because I'm an immature dipshit. I hate living alone,
and so I have a lot of pets, but they're not all the "normal"
kind, which might be why no one wants to be with me, let
alone live with me. Or maybe it is only because I am an
immature dipshit, which now seems like the more plausible
reason, after more thought and soul-searching. I hope this
helps you feel less antipathy towards me.
Sincerely,
Evan

Dear Maxine,
Maybe I could knock on your door? Please let me know if it's
okay for me to knock on your door tomorrow morning.
Sincerely,
Evan

@@@@@@@@@

PROGRESS REPORT:
LEYANNA WELLINGTON

Language Arts 11%

(0/10) Rough Draft - Defining Moment Essay

(10/10) Journal 1 - Choice Novel

(10/10) Journal 2 - Choice Novel

(0/100) Essay: Defining Moment

(0/50) Presentation - Choice Novel

Math 98%

(10/10) Chapter 3-1 Homework

(10/10) Chapter 3-2 Homework

(10/10) Chapter 3-3 Homework

(24/25) Quiz 3-1:3-3

Social Studies 71%

(0/10) Discussion Week 1

(0/10) Discussion Week 2

(20/20) Chapter Review

(0/10) Discussion Week 3

(55/55) Chapter Test

Science 68%

Orchestra 100%

Art 97%

@@@@@@@@@

Leyanna Wellington
Language Arts 6
Hour 2
October 25
Defining Moment Rough Draft

The only defining moment that I've had that I can think of is being born. I'm only twelve. Why would you think I would have already had some major moment that I've chosen to define who I am yet?

Leyanna, defining moments are relative. Remember, we are only examining our defining moment "so far," and we can have more than one in our lifetime. Maybe you want to choose being born if that was a remarkable moment. Was it? Please refer to the list of guiding questions on the assignment sheet, answer as many of those questions as you can, then see me so we can look over those answers together to help you create a true rough draft. -Ms. Z

@@@@@@@@

Sent October 25
To: Jessamine Lewis <steamyenergy@gmail.com>
From: Naomi Wellington <myownperson02@gmail.com>
Subject: homeless (not me, obviously)

One of my students wrote to explain why he hadn't logged on for the past two weeks. It was because he and his dad were evicted from their apartment for being way behind on the rent. His dad has been looking for work for three months, and they have been barely getting by. My student's been working during the day at a White Castle and only today was able to get to the library while it was still open.

This could have been me at any time, from kindergarten through senior year. My parents were always so unpredictable, floating from job to job until they'd get fired for stealing, arrested for stealing, or making me go to the store with an obviously bad check. (Do you remember the time I came home and discovered most of our furniture disappeared? I still don't understand how that even worked. Who buys a bunch of junk furniture in the span of a few hours?) I have the social worker from our middle school to thank for helping me figure out the food shelf, the volunteers for making it look like it came from our local grocery store, and my next-door neighbor for the best ways to hide the good stuff from my mom and dad.

Do you remember when my mom showed up at your place, looking for me, and then trying to make Momma Junie look like the bad guy? I was mortified. I dragged her away and threw up as soon as we got home, all while listening to her spout out how she was my REAL mother and knew what was best for me and who did Momma Junie think she was, trying to act all high and mighty about "helping" out with me. "You're MY kid, and the key word in there is KID, and you ain't got any say in who gets to be your mom. You came out of ME." And on and on. All because Momma Junie stood with a thousand times more class in front of my sorry-ass "mom" to say, "Naomi can stay with us anytime she chooses." I think it was that "choice" thing that got to her. She knew I'd choose your family any time over her.

Did I tell you she called me again a few days ago? Sober this time. She's been clean for all of a week and telling me, "this time is for real." God. Whatever. I don't know why I ever gave her my phone number.

Our counselors are taking care of our homeless student and his dad, btw. Interim Idiot hasn't wrecked that part of our program yet, thank God.

-N

Sent October 25

To: Naomi Wellington <myownperson02@gmail.com>
From: Jessamine Lewis <steamyenergy@gmail.com>
Subject: Re: homeless (not me, obviously)

Oh, I remember that day, for sure. Do you know what Momma said to me after you left? "Jessamine Louise, the next time you pick a fight with Naomi, I want you to remember how hard she works every day to just BE. She fights in ways, praise the Lord, you have never had to do. You got that?"

You were always in her prayers. Except, I'm pretty sure she didn't understand how amazingly irritating your random history fact-sharing was. I am 100% in the right for arguing against this obsession of yours. One. Hundred. Percent.

I'm sorry your mom's trying to rope you in again.

-N

Sent October 25

To: Jessamine Lewis <steamyenergy@gmail.com>
From: Naomi Wellington <myownperson02@gmail.com>
Subject: Re: homeless (not me, obviously)

Did you know that around this time back in 1962, the whole Cuban missile crisis took place?

(Don't shoot your own missiles at me, please?)

-N

@@@@@@@@

Sent October 26
To: Jessamine Lewis <steamyenergy@gmail.com>
From: Naomi Wellington <myownperson02@gmail.com>
Subject: craving cherry jellies

Why is it so hard to find plain cherry jellies? Why do they all have to be cinnamon? I like cinnamon-flavored stuff, but those sugar cherry slices are soooo good. I remember when Jackson drove the hour and a half round trip to Minnesota's Largest Candy Store to get me a few containers of them back when I was pregnant with Leyanna. And him with a final the next morning. Sometimes I kind of wonder... IDK, like what if we had tried to be together back then after all?

Anyway.

Lanh obviously doesn't have the same sweet tooth I have, although at least he hasn't acted all judgy around my coffee shop orders. He says sugar makes him too jittery. Like he has an extra sensitivity to it. He eliminated most sugary things a couple of years ago and discovered he felt so much better. Way more calm.

"Do you miss it?" I asked him. "You know, like when people bring in donuts on Fridays? Or birthday cake?"

"Kind of. I don't *not* eat stuff like that. When I eat it now, though, I tend to feel a little sick, so I watch how much I eat at special occasions." He smiled when he added, "I miss the idea of how eating something sweet can make you happy. Like how you are when you lick off all the whipped cream from your coffee each morning."

"I *try* not to order it," I said defensively. "Sayeed keeps adding it back in."

"Because it's obvious how much you love it!" Lanh laughed at me.

It's true. I love all the extra whipped cream almost as much as I love my kid. And cherry jellies.

Jackson's birthday is coming up. Maybe I'll be the one to make the big trip to the candy store and get my cherry jellies along with those Pop Rocks he loves.

-N

@@@@@@@@@

Sent October 27
To: Jessamine Lewis <steamyenergy@gmail.com>
From: Naomi Wellington <myownperson02@gmail.com>
Subject: things heard at a Sunday dinner

"Leyanna, baby girl, you keep getting so tall and beautiful. Did you take some of Gramps' growing beans?" (Gramps, as though he doesn't ask that question every single week. 🩶)

"Naomi, honey, when you gonna find yourself someone to settle down with, hmm?" (Auntie Sadie, naturally.)

"Jackson, your cousin Antwann says people don't fix their techy gadgets anymore. Instead, they buy something new. Is he right? Are you about to go outta business?" (Grams, bless her heart.)

"Oh my, Whitney, is that some of your amazing cheesy potatoes? You know they're my favorite." (Momma Junie.)

"Naomi, baby, if you grew your hair out, bet those single men and women would come a-running." (Momma Junie, and every man I've ever dated.)

"Junie, you've outdone yourself with this ham. It's cooked to perfection." (Pops. And all the rest of us because your momma's ham is always PERFECTION.)

"I'm so glad at least one of my children learned how to create something delicious in the kitchen." (Momma Junie about Jackson's rolls, of course. You know she's not all wrong on that, either!) (Also, at least I'm not the only one getting slighted here, though it would help if you were present to commiserate with me.)

"Those earrings are beautiful, Whitney! You are so talented with those beads and colored glass." (Momma Junie.)

"Why haven't you brought someone 'round here for Sunday dinner lately, Naomi, baby?" (Pops. I mean. HIM, too?)

"I made you some dark chocolate brownies to take home with you, dear." (Grams to me. Have I mentioned lately how much I adore Grams? She's my favorite.)

"Tell me about the new workouts you've been trying, Whitney. I need some way to shape up these flabby arms." (Auntie Sadie, conveniently right after Grams telling me about her melt-in-your-mouth brownies.)

"Whitney, can you get me a deal on a new set of stylin' hubcaps? I need something smooth for my truck." (Uncle Casper finally chiming in.)

"Auntie Junie, you know I need more slices of ham than that. And more rolls. Why you skimpin' on the rolls?" (Cousin Lance, of course.)

"Jackson, honey, after dinner, can you help me with the printer? It keeps making noise, and nothing comes out of it." (Pops. Why is he so hopeless with computer stuff? He's an engineer, for pete's sake.)

"Leyanna! Did you make that necklace with Whitney? It's perfectly gorgeous." (Momma Junie.)

"Naomi, baby, you look a little tired. I hope you're not working too hard." (Momma Junie. I can't tell if she means well or if it's a passive-aggressive insult. At least it wasn't about hooking up with anyone.)

"You need to take a break and get out there if you want to settle down with some nice young man or woman." (AH. Spoke too soon.)

"Dad, can you and mom talk more about letting me do online school?" (Leyanna, not really during dinner, but during our hand off. She is nothing if not persistent.)

I miss you.

-N

Sent October 27
TO: NAOMI WELLINGTON <MYOWNPERSON02@GMAIL.COM>
FROM: JESSAMINE LEWIS <STEAMYENERGY@GMAIL.COM>
SUBJECT: RE: THINGS HEARD AT A SUNDAY DINNER

Mimi,

That email made me sooooo homesick. You don't even know. I miss Momma's ham and Jackson's rolls and Gram's hugs. I'd be willing to be slighted all night long if it meant hanging with all of you back home.

Faith didn't grow up with Sunday dinners, and back when we first moved away, I tried to get us to carry on with the tradition, thinking she might have been on board after a couple of years of it with our family, but it didn't really work. I'd suggested we start inviting our coworkers as a way to make it feel homey and to get to know them all better, make some friends. She thought it would look too informal or familiar for her Ph.D. colleagues, and I said the familiarity was kind of the whole idea.

Anyway, now our Sundays are all about laundry, cleaning house, running errands, and getting some kind of takeout for dinner, and while it's nice not to have all the cooking and cleaning for a big deal, it doesn't have the same atmosphere. For all of your message making it sound like no one loves you, I know you don't feel as though they don't. You left out all the jokes, the story-telling, and the laughter.

We've lost some of the laughter here since Faith broke her arm. To be perfectly honest, it's been going away before now, but with Faith in so much pain all the damn time, I'm stressed out and almost as short-tempered as she is. I would have thought some of the pain would have eased off since she isn't supposed to need the cast for much longer.

Maybe I'll do us up a Sunday dinner next week, with or without Faith. I'll invite my department managers and Mina and her family, and if Faith is too high and mighty to invite her colleagues, it's on her.

Hugs to you, and maybe soon you'll be able to bring hottie guy from the coffee shop, and you can get a little extra love, thanks to him.

<3

-Jess

@@@@@@@@@

Sent October 30
To: Naomi Wellington <myownperson02@gmail.com>
From: Jessamine Lewis <steamyenergy@gmail.com>
Subject: OMFG HALLOWEEN

Mimi, I am the worst mother ever.

Halloween is two days away, and I have nothing ready for the kids. Nothing. Both kids told me earlier this month about what they wanted their costumes to be, and the very next day, Faith broke her arm, and everything's been kind of a shit show since then. Faith has been absolutely worthless, and I go back and forth between huge worry for her—because this pain thing is *not* normal, and being utterly pissed at her for acting like a big baby. I've been doing pretty much everything for our household—and her—while she puts all her energy into barely hanging on with her teaching and committee duties.

She only makes it to the dinner table with the kids and me about half the time. Sometimes she starts making the kids' lunches or snacks, and then I'll come in to see they're only partially done. (Is it cruel of me to tell you it reminds me of your lunches back in those early middle school days? Those were sad, babe.)

I've been so overwhelmed with taking care of everything that I've forgotten the things that will crush my kids if I don't have them.

Mina—you know, my barista friend at Starbucks—is saving the day by bringing a couple of her kids' costumes from last year. One is an Elsa one which makes me want to vomit, but I think Olivia will love it if we can't find a Jasmine one (which also kinda makes me gag). Mina also has a dragon, which wasn't one of the things Isaac wanted, except now he thinks it's the best thing ever, so it's like a miracle.

I'm not going to bother with candy for trick-and-treaters coming to our door. I can guess already Faith won't be participating in anything, least of all putting on a happy face for kids coming to our door. As for me, I only hope I'll have enough in me for Livvy and Isaac's sake.

I wish you were here. You always made Halloween fun. I could really use some of that fun about now.

-J

Sent October 31
TO: JESSAMINE LEWIS <STEAMYENERGY@GMAIL.COM>
FROM: NAOMI WELLINGTON <MYOWNPERSON02@GMAIL.COM>
SUBJECT: RE: HALLOWEEN

Mina saves the day! Please send pictures! Despite everything, your kiddos will make it so you will smile today; I know it (at minimum, I desperately hope it). They can't help themselves around all that sugar.

Leyanna is sort of apathetic today about Halloween (I've had to do most of the decorating myself), and I hope it isn't a new teen thing. However, she showed me a bit of her old self last weekend at Powderhorn's Spookarella event. We went as hipster princesses. IT'S A THING. We got tenth place in the couple's costume contest (!), and I haven't seen Leyanna smile like that in a long time. This is how I know Olivia and Isaac will boost you right up.

<3

-N

Attachment <IMG_465.jpg>

@@@@@@@@

Sent October 31
To: 'Reese Vaskin' <notthatreese@mail.com>
From: "Naomi Wellington"
<naomi.wellington@aesamn.edu>
Subject: checking in

Hi Reese,

Your latest exam concerned me. How are you feeling? Exhaustion can really hit you when you're pregnant; the baby takes a lot of energy to grow inside of you! And I remember how difficult it was when an arm or a leg would get jammed up into the rib cage. Talk about uncomfortable and sometimes downright painful!

I always enjoyed the occasional kick—it was kind of cool to know I wasn't ever alone. I hope you feel the same way, especially when your family isn't always as supportive as you want them to be. I was very lucky, which is why I knew I'd be able to keep my daughter and raise her. I had lots and lots of help. Plus, her daddy has always been there for her, even though we aren't together.

You have not directly said what your plans are when the baby is born—and I know this is a pretty personal question, so please don't feel like you have to answer. However, I want to help you find the resources you need for whatever the answer is. Will you keep your baby? Will you have a safe and supportive place to live and raise her if you do? Or are you considering adoption?

There isn't a right answer. This isn't a test. But maybe it will help you to talk it all out.

-Ms. W (Naomi)

@@@@@@@@

Dear Evan,
If you knock on my door tomorrow, I might open it (although I'll peek through the window first). BTW, I'm not morbidly obese.
Sincerely, Maxine

@@@@@@@@@

BOARD: THE LITTLE PRINCE by Antoine de Saint-Exupéry

▽ **TOPIC:** Do you think the prince is real? Or is he a part of the narrator's mind?

Maxine: Oh my goodness, I never even considered that he wasn't real! He's such a dear little heart.

Lisa: Susette! What a great question!

Chester: Why you acting so surprised?

Lisa: I'm not. That inference is all on you. It was me getting excited, dumbo. Anyway, I think it makes perfect sense for the prince to be in the narrator's head. He's stranded and water-depraved. He's feeling desperate and nostalgic.

Chester: You know what, you're right, Lisa. My bad. Also, I can see how the prince could be in his head, but I see it more as he's "real," and the whole story is basically a metaphor.

Naomi: A metaphor for what? I'm thinking something about how you need to focus on the little things because everything is important.

Chester: Yes! What makes those things important is the energy we put into them. The rose is a single flower, but it deserves care and attention like anything else.

Maxine: Maybe if we used emojis more, we wouldn't misinterpret each other's comments.

Grant: I'm with you, Maxine (about the book, not the emojis - but you do you, Maxine). I had no idea that the prince being a figment of the narrator's imagination was a possibility. I like it. I look at my own kids and the kinds of questions they ask and wonder when and how we lose that innocence.

Naomi: So true! For a lot of my students, they lose that innocence waaaayyy too young. They're pretty savvy about how the world works. And yet, their behaviors are still immature. They still only think a few hours ahead and only to what directly surrounds them. They might see the flower that Chester talks about needing care, but not see the big picture in *how* to give it the care.

Maxine: I'm so glad your children have you, Naomi. And you, Grant. And whoever else in this group has or works with children.

Naomi: Well, don't speak too soon, Maxine. I'm not sure I'm doing too great with my kid. Her progress report came home a couple of weeks ago, and some of those grades were NOT good.

Susette: It always feels like a reflection of our parenting when the kids get bad grades, doesn't it? Like, how could we have possibly let it happen?

Naomi: Right? You guys, I'm a *teacher,* and it doesn't seem right at all when my kid isn't doing the basic stuff (such as turning work in). Surely I've taught her better, haven't I?

Chester: Kids are still gonna do what they're gonna do. We like to believe we have control over how they think and act, but all we've got is example. Being a model for them.

Grant: I know I learned early on about modeling. I remember when I first met my kids (long story) and discovered how much my kids looked to my wife for an example of how to act. Every toy, food, drink, whatever—if it was new, they'd look to her and see how she reacted.

Naomi: Great, so what you're saying is I'm modeling the wrong things.

Chester: Nah, Nay. That's not it. She's still working out what you're putting down for her. What will you accept? What won't you?

Grant: Exactly. My daughter? As she's grown older and more secure, she pushes ALL the buttons. ALL of them.

Susette: My daughter tests me all the time, too. Comes home an hour past curfew. Skips class. Slams doors. < — A lot of this today since I've taken away her car keys...

Naomi: Okay. I don't accept the poor grades when I know it's from simply not doing the work. I will put down for her what I want her to take. BTW, Chester, "Nay"?

Chester: My bad. Shouldn't have turned your name into a nickname.

Naomi: It's okay. Not many people go that route with the nickname. I was just surprised.

Lisa: My nickname for Chester is "dickhead" or sometimes "douchebag," which feels like a completely natural shortening of his name, tbh.

Chester: Welcome back to the conversation, witch.

Lisa: 🧹 帚

Naomi: Hey Maxine, whatever happened with your newspaper and the idiot neighbor? Did you talk to him?

NOVEMBER

Sent November 2
To: Naomi Wellington <myownperson02@gmail.com>
From: Jessamine Lewis <steamyenergy@gmail.com>
Subject: not a bad day

Mimi,

We celebrated Faith's birthday today (btw, I don't know if she texted you yet, but she liked the earrings), and it kind of went... well! I don't want to jinx anything, but maybe her arm is finally healing? We sort of took on some kind of unspoken agreement to not talk about it tonight, so I didn't ask her. I couldn't bear to break the spell of a Faith who smiled (a little, anyway) and spent time with all of us. We all went out to dinner and then came home and watched *Moana* together, and granted, she fell asleep halfway through the movie, but sleep is something she hasn't been getting much of, so I was grateful it came.

I hope this all means she and I can go out as only the two of us sometime soon. I feel like this past month has gone by in a blur, and we need to reconnect. I don't know what's been going on with her at the university, and she hasn't heard anything about my days at work, either. We've barely spoken more than a few words to each other each day beyond catching up (sometimes) about the kids and managing the pain she's been experiencing. Mina knows more about my life right now than Faith does. (And obviously, you know more, too—thank God for sister-friends!)

I'm also glad for the reprieve because this month starts the retail season of chaos. All of the weird, you-can-only-find-this-shit-during-Christmastime has been arriving, along with holiday displays, and at least three new clothing lines. The college students we've hired are hit or miss on how many hours they are willing to take on, and my scheduling manager is going insane with how often they call in "sick" or beg to trade shifts with someone. I'm now officially in the "you better believe I take Fridays off in the summer because I work five billion overtime hours in November and December" zone.

I kind of love the rush of these two months, tbh. You know I'm not a fan of Christmas itself, but the energy at the store is the best. Yeah, those college kids are blowing off shifts, and yeah, it's a lot of extra hours, and yeah, next month we'll see a lot of crabby customers... but I love digging in and making the magic happen around balancing everything and seeing what ends up being the big hits of the season. I like how I can usually be unapologetically chin-deep in work. I wouldn't want it to be like this all the time because I love my kids, but for a couple of months a year? I feel like I get to show off how good I am at my job (although I still haven't found a new department manager, so it's a little bit much this year).

I'd like to go bigger one day like Macy's, except this town is too small to do it close by. Lewiston is a forty-minute drive one way with no traffic, and with my hours, adding the commute feels impossible. Maybe when the kids are older.

IDK why I'm thinking about all of this now, especially when things are good for the moment. I guess all the talk from you about changes has kinda had me thinking. My job is good—why am I reaching?

-Jess

Sent November 3
To: Jessamine Lewis <steamyenergy@gmail.com>
From: Naomi Wellington <myownperson02@gmail.com>
Subject: Re: not a bad day

Jess,

Why wouldn't you reach? You rock at your job and will rock at the bigger and better career moves ahead of you.

I think it's totally natural to think "what's next" after a certain amount of time in a job. If Leyanna's asthma hadn't kicked in when it did, would I have been feeling stuck in my school teaching only ninth grade geography and government courses? And now, three years into the online job, I'm looking forward to challenging myself by being on the curriculum team, and by being part of change instead of going with the flow.

I think you should go ahead and let your brain explore.

What does Faith think? If she's on the upswing, hopefully she'll be ready to hear you, and you can work together on what to do next.

<3

-Mimi

@@@@@@@@@

Sent November 4
To: NAOMI.WELLINGTON@AESAMN.EDU
From: MARY.SLAUSON@AESAMN.EDU
Subject: OUT-OF-OFFICE-REPLY RE: THINGS ARE FALLING APART

Thank you for contacting me. I am currently on leave from Alternative Education Solutions Academy in order to deal with a family matter. Please direct all questions to our Interim Director, Mark Sumner, at mark.sumner@aesamn.edu or to his assistant, Madeline Lerner, at madeline.lerner@aesamn.edu. Thank you.

Mary Slauson
Director
Alternative Education Solutions Academy

Alternative Education Solutions Academy seeks to provide a safe learning environment where all students can meet success on their own terms.

On Tue, November 04, Naomi <naomi.wellington@altedsolutions.com> wrote:

<<< *Hi Mary,*

I'm sorry to interrupt your much-needed time with your mother. I wouldn't message you, except things are turning into a mess here at the Academy without you. Mark and Nick have made a few changes, and I worry about how many more are coming down the line. They are turning us into one of those big for-profit education online vendors, and that's not who we are.

Is it?

Please call when you can.

-Naomi >>>

@@@@@@@@@

Sent November 7
To: naomi.wellington@aesamn.edu
From: Nick.Jones@aesamn.edu
Subject: Curriculum alterations

Naomi,

After the incident last month, I had hoped I would have seen a marked change in your weekly Current Events Seminar. However, as I've been reviewing them each week, I see you are still using social media, entertainment, or sports stories as topics of discussion.

Please adhere strictly to the provided curriculum.

I will contact you again in two weeks' time to review and consider whether or not we will have to transfer this course to another instructor.

Best,

Nick Jones
Department Chair
Society and History Studies
Alternative Education Solutions
Management is doing things right; leadership is doing the right things.
— Peter Drucker

@@@@@@@@@

Sent November 7
TO: NICK.JONES@AESAMN.EDU
FROM: NAOMI.WELLINGTON@AESAMN.EDU
SUBJECT: RE: CURRENT EVENTS SEMINAR ISSUES

Hi Nick,

I'm confused. You told me I needed to follow a more "traditional" path with prescribed topics. I have been using each of the topics you've sent to me for all of the Seminars. It's true my students do not always have as much to say about those headlines, even with your guiding questions. (Kudos, btw, on finding this resource on Matthew Larson's "Teaching Our Kids the World" website!)

I have merely segued into related topics for those who are interested (NOTE: these are not "bonus" questions or "add-on" since those are not allowed, correct?). Often I can find something linked to the assigned curriculum event, and I wonder if you noticed how much more engagement occurs when we make those connections? Our discussions have been so fun and interesting! I love hearing how well-informed our students are and hearing their strong opinions.

I hope you will reconsider narrowing our students' discussions as I think it will be a disservice to their learning and their global perspective.

Cheers,

Naomi

Naomi Wellington
she/her
Society and History Studies

Alternative Education Solutions Academy
"We realize the importance of our voices only when we are silenced." -
Malala Yousafzai

@@@@@@@@@

[Submitted by Reese Vaskin on November 7 at 11:53 PM]

Modern World History

Essay Response

3. How did the Enlightenment lead to a more secular outlook?

It's kinda like The Wizard of Oz. Once you see the old white guy behind the curtain, you figure out God ain't doing shit for you. My mom can say it was the devil that got me pregnant, but I'm pretty sure the devil had nothing to do with it (unless you consider my ex-boyfriend the devil). I'm in a full on enlightenment here the way things have been going. I used to be a daddy's girl, you know? Not like a lot of my friends are cause my dad, he's not so showy with how he feels about me, but he used to take me to work and brag about me, saying how smart I was and how I'd be everyone's boss one day, including the boss of him. He liked how I never complained about doing schoolwork and always put my report card on the refrigerator. Now? He says, "scuse me" if we accidentally bump into each other, and that's it. I don't exist. I used to think he'd get over it and forgive me, but it's been three months, and he's near erased me from his line of sight. Mama keeps telling me I need to give my devil baby up for adoption (that's what she calls it, devil baby. Damn.). I tell her I want to keep it, and she asks me who's going to take care of it? I am! How are you going to pay for everything? I have a job, Mama! Who's going to take care of the baby when you're working? Mama, you're not going to help me at all? It will be your grandbaby! If you're old enough to have sex and old enough to make the decision to keep your baby, then you're old enough to figure out how it's all going to work. She says she'll bring home information about adoption next week. I can't raise this baby on my own, but I don't want to give my baby up. I know you've been emailing me about all this stuff, but please, can you use the grading comments instead? Daddy is ignoring me, but still checking up on me by reading my emails. I've had to delete your messages without even reading them as soon as you send them. He doesn't see all this stuff in the grade book, though. I'll be Galileo and make him think I don't have anyone on my side, even though I do. I have you on my side, don't I, Ms. W?

@@@@@@@@

Jocelyn Thurman
Current Events Seminar
Naomi Wellington
This Week In the News
November 11

"Remodeled Rest Stop"

Next week the rest stop off the freeway near our town will open up after being closed forever for remodeling. One of the officials interviewed called it a "boondoggle." Seriously. That's the word she used. That's how you can tell I live in the middle of absolutely nowhere. Anyhow, I chose this article because I don't think many people realize how important nicely made rest stops are. I have to drive me and my sister to my mom's house every weekend, and she lives four hours away. Sometimes, I don't leave her house until after dark, and a nice, well-lit, and well-maintained rest stop is a big deal for a couple of young girls on their own. I wouldn't stop at all most of the time, but my sister is only six and can't hold it like I can. Lots of people commented on how dumb it is that so much money was spent on it, but I think it's money well spent, especially since they cited statistics on how thousands of people use this rest-stop every year.

@@@@@@@@

Sent November 12
TO: JESSAMINE LEWIS <STEAMYENERGY@GMAIL.COM>
FROM: NAOMI WELLINGTON <MYOWNPERSON02@GMAIL.COM>
SUBJECT: ODE TO A LIBRARY

I decided to work at the library this morning, and I sat in the Young Adult section because it always feels like home. This library doesn't have Miss Jackie, but it DOES have Drag Queen story hour every third Saturday, and let me tell you, I would have loved that kind of thing so much when growing up. Leyanna and I sometimes plan our library visits around it and sit in the back to listen in.

Anyway, I was just reading a student's "Current Events" summary (about the need for well-lit and well-maintained rest stops and, I mean, YES), and it reminded me of our senior year in high school when we drove out to Eau Claire, and you were all exasperated with me for telling you maybe we should let someone know where we went? (And then you only agreed to let me text Jackson because you thought if it came from me, he wouldn't rat us out, which turned out to be a wrong assumption, unfortunately.)

All of our made-up headlines came back to me:

"HIGH SCHOOL GIRLS IN HOSPITAL AFTER MOMMA RIPS THEM A 'NEW ONE.'"

"PLANNED THELMA AND LOUISE STUNT OVER UWEC FOOTBRIDGE THWARTED BY SNITCH BROTHER."

We may not have made it all the way to Eau Claire, but it was still a pretty good time, wasn't it? I felt free and independent of my home life for a day.

I mean, until we got home and Momma Junie laid into us and said we hadn't graduated yet, and you were still living under her roof and therefore she made the rules and no, you could *not* borrow the car again until you were forty-two years old.

What will I do if Leyanna decides to go on an unannounced road trip?

@@@@@@@@@@

Sent November 12
TO: NAOMI.WELLINGTON@AESAMN.EDU, LAUREN.HEISLER@AESAMN.EDU, CORYNN.JEFFERSON@AESAMN.EDU, ADAN.SALAZAR@AESAMN.EDU
CC: DANIEL.TOWERS@AESAMN.EDU
FROM: LISETTE.GARCIA@AESAMN.EDU
SUBJECT: OVERLOAD WITH LATE WORK REQUESTS

Hi all,

Daniel and I are flooded with your late work exemption requests. We won't stop accepting them, but please know we are a bit overwhelmed with this commitment on top of our other tasks, and it may take a couple of weeks before you get approval.

Keep up the good fight,

Lisette and Daniel

Lisette Garcia
she/her/hers
Academic Counselor
Alternative Education Solutions Academy

@@@@@@@@

Sent November 12
To: NAOMI.WELLINGTON@AESAMN.EDU
From: NICK.JONES@AESAMN.EDU
Subject: Late Work Policy Breach

Hi Naomi,

When spot-checking your grade book, I noticed several instances of full credit given to work submitted late. I would tolerate a few events of "letting it slide" or "forgetting" because our students are still learning. However, given your tendency to push back and skip meetings, I have less patience for your own learning curve. Some of these assignments were submitted well over a week late, and to offer them full credit in such an egregious act of ignored deadlines is unacceptable from the student, but more so from you.

If you continue to accept late work for full credit, I will have to act accordingly and put a formal reprimand in your evaluation record and consider other consequences as necessary.

Best,

Nick Jones
Department Chair
Society and History Studies
Alternative Education Solutions
"Control your own destiny or someone else will."
Jack Welch

@@@@@@@@

Sent November 13
TO: JESSAMINE LEWIS <STEAMYENERGY@GMAIL.COM>
FROM: NAOMI WELLINGTON <MYOWNPERSON02@GMAIL.COM>
SUBJECT: UNREQUITED LUST

I don't know how she gets away with it, but today at Polar Cafe, Elton John's "Sad Songs" was playing on repeat. Maybe it's because the manager is hardly ever there. Elton John is Tracy's elegiac response to all break-ups.

"What happened, Tracy?"

She sagged onto the register. "He said I didn't have enough ambition."

"Isn't he a valet? At a suburban mall?" This was from Lanh, who was behind me, and joins in with Polar chats now that we often sit for a while talking up books. (Our latest, btw, is *Hotel on the Corner of Bitter and Sweet* by Jamie Ford. The story maps the separation of two friends by means of the Japanese American internment camps.)

Tracy sighed. "Well, yes."

"What a hypocrite!" <<= Sayeed.

"Of course, he also told me he and his ex-girlfriend had been texting, and maybe they decided they should get back together," Tracy added. "But it was the whole 'lack of ambition' that hurt." She pressed both palms to her heart. "Right here, you know?"

"What does he know?" Sayeed punched his fist into the air (he can get really animated; I love it). "You have many years to figure out what you want to do! And then! You can change your mind! It is your prerogative!" Did I tell you Sayeed is madly in love with Tracy? He always takes her side in every debate and even pretends to enjoy hearing all about her latest boyfriend—well, boy*friends*. She does go through them. When I told Lanh about this later—the part about Sayeed, I mean—he surprised me.

"Isn't he gay?" (We were sitting far away in a corner, so neither Sayeed or Tracy heard us, don't worry!)

"Huh. Really? You think so?"

He shrugged, leaning back into his chair to sip out of his coffee like some sort of queer expert.

"Wait," I eyed him suspiciously and tried not to show him how my heart was sinking. "Is it because you hope he is because you're interested in him?"

Then he gave me that huge grin of his, full of beautiful, almost-but-not-quite-straight, white teeth and shook his head. "Nah. You?"

"No!" I admit I said it a bit too emphatically. Hadn't we been flirting with each other? Wasn't it obvious? And then, when I thought about how it might not be obvious to Lanh that I am definitely interested in *him*, I realized maybe Tracy wouldn't recognize Sayeed's fawning after all.

"You look troubled," Lanh told me, leaning back into the table, and then all other thoughts left my head. He was just so...near.

"I'm..."

Then, nothing. I kid you not, I couldn't create another coherent word to force out of my mouth. I started sweating, but my mouth went the opposite direction and dried up. My heart raced, and then he said, "We should go out on a date."

"Yes."

And so we are going on an actual date. Not a coffee shop thing. A real thing. Dinner at Louisa's Diner right here in the gaybor-hood next week.

AAAHHHHH.

-N

@@@@@@@@

Sent November 14
To: Jessamine Lewis <steamyenergy@gmail.com>
From: Naomi Wellington <myownperson02@gmail.com>
Subject: Re: fanfiction revival

So much for the upswing. What type of prescription meds is she taking? It seems like regular stuff isn't doing the trick. What about some kind of meditation? Doesn't she do yoga? I feel like everyone says yoga pretty much solves everything. But I don't mean to joke because it all sucks, Jess. I can't believe what was supposed to be a common break is turning into the most difficult injury for all.

I love the idea of you taking a day off and just hanging with Isaac. Maybe some of that special time with Momma where he gets 100% of the attention will make it so he'll remember home is fun, too. Don't you hate the double-edged sword of a good daycare? We want our kids to be well cared-for and super loved, but you know, not TOO much so that it's better than their momma? Ugh. The Momma-Isaac day will be fun. I remember those younger days with Leyanna when I'd have one of those conference comp days, and she and I would go park-hopping, eat ice cream for lunch, chicken nuggets for a snack, and snuggle on the couch for a movie and microwave popcorn.

I miss those days. Leyanna is already turning into a teenager even if she doesn't have the "teen" in her age yet. She's not all snotty or argumentative like teenaged girls can be, fortunately. Instead, she doesn't talk to me. She doesn't even talk books with me much. She'll still tell me what's she's reading and take my recommendations when I have them, but we used to dive into how much we loved or hated the different characters. I've stooped to binge-watching "Sugar Girl" with her in an effort to "bond." (The struggle is real, Jess.) School isn't going as well for her as I hoped. I knew it might be tough with her friends going to the other middle school, but it's like she's not even trying to make new friends, which wouldn't be *so* bad, except I also don't think she's in contact anymore with her old friends. When I ask her about school, she shrugs. She asked me about doing online classes—again—and I thought about her current grades and would she be a kid who tanks trying to do the intensely independent direction of online school? I told her I needed to see more from her before I would consider it. More what, though? Shouldn't I know what I'm looking for?

She has some friends she hangs out with at lunch, I guess. And during homeroom. Nothing has panned out to do anything with them outside of school, though. I don't want her to lose the social connection. Some of my students already have a strong social life (and sometimes, this is what distracts them from their schoolwork). Others are super isolated. If Leyanna is already on the semi-isolated end of the spectrum, I feel like online school might only intensify the isolation rather than lessen it.

Nab that day with Issac.

Hugs,

-Mimi

P.S. Since we are both falling back into the fanfiction hole, I explored some stuff for *Sugar Girl*. ABORT. Don't go there, Jess. I think it's all written by twelve-year-olds, and I love them for trying, but it's So. Bad.

@@@@@@@@

Sent November 15
TO: NAOMI WELLINGTON <MYOWNPERSON02@GMAIL.COM>
FROM: JESSAMINE LEWIS <STEAMYENERGY@GMAIL.COM>
SUBJECT: ADDITIONAL BRAINS NEEDED AT REGISTERS

Some days I have zero patience. ZIP.

Sales associates have a button they press when the checkout line gets too long. The standard is to use the button with three customers in line beyond the one you are currently helping.

I have a sales associate who presses it when one person is waiting. ONE. By the time anyone arrives to help, she is already working with that one person who had been waiting. She is hopeless. She's been on the job for almost a month and still panics at one person waiting in line as though it's rush-hour traffic time at a Boston roundabout. And don't even with this idea she must have some kind of anxiety. Sometimes "not right for the job" means she is NOT RIGHT FOR THE JOB. I promise you our Sales Leads have worked with her, and it is not anxiety.

Do you remember when you convinced me to work at the State Fair, and I had to work at one of the concessions stands in the coliseum? You know how sensitive my sense of smell is, and all those animal smells from the horse shows made me gag, and I threw up TWICE during the first day. Not. The. Right. Job.

One time a couple of the floor associates grabbed a few items and stood in line with their back to her so she wouldn't notice who they were right away just to mess with her (not my idea and I put a stop to it). Do you know what they found out? Turns out she is a pity-attention addict. When the announcement of "additional assistance requested for north sales" goes out and no one comes (or rather, they get there and catch on to what's happening), they overhear her telling the customer, "I'm *so* sorry for the wait." Then she sighs (you should hear one of my sales leads,

Gilly, imitate her), "they never come when I need help. I just do the best I can and figure it out on my own. Thank you so much for your patience." Most of the time, the customers respond sympathetically and say what a wonderful job she's doing. Gilly heard her do this *seven* times in two weeks. If I never put her on the register, how would she get her attention on the sales floor?

I would have searched for a way to encourage her to find something else if I wasn't worried about having enough people as we get closer to the holiday season. She made it to the one-month mark, which meant she probably wouldn't ghost, so here's what I did. We overstaffed the registers during shifts we had her ringing sales. The other associates brought a bunch of tagging projects with them so they wouldn't get bored (let's not get started on how the drama girl can't seem to multi-task). Within a week, Drama Girl (<— see what you've done to me? I'm nicknaming my employees now) whined about how she didn't have enough to do, and everyone else was taking her customers and "I thought we only had extra people up here when there are three people in line?"

Gilly said, "Oh, it seemed like you still needed a little more time adjusting since you were calling for assistance so often. Are you feeling more comfortable with the workload now?"

Suddenly, Drama Girl was all, "Oh yes, of course. I want to do more. I know I can handle it."

And now? No drama. Well, almost no drama. She can't go too long without some ego-boosting shit, but I'll take it. She's good with customers (even better now, without drumming up false attention), and God knows, we need that right now.

I need it right now. Things are falling apart at home, and at least something is going right at work.

-J

P.S. Check out jsq's latest fic for *Never Now, Always Then*. I love her stuff and this new story? SO GOOD.

@@@@@@@@@

Sent November 15
To: Jessamine Lewis <steamyenergy@gmail.com>
From: Naomi Wellington <myownperson02@gmail.com>
Subject: wobbly

Jess, I am super nervous for this date with Lanh. I don't remember the last time I felt this way. Lucinda, maybe. No, I was only nervous about her coming to her senses about how hot I was *not* in comparison to her. So, Ben. Five years ago. He was the first and only guy I ever saw a future with. What happened to us? Wasn't I madly in love with him? Oh, wait, right. He was a "midnight toker."

Not Lanh. He's too healthy.

TOO HEALTHY. Do I have to order a salad at dinner tonight? DO I, JESS?

I regret all my food and non-exercise choices in the past fifteen years.

-N

Sent November 15
To: Naomi Wellington <myownperson02@gmail.com>
From: Jessamine Lewis <steamyenergy@gmail.com>
Subject: Re: wobbly

Eat all the good food, Mimi. Don't waste salad on him. Test him right away since you know you won't be able to keep up the healthy façade beyond the second date anyway.

Also, wear your orange and blue jersey dress. Those stretchy fabrics cling to you in the best ways. Plus, you are the only white person I know who looks good in orange.

-Jess

Sent November 15
To: Jessamine Lewis <steamyenergy@gmail.com>
From: Naomi Wellington <myownperson02@gmail.com>
Subject: Re: wobbly

This is why we're friends.

@@@@@@@@@

[12:17 16 Nov]

NAOMI

KISSING. THERE WAS KISSING.

JESSAMINE

OMG. Tell me more! I need more!

NAOMI

Not yet. I can't. It's too…perfect right now.

JESSAMINE

@@@@@@@@@

Sent November 16
To: Jessamine Lewis <steamyenergy@gmail.com>
From: Naomi Wellington <myownperson02@gmail.com>
Subject: DATE

Jess,

First of all, WARNING: SUPER LONG EMAIL AHEAD.

Last night was...fabulous.

Where do I start? Oh, right. BOTH of us brought a book. Because, of course, right? This is how we've been connecting so far. He brought *The Bone Season* by Samantha Shannon, and I brought *Landline* by Rainbow Rowell. His was definitely the more intriguing choice (i.e., I think I might have a new series??) I started it last night before bed, and it's steampunk/urban fantasy—a new genre for me, and now that I've started it, I feel like I gave him a cotton ball in comparison. Anyway. I will stand by my choice, though, given how long we talked and how much stuff we covered.

Because, Jess, we talked about So. Much. He has a lot of experience with online learning. He says it saved his life. Being trans now is still hard enough—you can imagine what it must have been like for him to try to be even a part of himself in high school twelve years ago (he's a little younger than us). His mom was a huge advocate for him and found an online program just as online learning was starting to gain some momentum.

"My mom has been an amazing supporter," he told me. "She would march into the office and demand to speak to the principal and chew him out for all kinds of shit. She pretty much demolished his stereotype vision of a 'quiet, smiling, Asian woman.'"

"Had you started transitioning then?" I asked.

"I tried. I cut my hair. Bound my chest—fortunately, I didn't have much going on there, yet—and stupidly tried to wear clothes that made me look like I was part of some gang instead."

Naturally, I eyed his current clothing choice: Plain blue t-shirt tucked into black jeans. Hot.

"Yeah?" he said, grinning. JESS, I SAID "HOT" OUT LOUD.

Whatever. I leaned into it. "Oh yeah. Definitely. What you're wearing now, I mean. Not the gang stuff."

He shrugged. "How do you know I didn't look hot then?"

I lifted an eyebrow—you know how effective my eyebrow lift is—and he laughed. "I *might* have looked hot if I were a little bigger. Instead, I was still barely passing five feet tall with no muscles whatsoever." (He's not all that tall now, around 5'5", I'd guess—a smidge shorter than I am.)

"Was it bad? The stuff you went through in high school?"

He looked away from me at that question, and we let some silence sit between us. "Maybe we don't have to cover *everything* about our lives during this first date?"

"Of course not. I get it. I'm sorry." I was, too. Obviously you, me, and Faith can easily guess a lot of the bad stuff.

"I could tell you some of my shit history if it would make you feel better," I offered, thinking he might smile, but the poor guy only looked sympathetic. "It's fine!" I told him. "It is! I had a safe place to land."

"You needed one?"

"Yep," I nodded without hesitation. "My mom's an addict—though she wasn't always one. My dad disappeared a long time ago, back when one of his and my mom's pyramid schemes went wrong."

"I'm sorry."

"Me too, but not super sorry. I used to wonder if my mom would have stayed off drugs if my dad had stuck around, but then I realized it's quite possible he left her because she started using. I don't know. To be honest, I've always been pretty much an afterthought with them. I used to think it was me, but, you know, counseling. I was unplanned, and they weren't ready. They weren't married or living together or anything."

I mean, dear old dad was no "hold-your-hands-in-the-shape-of-a-heart" guy, you know? (BTW, I made this comment to Lanh, and he joked back how he only half-heartedly does this. You know, because he only has the one hand?)

I told him about basically having to fend for myself most of the time. Surreptitiously, of course, otherwise mom would get all defensive and do something like demand my teachers' phone numbers so she could pretend to be concerned about...what? IDK, a worksheet I turned in a day late? Anyway, it didn't matter anymore after I met you. If home is where the heart is, I told him, then my home was definitely with your family.

We closed out the restaurant and meandered around Powderhorn Park for a bit, holding hands, no more talking. It's a rare person you can just "be" with like that. We walked to the end of the dock, and right there, he turned to me, put his hand along my face, pressed his other arm gently at my side and kissed me.

It was perfect. I've got that swoop in my stomach and the flutter in my heart remembering it.

And it warmed me up because dang, it's getting pretty cold already. Holding hands was a form of weather-proofing, among other lovely things.

We plan on talking about our first impressions of our exchanged books over coffee on Monday.

I've missed this feeling. Maybe I'll finally have...more, this time around.

--Mimi

@@@@@@@@

ORDER [13] *07:59 AM*
-Lanh-
[1] 20 oz
Chai tea
[1] 16 oz
Breve
x-tra Whip
[1] bagel
mple fr toast
[1] scone
cran-orange
[1] apple chips

@@@@@@@@

[Submitted by Josiah Cornell on November 18 at 10:16 PM]

American History

Short Response

1. List the primary causes of the Civil War.

Is this, like, a trick question? I know the readings kind of tried to talk about other stuff, but you said you agreed with us in the discussion thing that the only real cause was slavery, right? I'm just gonna say that for this list. Slavery.

@@@@@@@@

[Submitted by Reese Vaskin on November 19 at 11:53 PM]

Modern World History

Essay Response

3. Discuss the idea of "power" as it meant to France before Napoleon's rule and after it.

Ms. W, this is the first exam question I've seen so far that isn't ridiculous. Doesn't the book *Animal Farm* have a character named Napoleon? He's supposed to be like Stalin, but I can see him like the real life Napoleon, too, who ended up taking everything he wanted by force. You know who else is like Napoleon? My former best friend. She's been starting all kinds of rumors about me, and then that bitch is now dating my ex-boyfriend, which is obviously why she's bad-mouthing me. He's telling her all kinds of lies about how I tricked him into getting me pregnant and how it's probably not his anyway. I thought she was smarter than that fool boy. I may have been the fool to let him not use a condom the one time, but she KNOWS all about him, and still, this is what she does. You know what? They all can go on believing it ain't his baby. I'm sorry as hell it IS his, but I don't have to let him lay claim to it anymore.

@@@@@@@@@

Leyanna Wellington
Language Arts 6
Hour 2
November 15
Defining Moment Rough Draft

I remember the first time I had an asthma attack. I was so scared because I didn't understand how I could feel like I was suffocating when I didn't have anything blocking my face. I was pretty lucky because my gym teacher saw right away what was going on. He had me sit down and got me to breathe through my nose and then got me to the nurse.

My dad took me to the doctor, and that's when I found out I had asthma, and that changed everything. Suddenly I had to carry around an inhaler and be one of those kids where the teacher has to lug around a bag full of medications when going on field trips. I had to be careful during outdoor activities and slow down during gym class—or sometimes sit out from gym altogether. Viruses were especially bad, and I stayed home sick for longer than I used to.

The biggest change was that my mom, who is a teacher, had to change jobs because I was sick so much. My dad said he could take more time off since he owns his own business, but my mom said it would be easier if she just started working from home because my dad's business was so new, so she got a job teaching online. Some of the kids she teaches are like me, kids who miss too much school for lots of reasons. It's an alternative learning high school.

And so, that's how my life changed after being diagnosed with asthma. The doctor said I might grow out of it, and I think she's right because I don't have near as many attacks as I used to.

Leyanna, finding out about something affecting our health can definitely be a defining moment. What is missing from yours, however, is how it directly affected you and changed your life. You talk a little about it with your gym class behavior. If this truly is your defining moment (I'm not sure it is, to be honest), then I want to know more about your perspective and not how it affected others. You're getting there! Keep at it, and let's talk! -Ms. Z

@@@@@@@@@

Sent November 20
TO: NAOMI WELLINGTON <NAOMI.WELLINGTON@MAIL.COM>
FROM: MELANIE ZELLER <MZELLER@PVMS.K12.MN.US>
SUBJECT: LEYANNA'S PROGRESS

Hello Ms. Wellington,

I want to check in with you about Leyanna's grade in Language Arts. I believe you saw her progress report last month, yes? Since then, she has been working more on her Defining Moment essay, and as that is the case, I will be exempting it from this semester's grade and including it as part of her full-year grade. She has also been submitting strong work with reading assignments, but we still have an issue with her incomplete Choice Novel presentation.

Leyanna is clearly a strong and avid reader, so it surprises me she has not yet submitted her presentation. Perhaps you can check in with her about this and let me know what obstacles she's facing so we can help her work through them?

Thank you. It's a pleasure to work with Leyanna.

Melanie Zeller

@@@@@@@@@

Sent November 28
To: Jessamine Lewis <steamyenergy@gmail.com>
From: Naomi Wellington <myownperson02@gmail.com>
Subject: Thanksgiving

Thanksgiving without you is a major bummer. I wish we could have made it out to Washington this year, but all those car repairs this last summer zapped away that plan. I know lots of people think it's weird that I still do Thanksgiving with your family, even when you're not there (they think it will be weird with Jax and Whitney—and it usually isn't, but... well, more on that later). Y'all are my second family, and I love your parents and grandparents so damn much. And my mom... well, you know how it is. Sometimes (like this morning before we headed over to your place), I worry Leyanna is, IDK, missing not knowing her other grandparents, but then I see how happy she is with your mom and dad—how *relaxed*—and I'm okay about it again.

Grams crocheted me a pair of gloves without fingertips because she knows my hands get cold as winter comes.

"You could afford to turn the heat up during the day if you hadn't spent all that money on a fancy new car," your mom told me. Ouch! (Although she's right, I'm broke these days, but don't tell her I said so!)

"Everyone deserves a sweet ride, baby," Gramps came to my rescue.

"What does she need with such a big ride like that, though?" (Yo, I had no idea she had such a problem with me buying a brand new car. She knew my old car was about to fall apart. And I'm 32. Don't I deserve a brand-new car? What am I missing, Jess?)

"Don't be like that, Momma. It's only an SUV, and it's safe," Jax jumped in. "It's protecting your grandbaby."

"Whitney hooked me up with one of her sales colleagues, Momma Junie," I said. "And by referring me, she got a bonus check."

"Oh, did she now? I didn't know that."

And just like that, we were right as rain.

I thought I caught some looks she kept giving me, Jackson, and Whitney, though. They were looks like...IDK, disapproval? There wasn't anything different in how we all were around one another. All things considered, Whitney was doing well in spite of the pregnancy difficulties and the miscarriage, you know? The only weird thing, I suppose, is that it usually *isn't* weird with all of us. Whitney's always been pretty cool, and she and Jax are really good together. So why is your mom giving me the side-eye?

Lanh and I are going on our second date tomorrow night. We're going to the Fitzgerald for an author talk. How perfect is that?

I hope you got Isaac and Livvy to eat more than rolls for your dinner (although, if they were Jax's rolls, who could blame them? I could live on those.) Hugs to those adorable kiddos, you, and Faith.

<3

Mimi

Sent November 28
To: Jessamine Lewis <steamyenergy@gmail.com>
From: Naomi Wellington <myownperson02@gmail.com>
Subject: Re: Thanksgiving

P.S. Just got off the phone with Lanh, who called to wish me a Happy Thanksgiving, and so much stomach swooping. He's picking me up at midnight so we can go Black Friday shopping. I hope you don't mind. I haven't been Black Friday shopping with anyone since you moved away, and I know it won't be the same, but it sounds fun again, so I thought I'd try it.

I'm sorry you probably have to work with crazies like us invading your store! 😾😾

Sent November 28
To: Naomi Wellington <myownperson02@gmail.com>
From: Jessamine Lewis <steamyenergy@gmail.com>
Subject: re: thanksgiving

My momma is the queen of side-eye, so I'm impressed you made it through the day in one piece. I think she's feeling a little closer to Whitney these days because of the miscarriage. Jax is doing good, but you know it isn't the same for men as it is for women. Even if they never heard that baby's heartbeat, you know Whit felt all there was to anticipate since finding out she was pregnant. Momma's feeling overprotective, that's all.

It's a real miracle I am typing up this email right now instead of using my one phone call in prison to call you and tell you how I murdered both my wife and her parents.

Seriously.

You think Momma is overprotective? She only dabbles when compared to Lance and Yolanda. One minute they are all "baby girl this" and "baby doll that" when getting more of the story about Faith's broken arm (which no longer has a cast, but still doesn't seem to be quite healed), and the next, they are telling her to get over herself when she escaped to our bedroom in tears because the pain in her arm has flared up (the pain seems to take over her entire arm and shoulder, Mimi, I don't get it. Can a nerve get broken? Or nicked or something?) She's crying, and they're blowing her off. God forbid I come to her defense, though, because Faith then yelled at me to stop talking to her parents "that way" and, well, you know how her parents feel about me. No penis, no power.

The kids are with them now, seeing a movie, allowing me to breathe for two seconds. Faith and I argued, but then she broke down.

"I'm so tired of being in so much pain, Jess. I don't know what I'm saying half the time. I'm sorry."

"Please go back to the doctor," I told her. "There has to be something else going on with your arm. Maybe it didn't heal right."

Because Mimi, this can't possibly be normal. She got her cast off last week, but it's almost as if she is in more pain than when it was on. Plus, it still looks swollen and a couple of her fingers are a weird color. I got her to agree to call on Monday to schedule an appointment.

Until then, remember you promised to be the kind of friend that would help me bury bodies because lord help me, I've got two more days with the in-laws from hell.

-Jess

P.S. I'm headed to work in about two hours to deal with crazy people like you and Lanh. Like the crazy person I used to be when we'd do it together. Have fun. I mean it.

@@@@@@@@@

Sent November 29
To: naomi.wellington@aesamn.edu
From: josiah.cornell@student.aesamn.edu
Subject: make-up exams

Hi Ms. W,

I'm sorry I've been missing tests. I dropped my laptop a couple of weeks ago and I've been trying to do everything on my phone but I ran out of data and we don't have internet at the apartment I'm renting with three other people and I can't afford more data because all of my paycheck from the grocery store goes to rent and food. Thank you for letting me make them up past the regular due date I appreciate it so much I'll try to do better this next month.

Josiah

@@@@@@@@@

Sent November 29
To: Naomi Wellington <naomi.wellington@mail.com>
From: Voice Messaging <voicemessaging@clear-voice.com>
Subject: New Voice Message from 612-555-3655

Naomi, it's your mother. Remember me? No, I guess you wouldn't since all those years ago when you went and got yourself a new family. I burned a turkey yesterday waiting for you to show up, but you never do show up, do you? I even went through the effort of staying sober until the goddamn smoke alarm went off from the goddamn turkey. I hope your new bitch momma Junie's meal was—

@@@@@@@@

BOARD: MOBY DICK by Hermann Melville

▽ **TOPIC:** Discussion Question 1: Why does Ahab pursue Moby Dick so single-mindedly?

Naomi: Alternate Discussion Question #1: Who cares why Ahab does anything? How far did you make it in this book before giving up?

Tyrell: 4 chapters

Grant: 10

Naomi: Wow, 10 chapters?

Grant: No, 10 pages.

Susette: 1

Tyrell: Susette, one chapter, and you're the one posting the first discussion question?

Susette: Sure, why not? Sounds like hardly anyone else read much more than I did, so doesn't matter much since nothing's really going to come of it.

Lisa: The whole thing. What is wrong with all of you?

Susette: Oh, well I guess Lisa could have started us out after all. SORRY.

Chester: Of course you read the whole thing. Of course.

Lisa: Kind of hard to have any intelligent things to say about a book if you don't read it, dipshit.

Chester: Nice. FYI, I read almost half the book, asshat, and my intelligent thing to say about the book is that it's way overplayed in its symbolism. I don't need to read the whole book to know where it's going and how it will end up. (Although to be fair, I already knew some stuff about it before starting out.)

Lisa: Well, douchebag, I'll grant you Melville is a bit heavy-handed in the symbolism and allusion categories, but it's kind of refreshing to read someone who seems to have really done this on purpose. I can't believe how often other authors kind of accidentally fall into something like that, and we give them way too much credit.

Chester: Gee, thanks, jerk face.

Tyrell: There's a kick-ass song by Led Zeppelin called Moby-Dick, and it's less than five minutes long. I vote we analyze that instead of the book.

Naomi: Amen to that, T.

Chester: I can get behind that.

Grant: Done. I'll start by saying Bonzo's drumming in Achilles Last Stand beats out that long solo on Moby Dick by far.

Tyrell: My man, you're not wrong, but the longevity going on in Moby Dick. That's gotta count for something.

Naomi: Wait, we're analyzing Moby Dick, not the whole Led Zeppelin collective, right? That being said, the opening riffs in Moby Dick surely make you think of that whaling boat just zipping along in pursuit, doesn't it?

Grant: Yeah, I can see that. Then the drum solo starts in on Ahab's introspection and obsession, yeah?

Lisa: So, this is what we're doing?

Chester: Embrace it, Lisa. Let's all grab a packet of Pop Rocks and jam with it all.

Lisa: Fine. Bonzo's got some smooth shimmer riffs that amp up the tension that remind me of Ahab's and Peleg's quick thinking.

Tyrell: And the repetitive riffs are all about those long-ass sections that talk about sailing or whaling or whatever I skimmed through.

Susette: The only song I know by Led Zeppelin is Stairway to Heaven. Is that anything like Moby Dick?

DECEMBER

Sent December 03
TO: NAOMI WELLINGTON <MYOWNPERSON02@GMAIL.COM>
FROM: JESSAMINE LEWIS <STEAMYENERGY@GMAIL.COM>
SUBJECT: THANK YOU FOR LISTENING TO MY RAGEY SCREAM ON YOUR VM

I wish you had been available, but maybe it's for the best you didn't get more than just that scream. I would have been nonstop yelling before you even got out your hello.

Male doctors for female patients are fucking horrible. Add in white, and I can't think of anything worse. I took Faith to the doctor because she was in no shape to drive on her own today. She was on the last of her Percocet, which was a victory itself since she's been resisting the hard-core painkillers. The nurse gave me the side-eye when I got up to walk with Faith to the exam room.

"Only family members with permission, ma'am."

What bullshit. "No," I said, "*anyone* with the patient's permission. Also, I'm her wife."

She turned to Faith. "Ms. Baker? Am I allowing your friend—"

"—*wife,*" I interjected. What. The. Fuck. I swear to God I was ready to beat her down. We weren't at our regular clinic. Faith was looking for the earliest appointment with this doc she could get, and he didn't have any openings at our regular clinic.

Faith managed a nod. I wished she would have been able to do more, although she probably wouldn't have, even if she were in good shape. She's all about "measured responses." Fuck that.

The nurse started to take Faith's blood pressure—*by putting the cuff on her left arm.*

"Are you really this incompetent?" I yelled. "That's the arm giving her so much pain!"

"Jess," Faith warned me, even though she looked like she was going to pass out.

"Damn it, don't 'Jess' me." I turned back to the nurse. "Stop. Touching her. We would like a new nurse."

"There's no need to overreact."

"We want a new nurse."

"I'll simply—"

"We want a different nurse. Not you. A nurse that is not you. A completely not-you nurse."

"Maybe we should just go, Jess," Faith whispered, and my heart near broke.

"Not until we see the doctor. And a different nurse."

The bitch nurse finally caught my rage-filled glare and left the room.

We waited twenty more minutes until a different nurse came in. Black, thank you, baby Jesus.

By the time we finally saw the doctor—thirty minutes later—Faith was lying on the floor with her head in my lap. The first thing Doc Asshole did was scold me for letting Faith lie on the floor instead of the bed. As if I didn't try that already. As if he didn't know we were all alone for a half-hour. And what about being worried or concerned? Shouldn't he be ALARMED at what he walked in to see?

No. I guess not. He told Faith to get up and sit on the table. He didn't even help us. No way he was this awful when he treated her before. She would have told me. She would have made sure to see a different doctor. That bitch nurse must have told him he was about to walk in on an Angry Black Woman.

He examined Faith's arm. She cried out each place he touched from her wrist up to her elbow. His conclusion after that two-minute exam? He said it was probably high blood pressure (because obviously, it was super high when the nurse finally took it), and she was probably over-using the arm. She needed to take it easy and do the recommended exercises he gave her after they took the cast off.

"Aren't you going to take another x-ray?"

"I don't see any reason to. We took one when we removed the cast, and everything had healed up nicely. If she were treating it correctly, I'm sure she'd no longer be experiencing any pain."

And that was it.

Mother. Fucker.

Faith is locked in our bedroom again and Isaac's crying. Gotta go.

-J

@@@@@@@@

GENERAL OFFENSE POLICE REPORT
PUBLIC INFORMATION RECORD

Bkg date	Bkg time	Name of Suspect	Age	Address
12/03	3:44PM	KRISTINE WELLINGTON	48	000 block, Eastbound 6th St. SE
Offense 1		**Offense 2**		
MOV-RECKLESS		DWI-DRIVING WHILE INTOX		

@@@@@@@@

DRAFT

To: Jessamine Lewis <steamyenergy@gmail.com>
From: Naomi Wellington <myownperson02@gmail.com>
Subject: MOM

There is nothing more that I dread than a call from the police about my mother. I will say this, though, she's excellent at not getting caught for the same thing twice, usually.

Except for this time. Another DWI. At least she didn't hurt anyone.

I hate walking into the police station. Half of the people stare at me with pity, and the other half paint me up and down with disapproval, as though I should be able to keep my mother in line, make her a better person.

I've never learned how to fix her. For as long as I can remember, I've only been a prop to help run all of her schemes, a display case for all the fake shit she and my dad used to sell, a scapegoat for all the failures in her life. Why couldn't I be the model instead of the box full of blame?

Is it wrong of me to want the attorney to advocate for jail time so I could have a couple of months' peace from having to deal with her? Instead, she'll wander free, and I'll be the one paying all the fines. Maybe I shouldn't have gotten that new SUV after all.

And now I'm re-reading all I've written while remembering your email about the doctor visit.

I can't send this message to you. You have too much on your end to deal with rather than put up with all my stale baggage.

@@@@@@@@@

Sent December 04
To: Jessamine Lewis <steamyenergy@gmail.com>
From: Naomi Wellington <myownperson02@gmail.com>
Subject: Nick the Dick, Volume 37

First, I am SUPER relieved to know that you have an appointment set with Faith's regular doctor. The other guy was a complete tool. All I want for Christmas is for things to settle down for you both. I hate how tired and stressed out you've been. I wish we didn't live so far away from each other.

On the other hand, if you lived too close, you'd have to put up with me vomiting constant complaints about Nick the Dick IRL instead of through email (and texts)--probably over coffee at the fabulous Polar Cafe, obvs.

And speaking of Nick the Dick. Have I told you lately how annoying he is? Yes, yes, but seriously. How does a teacher who clearly doesn't want his students to succeed become a teacher? Or stay a teacher? I hate to say he fits the stupid phrase, "those who can't, teach" because OMG, he "can't" at anything. What I'm discovering to be worse is our interim director. It's like he and Nick are in cahoots. I guess idiots find other idiots pretty quickly?

Nick's newest initiative required students to log in for a minimum amount of time during "regular school hours," All the other department heads shot that idea down so fast; I regained a little hope.

For book club this month, we were initially thinking of reading Charles Dickens' *Great Expectations*, but then Susette thought it was too long of a book to tackle in December, which is such a busy month with Christmas and all. Of course, Lisa chimed in with NOT EVERYONE CELEBRATES JESUS, FFS, and Chester (who I think might have a thing for Lisa because he loves to yell back at her) said, JFC, NO NEED TO NAIL SUSETTE TO THE CROSS ABOUT IT (*snort*). Then Grant, ever the mollifier, stepped in and suggested *The Great Gatsby* because that was on the list, it's shorter, and isn't it supposed to be about excess? I agreed, mainly because, as you know, I might be a little bit in love with him (don't tell Lanh). And then Maxine said Fitzgerald was from Minnesota, which sealed the deal.

Speaking of Christmas, even though Lisa clearly doesn't celebrate it (FFS) and Faith only tolerates it, can you please send me Olivia and Isaac's deepest desired wishes? I have to maintain my reputation as the Bestest Auntie.

Love and hugs to you and the fam (gentle hugs for Faith, of course, as I don't want to set off any pain triggers!),

Mimi

@@@@@@@@@

STATE OF MINNESOTA
DISTRICT COURT
COUNTY OF HENNEPIN
05 DECEMBER

* * *

State of Minnesota, Plaintiff

v.

KRISTINE WELLINGTON (DOB: 08/11/71), Defendant
CRIMINAL COMPLAINT:

_X_ Summons ___ Warrant___ Order of Detention

_X_ Plea Agreement

The Complainant, being duly sworn, makes complaint to the Court
and states that there is probable cause to believe that Defendant
committed the following offense(s):

Count I
Charge: Moving Vehicle Violation: Reckless Driving
Offense Level: Misdemeanor
Offense Plea: __ Not Guilty_X_ Guilty
Sentence: Waived

Count II
Charge: Driving While Intoxicated (2nd off)
Offense Level: Gross Misdemeanor
Offense Plea: __ Not Guilty_X_ Guilty
Sentence: $2000 fine. Plates – impound. Driving privileges revoked:
1 yr or 3 consecutive successful chemical health assessments

@@@@@@@@@

Sent December 05
To: HISTORYSTUDIES_GROUP@AESAMN.EDU
FROM: NICK.JONES@AESAMN.EDU
SUBJECT: DECEMBER DEPARTMENT MEETING RECORDING

Hello colleagues,

Here is the link to yesterday's Society and History Studies department meeting. A reminder that if you missed the meeting, you are required to view the recording within 24 hours and complete the form with the code phrase used within the meeting, and are immediately responsible for any and all decisions and policy changes made herein.

Special note to key issues that arose when discussing re-takes and re-doing assignments:

If a student has willfully left answers blank or given answers that do not match the parameters of the questions, the student has demonstrated a lack of preparation or respect when opening the exam and may not re-take it.

Assignments may be resubmitted at the instructor's discretion; however, completion must still reflect the nature and directions of the original assignment.

It is essential we all adhere to these policies to achieve consistent expectations for all of our students.

Please reply directly to me with any questions regarding these issues.

Best,

Nick Jones
Department Chair
Society and History Studies
Alternative Education Solutions
"Without continual growth and progress, such words as improvement, achievement, and success have no meaning." - Benjamin Franklin

@@@@@@@@

Sent December 06
To: NAOMI.WELLINGTON@AESAMN.EDU
FROM: JULIETTE.SORENSON@MAIL.COM
SUBJECT: CARSON

Dear Ms. Wellington,

My son, Carson Jennings-Sorenson, is a student in your American History course. As I've been monitoring his grades, I've noticed Carson turning in many late assignments and getting full credit for them. I do not know what kind of sad songs he's been playing for you, but I assure you he is not taking courses through this school due to being a juvenile delinquent. He has severe allergies to both foods and materials, preventing him from easily leaving the house. He should never need any sort of leeway or extension for his work as his time is well-structured and, to be honest, rather limitless should that structure not be open enough.

We had several options for online learning for our son and were assured your curriculum was rigorous and would offer challenge. I'm not sure we have seen either of these selling points. Back in October, we received communications about the late work policy, and we helped Carson re-structure his time, allowing him ample opportunity to complete and submit all his American History work on time. Firstly, to find out he's been submitting work late and not finding this out until now is troublesome. Secondly, to offer him full credit for this same late work certainly de-incentivizes him, and thirdly, it encourages poor work ethics.

If we cannot expect you to hold our son to high standards, we will have to take other measures to either remove him from your class or, if necessary, remove him from this school altogether.

Regards,

Mrs. Juliette Sorenson

@@@@@@@@@

Sent December 07
To: Jessamine Lewis <steamyenergy@gmail.com>
From: Naomi Wellington <myownperson02@gmail.com>
Subject: snow day

I remember when snow days were the best days. Unfortunately, when you teach online, there's no such thing because no travel means no worries about the weather. And today is worse because I don't have Leyanna staying home to keep me company since it's Jackson's week. I slogged through the snow to the cafe, though, because no way I'm making it through this day when all my former F2F classroom colleagues are eating bonbons while watching the latest episodes of *Big Little Lies* on HBO On-Demand. Is "eating bonbons" still a thing? Maybe it's eating cake pops instead.

Disappointingly, Lanh worked from home today, leaving me to fly solo. When I arrived, Sayeed and Dark-Haired Indian Man of the Brilliant Colored Shirts (DHIMBCS) were highly engaged in conversation. I mean, the flirty kind of engagement. Maybe Lanh's right and Sayeed is gay, although I'm still going with at least bi because I know I'm not wrong about his secret flame for Tracy. Watching him talk to DHIMBCS, I saw a definite connection, though. And Tracy? She was kind of testy when taking my order, which was a first. "I'll type in 'no whip,' I guess, which we all know is a farce since Sayeed will fill you up on it anyway." Bang-bang-bang on the keys of the register.

"It's sort of a sneaky fun," I told her half-heartedly.

"Whatever."

I suppose it didn't help we were the only three people in the cafe, which highlighted Sayeed and DHIMBCS' laughter and obvious enjoyment with each other. When Sayeed handed me my Breve, I leaned in a little extra and whispered, "Nice going! You should give it a go with him."

"He's nice, but—" and then he glanced over at Tracy.

"You don't have to marry him. If you're not going to take a chance on her, you might as well have some fun with *him*."

He only shrugged at me.

I brought my computer and worked at the cafe, figuring it would be dead. It was a nice change of pace, and Tracy eventually stopped banging around on things after DHIMBCS left.

She came to sit with me a bit, splitting a piece of lemon cake because it was a snow day and why not. She finished up an online course last week and didn't know if she'd take another one. She thought it was cool to interact with others on a discussion board, but the teacher barely did anything at all and hardly gave any feedback on her work. "Did I earn the 'A' or was it her way of making her life easier if she didn't have to tell me what I did wrong?"

Sometimes I wonder if my students would rather I simply slap a number into the grade book and be done instead of making them re-do stuff or calling on them to do more—well, naturally they'd rather I do the easy thing, let's be real. I hope they are old enough to kind of appreciate the attention I give to their work in spite of a willingness to admit it out loud.

I mean, that was me. One of the ones appreciating the time teachers gave to me. No one was checking on my grades or anything, except for Ms. Stone, my World Studies teacher, and Mr. Warner, the school counselor. In hindsight, I'm betting Mr. Warner pretty much knew what was up with me and what I had going on at home. Probably he and Ms. Stone worked together to keep me following my goals, you know? I didn't know how I was going to do college, and they helped me figure out the community college thing and apply for scholarships and figure out how I could do it all, even if I didn't complete my degree in four years. They helped me see beyond the next day and to have hope. Hope of getting away from my mom and dad. Hope of being surrounded by health and positivity all of the time and not only in the bubble of your house.

This is what I want for my students. I want them to see further than tomorrow. I want them to get a glimpse of what can be instead of only what is. I don't know if it's working. I only know I have to keep trying.

-N

@@@@@@@@@

[6:38 08 Dec]

NAOMI

Do you cook?

LANH

I am an amazing cook

NAOMI

Like, you have the perfect proportions for mac and cheese amazing? Or Food Network amazing?

LANH

Yes

NAOMI

Hm

LANH

Expand upon this "hm"

NAOMI

I was kind of hoping you were more like Food Channel good, not Food NETWORK good so I could show off my new Test Kitchen recipes.

LANH

You can still show off. Come to my place on Friday, and we'll cook together

NAOMI

@@@@@@@@@

[Submitted by Lucy Clark on December 09]

American History

1. How has the United States benefitted from the idea of Manifest Destiny? What have been some drawbacks?

Uh, "some drawbacks"? The whole thing is one huge drawback. Is this really how we are looking at it? I thought all of our research made it clear that Manifest Destiny is 100% racist? The whole thing is a drawback.

Oh wait, we white people have gotten ALL the benefits. But who IS the United States? White people or Every People?

@@@@@@@@@

Reese Vaskin

Current Events Seminar

Naomi Wellington

This Week In the News

December 11

"Another Insta Pot Explosion"

And by Insta Pot, I mean this baby cooking in my stomach, and by explosion, I mean I've about had it with my parents. My dad is still the Parent Who Would Be a Brick Wall, and now my mom is insisting I give my baby up for adoption. Look, I'm not stupid. I know adoption is a good choice, maybe the smarter choice. But I can't. I know I can be a good mom. I can make it work. This is MY kid. MY choice.

Right?

BTW, the headline is real. People are dumb. This woman stuffed it full of potatoes and beans, and the beans got so big it blasted the lid right off. I would never be so stupid. No risks with my baby because no way is she going to think I'm dumb. It's why I'm still doing this online stuff. I'm going to get my diploma. I don't know about college yet, because I don't know where to stay since I don't think my daddy will let me live at home with the baby, and my mom obviously doesn't want her grandbaby girl.

It's a girl. Did I tell you that yet? I already know her name. Fabiola, like in *American Street*? Then I can call her Fabulous, just like in the book, too.

@@@@@@@@@

Sent December 12
To: Jessamine Lewis <steamyenergy@gmail.com>
From: Naomi Wellington <myownperson02@gmail.com>
Subject: Leyanna sick again

Even though Leyanna seems to be growing out of the asthma (thank all the beings in the universe), she still gets sick a lot. I don't know if it's because her immune system is still so weakened or what. It's mostly stomachaches, although she hardly ever throws up, and by late afternoon or dinner time, it starts to go away. We have enough saltine crackers in this house to feed twenty snacking women in their first trimester of pregnancy.

On the plus side, I have gotten super good at making homemade soup! Beans, noodles, rice, vegetables, you name it, I can soup it up! Leyanna always raves about Jax's breads (I'm not arguing this point because we all know that Jax is the God of Gluten, bless that man for always sending extra loaves back with Leyanna after her weeks with him), but finally, *finally*, I heard from him that she now sings the praises of my soups. There is hope for me, yet! I've been starting to watch *America's Test Kitchen* during my lunch hour, and yesterday I made Jerk Chicken (to go along with the cornbread Jax dropped off), and it was pretty tasty. There were leftovers, so you should come on by for lunch (I WISH).

I am bringing today's vegetable soup to Whitney and hoping I don't say anything stupid. I don't think she's happy that Jax shared with Leyanna and me that she is pregnant again. I know he's your brother, but I can't say I blame her for being upset with his loose lips on this one. All of the extra exaggerated, sympathetic tones have to be the most annoying thing ever. Fortunately, she has an interesting job, and I can ask her to vent about all the ways customers dealt with their car repairs at the dealer today. One day, I'm going to be there to witness a guy's face when he tries to talk down to her about car shit, and she'll talk circles around him with how much she knows. I love how Leyanna is learning how to maintain my car, even though she's years from driving one.

Metaphorical piles of exams await my grading. I'm off to check on the girl, then slam my head against the wall for each clueless answer to the differences between socialism and capitalism.

-N

@@@@@@@@@

Sent December 12
To: Jessamine Lewis <steamyenergy@gmail.com>
From: Naomi Wellington <myownperson02@gmail.com>
Subject: big mistake

Shit, shit, shit. I should NOT have brought that soup to Whitney. She was über-pissed off at me. It's hormones, right? I'm going to go cry and hope to God that my freakishly perceptive daughter doesn't guess that I have wrecked the relationship with her step-mom.

@@@@@@@@@

[7:11 Dec 12]

NAOMI

God, Jax, I'm sorry about upsetting Whitney.

JACKSON

?

NAOMI

This afternoon? When I tried to bring over some soup?

JACKSON

You stopped by? Whit didn't say anything about it.

NAOMI

Oh, well, nvm, then.

JACKSON

Nuh-uh. What?

NAOMI

I brought soup. To maybe help her stomach. She got... upset with me. Probably because I'm not supposed to know she's pregnant. Probably because

NAOMI

she's stressed out about it. I get it! It's scary this time around, isn't it? Anyway, I'm sorry.

JACKSON

...

NAOMI

...

JACKSON

...

NAOMI

Are you mad at me?

JACKSON

No. I was thinking. I don't get why she didn't tell me about you coming by. She's probably embarrassed by her reaction.

NAOMI

Whitney? Embarrassed?

JACKSON

Yeah, I know, but you're right. She's scared. We both are.

NAOMI

I'm so sorry.

JACKSON

You're good, Nay, don't worry. Thanks for trying to connect with Whitney right now. Means a lot to me. Am I picking up Leyanna Saturday, or are you dropping her off?

NAOMI

I'm going out that night, so if you can pick her up, that would help.

JACKSON

Hot date with coffee guy?

NAOMI

Kinda.

JACKSON

"Kinda"? Damn, girl. 'Bout time.

NAOMI

It hasn't been THAT long.

JACKSON

NAOMI

SHUT UP.

@@@@@@@@@

Sent December 13
To: JESSAMINE LEWIS <STEAMYENERGY@GMAIL.COM>
FROM: NAOMI WELLINGTON <MYOWNPERSON02@GMAIL.COM>
SUBJECT: THIRD DATE

I know he's your brother, but OMG, Jax has the BIGGEST MOUTH. I was driving home from the store with Leyanna when he called about how he might be late picking her up tomorrow.

"I got an afternoon home call, so I might be a little bit later picking up our girl. But only, like, fifteen minutes or so, that cool?" he said.

"I can drop her off if you want."

"Won't that cut short your glam time?"

I mean. What. Does he even know what words are coming out of his mouth.

"My 'glam' time?"

"Yeah, you know. You gotta get ready for some possible down and di—"

"JACKSON!" OMG, Jess, he HAD to have known I was on speaker in the car. It gets all echo-ey!

"What? It's the third date, isn't it?" he said.

And now, Leyanna is at full attention. "Holy shit, Mom, you've been *dating* someone? How did I not know this?"

"Dammit, Jax!" And then I hung up on him.

And then Leyanna started giving me the third degree. She wasn't even mad. She was *excited*.

What's their name? Where did you meet him? When did you meet him? When do I get to meet him? Is he totally hot?

At that point, I couldn't help it, I smiled, and she shrieked. I mean, the highest-pitched, loudest thing ever, and I almost crashed the car into a neighbor's trash can that was sitting on the curb for pick-up day.

"Why did Dad make a big deal about it being the third date?"

And then Jax texted, and of course that came through on the display, and we almost got into another accident as I tried to hit "ignore" while Leyanna beat me to the "read."

"Sorry. Swear to God I did not know you were in the car with Ley. But seriously, tomorrow, GET IT, GIRL."

That's what he said. "Get it, girl." WHAT IS THAT? Your brother is the biggest weirdo. Also, listening to the female robotic AI voice say "get it, girl" is pretty much exactly how it would sound out of Jax's mouth, so he might as well have still been on the phone.

"Fix your dad," I told Leyanna, who by then was laughing too hard to even care about the fact that her mom was contemplating sex tomorrow night.

OhmygodI'mcontemplatingsextomorrownight.

CALL ME ASAP.

-N

Sent December 14
To: Jessamine Lewis <steamyenergy@gmail.com>
From: Naomi Wellington <myownperson02@gmail.com>
Subject: third date TMI

What was I worried about? #hotashell

Sent December 14
To: Naomi Wellington <myownperson02@gmail.com>
From: Jessamine Lewis <steamyenergy@gmail.com>
Subject: Re: third date TMI

Holy fuck.

Also, I feel like a total bitch for saying it, but I am so jealous of you right now. I miss my wife in so many ways.

@@@@@@@@@

Sent December 17
To: Naomi Wellington <myownperson02@gmail.com>
From: Jessamine Lewis <steamyenergy@gmail.com>
Subject: road trip

So here I was, checking in with Leyanna to see how things were after the social studies class discussion debacle and find out she wasn't even in on Monday because she was in some town I've never heard of in northern Minnesota with you and Jackson.

You and Jackson. No Whitney. And Momma didn't know he was on this secret trip because I talked to her yesterday, and she said she was going to drop off a casserole. Still, Whitney said she would be at her sister's place for a few days, so it would be just Jax, so she decided to just throw the dish in the freezer until Whitney would be back.

Jax isn't returning my texts.

What. Is. Going. On.

Sent December 17
TO: JESSAMINE LEWIS <STEAMYENERGY@GMAIL.COM>
FROM: NAOMI WELLINGTON <MYOWNPERSON02@GMAIL.COM>
SUBJECT: RE: ROAD TRIP

Wow, Jess, maybe you should have just texted me, then, instead of building everything up into some big suspicious, accusatory email. (And wait, what social studies class discussion debacle? Leyanna didn't mention anything to me.)

"Nothing. Is. Going. On." Geez. I mean, there was a thing, but it's not some big secret. Maxine from my book club told us she was trapped in her house. Completely snowed in, and she is kind of a hermit, I guess. Lives in the middle of nowhere and doesn't socialize much with most of her neighbors who, in other normal situations, would help her. She seemed pretty scared, so a couple of us jumped into a private chat and decided to head up her way to help her out. Dig her out, take her shopping, the whole nine yards. I asked Jax if Leyanna could stay with him and Whitney one more night, but he got all Neanderthal on me and said he didn't want me driving up alone.

"God, Jax, if I break down on the way up (which I won't because I have a brand new, rocking' SUV whether your Momma approves of it or not), I would do the exact same thing you would do. Use my 21st-century technology and call for help."

"That's not what I'm worried about. You've never met any of these online book club people in real life. What if they aren't who they say they are?"

I wish we had been talking F2F because if he had seen my expression, he would have been backing away slowly, then turning it high tail to run fast. Seriously, J. I know he's your brother but HELLO? Online teacher, here? We are all required to teach a one-week cyber safety course throughout the school year. Besides, no one is who they say they are online anyway.

I tried to force calm into my voice before I replied, "Jax. Really?"

He sighed out in that way he does. I could just see his eyeballs shooting straight up and out of his head. "Isn't there anyone else you can take with you? It doesn't have to be me."

I had thought about Lanh, but IDK, were we really at that point in our relationship? Were we even *in* a relationship? I mean, sure, we had sex, but does that *mean* anything? JESSAMINE, I AM SO OUT OF PRACTICE WITH DATING AND RELA-TIONSHIPS. Besides, I needed to get going ASAP, and I couldn't ask anyone to just drop everything for someone they didn't know, and it wasn't like Maxine had a medical emergency.

Anyway, we argued back and forth, and IDK how it happened, but suddenly Leyanna was coming with us, too.

And then we got up to Maxine's place, and oh, my heart sank so low, you don't even know. I don't think anyone had cleared her driveway or sidewalk all season yet (and that isn't even why my heart hurt). We spent all afternoon clearing the fresh foot and a half of snow and then chipped away at the other six inches of packed snow and ice. (I got to meet Grant, btw! He is as nice in person as he is online, and it turns out he lives in Richfield! Also, Lisa was there—you know, the one who is hypercritical of how women are written? She swears just as much in person as she does online, and even though she still did it around Leyanna, Lisa was so kind and friendly I didn't care at all—and shut up, I know you're laughing your ass off now, considering every terrible thing Leyanna has learned has come from me—SHUT UP.)

We worked forever to clear all that ice and snow, and afterward, she invited us in for hot chocolate, and that was the moment my heart squeezed so tightly. Maxine is a hoarder. I don't mean, "wow, she's got a lot of stuff." I mean an actual hoarder. We barely knew where to stand. It was like a maze. Every inch along the walls had stacks of something. *People* magazines. The local newspaper (super well-stacked; I can't believe how tall the stacks were, yet they were solid/sturdy). An entire four-shelf bookshelf holding Rubik's cubes instead of books. Most weren't even out of the original packaging. Drawers that weren't part of a dresser were stacked haphazardly and filled with spoons. Bunches of vacuum cleaners (ironic), floor lamps, and super odd: cat trees. Lisa asked if she had cats, and Maxine said, "no, never had any cats. I'm allergic." What. Which is basically what Lisa asked (well, tbh, Lisa asked, "why the fuck would you have all these fucking scratching post thingies, then?") to which Maxine only laughed, saying it was so much fun to *hear* Lisa talk that way in real life, to change up the voice she had in her head. (Me too, obvs, except I imagined a much lower voice—like if she smoked or something, but no, it's not high-pitched, although still much more modulated than I expected. Plus, Lisa is adamantly NOT a smoker. I won't repeat the tirade she let loose upon me when I joked about my online vision of her.)

Thankfully, Maxine gave us our hot chocolate in Styrofoam cups because I honestly didn't want to have to guess at whether or not her dishes were clean, which might not be fair since I was probably only projecting from what you see on TV, you know? That hoarding also equals gross. Her house was overwhelming, but I guess it didn't seem grimy.

It got a little embarrassing, though, when she tried to find places for us to sit. We all gave Leyanna the one chair that only needed two things removed from it while Lisa and I sat on the very edge of a loveseat, leaving Grant and Jax to say they were fine standing. I felt bad for them because they had to have been exhausted like we were from all the snow work.

There was a table holding HUGE stacks of Amazon boxes--the kind that holds a couple of books each. A few were open (with the books still inside). However, the majority were still sealed. It got me wondering how many might be duplicates because how would you know what you have if you never opened the package? I guess Amazon tells you if you've ordered something before, so there's that. In spite of the horrors of ridiculous tons of crap in her house, I nearly drooled all over that table. I wanted badly to rip open every single box and swim in the sea of crisp, lovely-smelling new pages. Jackson caught my lascivious glances towards that table and fanned himself. He's such a dork. Okay, fine, I'm the dork he was teasing, but whatever.

Maxine was so gracious, just like she is in the book club discussions. I don't know why she is isolated and a hoarder, but I am so grateful that she is still able and willing to interact with people. And then we found out the BEST story. Do you remember how I told you she had a shitty neighbor being mean to her? Turns out they're friends, now! She met him face-to-face, but they've been video chatting daily. He's taken on clearing her sidewalk and driveway, but recently broke his leg, and could we stop in and check on him before we left? Maybe clear his driveway, too?

Regardless of whatever you were thinking before, I'm grateful Jax came along after all. He lightened the load. Plus, I always love watching him and Leyanna together.

-N

@@@@@@@@

breathe

by leyanna

when you can't breathe

your brain shuts down

when you can't breathe

your brain goes into hyperdrive

when you can't breathe

you stare at all the faces

when you can't breathe

you are weak

when you can breathe

you are strong and yet

when you can breathe

you are still weak

when you can breathe

you are still trapped

when you can breathe

the faces remain

when you can breathe

it all stays the same

@@@@@@@@@

Sent December 18
To: naomi.wellington@aesamn.edu
From: Nick.Jones@aesamn.edu
Subject: roster change

Naomi,

I am preemptively transferring Carson Newhouse-Sorenson from your American History Section III course to Scott Cantor's American History Section I. I have been in contact with Mrs. Sorenson, and we agreed this switch was in Carson's best interests. Students first, of course.

Additionally, both Mark and I will be increasing our spot checks into grade books to ensure consistency of evaluation and adherence to policies. While I have not seen any issues with Carson's submitted work and subsequent evaluation and feedback (other than the lack of deductions due to late submission), I cannot discount Mrs. Sorenson's observations and complaints. Parents are our clients, too. She felt your response did not fully appreciate her goals and objectives for Carson, and I hope you will keep this in mind regarding future parent communications.

Best,

Nick Jones
Department Chair
Society and History Studies
Alternative Education Solutions
"One of the tests of leadership is the ability to recognize a problem before it becomes an emergency." - Arnold Glasgow

@@@@@@@@

[9:24 Dec 18]

NAOMI

My mom stopped by today, high as a kite. Guess she's not going to be passing any of those random "chemical health assessments" anytime soon

JACKSON

Damn

JACKSON

She looking for money?

NAOMI

As always. I guess it wasn't enough for me to pay her legal fees and fines

JACKSON

You okay with money?

NAOMI

Yeah, I mean, things are kind of tight, like usual, but we'll be okay.

JACKSON

Don't be a martyr about it

NAOMI

Shut it. I'm not. I'm good.

NAOMI

I'm glad Leyanna's back with you this week. At least my mom cares enough to know when Leyanna's not around

JACKSON

You think she's ever clear-headed enough for that?

NAOMI

My mom? IDK. She might keep watch. She's
done that sort of thing before

JACKSON

You okay?

NAOMI

I mean. Yeah. I guess. She said some stuff

JACKSON

None of it's true, Nay. Don't let her get into
your head like that

NAOMI

Yeah

NAOMI

I gave her some food, too. She'll probably only
sell it

NAOMI

Jess thinks I'm a fool to keep giving her
handouts. I know she's right, but...

JACKSON

Nah, she doesn't think you're a fool. She's only
looking out for you

JACKSON

Me too, Nay. Me too. Do you want to come
over? Whitney made lasagna. We have plenty
to share!

NAOMI

No, I'm all right

NAOMI

Jax?

JACKSON

Yeah?

NAOMI

Don't tell Jess about my mom, k? She's got enough going on right now to worry about my same old shit, different day, you know?

JACKSON

You know she gets it, but I got you.

JACKSON

Call your new man. That'll take your mind off things for sure

NAOMI

OMG JAX. BYE

JACKSON

@@@@@@@@@

[Submitted by Reese Vaskin on 23 December]

Modern World History - Unit 3, Chapter 9

Short Answer

1. How did industrialization affect the growth of cities?

My daddy brought home a Christmas tree today. An artificial one. He dropped the box by the fireplace and then walked out. He and my sister and I used to go out and pick out a real tree every year together. We'd do whatever dumb family activities the tree farm would have going on. Drink hot chocolate. Then sing Christmas songs in the car on the way home.

2. Describe the differences between capitalism and socialism.

I walked out, too. I went to the store, and I bought the cutest baby booties, little hair barrettes, socks with lace frills, and teeny tiny earrings. Then I bought my own little tree to fit on my dresser, and when I got home, I wrapped everything up and put the presents under my tree so I'd for sure have something to open on Christmas.

@@@@@@@@@

Sent December 23
TO: 'REESE VASKIN' <NOTTHATREESE@MAIL.COM>
FROM: NAOMI.WELLINGTON@AESAMN.EDU
SUBJECT: YOUR LAST QUIZ

Hi Reese,

I hope you understand my being unable to give you any credit at all for your last quiz. I can usually argue some points in your favor when you have partially answered a question. However, I won't be able to offer you a re-take on this one. Please schedule a time for us to meet and help you with next steps as you prepare for the unit exam.

Ms. W

Naomi Wellington
Society and History Studies
Alternative Education Solutions
"We realize the importance of our voices only when we are silenced." -
Malala Yousafzai

@@@@@@@@@

Sent December 26
TO: NAOMI WELLINGTON <MYOWNPERSON02@GMAIL.COM>
FROM: JESSAMINE LEWIS <STEAMYENERGY@GMAIL.COM>
SUBJECT: TRYING TO BE JUICED

Mimi,

You've got love going your way, some time on your own while Jackson takes Leyanna skiing, some time off, and I'm happy for you, for real.

But also, for real, I'm so tired, and I've been tryna keep it all together and making magic and shit, and I wish I could send my kids off skiing for a week. Instead, I've been scrambling to find care for the kids while I work during the busiest time of year for my job. I can't leave the kids at home with Faith anymore. At least, not for longer periods of time. Two hours is about as long as Faith can manage before she falls apart from trying to ignore the pain and not fold in on herself, at which point the kids could be on fire, and she wouldn't notice.

You know I don't love Christmas anyway, but this year was especially brutal. I'm only grateful that the kids didn't seem too affected by how stressed out Faith and I have been. Faith's parents and Momma pressured us so hard to come home for Christmas this year, and I wanted to try to come home—just the kids and me—because God knows I could use the break, except the other managers have already covered for me way too much. There was no way I could get away.

I need a vacation. So bad.

-Jess

@@@@@@@@

BOARD: THE GREAT GATSBY by F. Scott Fitzgerald

▽ **TOPIC:** Discussion Question 1: How does socio-economic class affect the characters' behaviors? The conflict?

Susette: I couldn't decide if I liked any of the characters. I mean, obviously you were only interesting to others if you had money of some sort.

Tyrell: Worse than that. If you are poor, you are stupid, like Tom Wilson. And then, when you're not stupid, you turn into a murderer. Talk about a whole book about stereotypes.

Maxine: Maybe that was the point, though? All the characters were over the top.

Chester: They were all dumb, though. "I hear he's an Oxford man" was said so many times with no real context, so I'm pretty sure the characters had no idea what it even meant. They could have just said, "He's a Little Caesar's Man," and then at least we'd have some real debate going on.

Tyrell: I'm a Ramblin' Man, myself.

Grant: Doing the best you can?

Tyrell: Yep, I was born that way.

Naomi: A Little Caesar's Man! How terrible! How rotten! Just suppose if you were someone else! Oh, the mere thought of it!

Maxine: What's gotten into you, Naomi?

Chester: Whatever has gotten into everyone, OLD SPORT? What does it all mean?

Naomi: It means nothing. It means *everything*.

Maxine: I'm very confused.

Grant: They're talking like the dramatic dialogue in the book.

Naomi: That's it, old sport. Will you see to the flowers?

Maxine: Oh, I see. Except, not really. Oh, wait, I guess sometimes I was a little lost in the strange conversations.

Chester: Now you have it, old sport! There's just one thing.

Grant: Never mind that one thing. Pull the car around, won't you?

Tyrell: Time for Gatsby to be a ramblin' man.

Lisa: Any chance we can get back to the question?

Naomi: Lisa, darling. Can we do it in character?

Lisa: If it means actually discussing the book, I'll try not to argue.

Chester: Then carry on, Lisa, old sport! We shall follow in your stead.

Lisa: That's all I'm asking.

JANUARY

Sent January 06
To: Naomi Wellington <myownperson02@gmail.com>
From: Jessamine Lewis <steamyenergy@gmail.com>
Subject: January is the worst month

Even in Washington, when it's not even that cold out like it is in MN. It's slushy wet snow and too many clouds. Everyone at work is dragging after the rush of holiday shopping, and the store is filled with trashed shelves and racks of clearance crap I wish we could simply burn.

Faith had a bad weekend, and I'm exhausted. None of the pain meds were working very well, and I tried to coach her through some breathing exercises like when I went through labor, but she drenched me in "fuck yous," which got a similar response from me, and I slept on the couch all weekend because fuck that.

Except, God, Mimi, I feel like a total shit now. I mean, what, I'm tired. So what. I get a headache, pop a couple of Advil and boom, it's gone. She takes hardcore prescription painkillers, and it still doesn't do the trick. She is in pain Every. Single. Minute. Of the day. And no one knows why or believes it's something real. It's killing me to see Faith laid out like this. It was only a few months ago she was laughing her ass off at me for not being able to keep up with her riding the hills with both kids in the trailer, and I had only me and my bike. She couldn't possibly hold herself up on her bike now with her arm like it is right now.

And then... Isaac wet the bed last night. He's only four, but he's been fully potty trained for almost a whole year. I can't remember the last accident he had. Thankfully, we've never gotten around to taking off the plastic mattress cover. Still, a 3:00 am wake-up call was not how I wanted to start my week. The laundry is out of control. What I wouldn't give to be living back home right now to have Momma. Take the kids for a few days or even just do the stupid laundry. I would even accept having Faith's mom here. That's how bad it is.

We have yet another doctor appointment later this week.

@@@@@@@@

Sent January 07
To: Naomi Wellington <myownperson02@gmail.com>
From: Jessamine Lewis <steamyenergy@gmail.com>
Subject: everything sucks

Faith's arm is red, swollen, and hot. We went to the ER, and they tried icing it while waiting on blood work, and she nearly passed out from the pain. Blood work came back negative for shingles, Lyme's disease, and some diabetic thing. They couldn't find any infection, even though the body reaction looks like one, so they sent us home with a prescription for antibiotics and Tylenol-plus-codeine.

They agreed with your suggestion for seeing an orthopedist, but said we needed the referral from her primary care doctor. Friday can't come soon enough.

. . .

Sent January 07
TO: JESSAMINE LEWIS <STEAMYENERGY@GMAIL.COM>
FROM: NAOMI WELLINGTON <MYOWNPERSON02@GMAIL.COM>
SUBJECT: RE: EVERYTHING SUCKS

Oh Jess, I'm so sorry about all this stress. What can I do? I wish I could come out there. I wish flights weren't so stupid expensive. I wish your mom didn't just have her foot surgery so she could come out. I wish Faith hadn't ever broken her arm.

All my love to you.

@@@@@@@@@

Sent January 09
TO: JESSAMINE LEWIS <STEAMYENERGY@GMAIL.COM>
FROM: NAOMI WELLINGTON <MYOWNPERSON02@GMAIL.COM>
SUBJECT: SERIOUS ENOUGH TO MEET THE KID

So, Lanh has reached Partner with Potential status. Or at least, it's what Leyanna thinks. Ever since the not-so-private conversation between me and Jackson in the car that one time, she has been asking about Lanh almost daily. "What are you and Lanh reading now?" (*Melissa* by Alex Gino this week, btw.) "What does he do to work out?" (running and weights) "When do I get to meet him?" (not until I know if it's serious!) "What if you don't know if it's serious until you know how he and I like each other?" (a good point, I had to admit, especially as there are two other guys she never did meet even though they had Partner with *Partial* Potential status)

TBH, he is still at the Partial Potential stage for me, although we've been spending tons of time together. I don't 100% know what is holding me back. He's great. My stomach still gets fluttery before I see him, which is at minimum almost every day at Polar Cafe, and we spend two-three nights together during Jackson's weeks with Leyanna. We cook together, I look over his papers for school, we do puzzles in front of movies of books we've read together, and then trash those same movies for not being nearly as good as the book. And we have amazing sex. (Obviously I had to share that part, right?)

It's easy to talk to him, and we talk about almost anything and everything. Well, almost everything. He hasn't told me much about his family beyond his mother, and I haven't shared everything about my mom. But maybe we'll get there. He's cool about Jackson and how close we are—at least he's cool so far. As you know, not every guy has been okay with our whole relationship, which I get.

Maybe Leyanna's right. Maybe I *do* need to see how she and Lanh hit it off before I can really let go and see where he and I are headed. It will be a good practice run, too, so I don't make the mistake of bringing him to Sunday dinner too soon. Trust me, I have *never* yet made that mistake again.

-N

Sent January 09
To: Naomi Wellington <myownperson02@gmail.com>
From: Jessamine Lewis <steamyenergy@gmail.com>
Subject: Re: serious enough to meet the kid

Oh yes, Jasper and Sunday dinner. I remember him. He's the one who said to you, "Wait, is Jackson your brother?"

I know you were pissed, but God, I still laugh out loud when I think of that day and how Daddy and Jax rolled with it. "That's how Black people do it, son. We keep it in the family."

"Yeah," Jax said. "This way, I know everything about my baby-mama."

Do you remember how big Jasper's eyes got? "Really? Is that a thing?" That fool BELIEVED him.

I'm sorry, babe, but What Were You Thinking with him?

Lanh sounds like the kind of person who could go right along with it all. I'll be sure to get the inside scoop from Leyanna after she meets him.

-Jess

@@@@@@@@@

[8:46 Jan 11]

NAOMI

I'm so sorry about Whitney's miscarriage

JACKSON

Thank you

NAOMI

How is she holding up?

JACKSON

Not good

NAOMI

And you?

JACKSON

Not good. It's not just the baby it's...we're barely hanging on, you know?

NAOMI

That bad?

JACKSON

For longer than I've wanted to admit

NAOMI

Shit

JACKSON

Yep

NAOMI

Anything I can do? Leyanna can stay with me for the rest of the month—to help give you and Whitney some time to focus on each other?

JACKSON

No. IDK. I don't want to do that to Leyanna. We'll figure it out

NAOMI

I'm sorry

JACKSON

I know

@@@@@@@@@

Sent January 13
To: Naomi Wellington <myownperson02@gmail.com>
From: Jessamine Lewis <steamyenergy@gmail.com>
Subject: we know what it's NOT

It's not M.S.

It's not Lupis.

It's not Parkinson's.

It's not cancer.

It's not neuralgia.

It's not any common blood disease.

What the fuck IS it? Can't any of these tests do more than one thing? More than only say what ISN'T wrong with Faith?

@@@@@@@@

Sent January 14
To: Jessamine Lewis <steamyenergy@gmail.com>
From: Naomi Wellington <myownperson02@gmail.com>
Subject: love is in the air

I think Pencil Skirt Woman and Sloppy Jock Brother are interested in each other. Sloppy Jock Brother hasn't been so sloppy lately. Part of it might be because he probably hasn't been running outside much because who in their right minds would run outside in January in Minnesota? Still, he wears newer tracksuit pants instead of sweatpants, and he arrives a little bit earlier than his brother (Super Suit) now. Jock Brother and Pencil Skirt (who is now Woolen Maxi Skirt woman although sometimes she still wears the pencil skirt with some pretty, patterned tights and leather boots (OMG those boots are glorious—I *need* a pair like them)) sometimes talk while they wait for their order. Occasionally, Sayeed helps with conversation, too. He and I have discussed this possibility of Jock Brother and Pencil Skirt (Juan and Elena are their real names. Sayeed and I also discussed whether or not that is confidential information, but I told him he calls out their name for when their coffees are ready, so it's not all that private) which is why Sayeed has upped his game in matchmaking.

Now, if he could only do the same thing for himself and win Tracey over.

Do you think I should help him out somehow?

Sent January 14
To: Naomi Wellington <myownperson02@gmail.com>
From: Jessamine Lewis <steamyenergy@gmail.com>
Subject: Re: love is in the air

Okay, I admit your coffee shop stories are kind of saving me right now, so let's do this.

Do you remember how Faith and I met? How I'd see her as she was leaving the Y at the same time I would arrive? Faith didn't magically think on her own to shift her workout schedule. It was all on the front desk people. Which is to say, yes, you (and Lanh) should definitely help Sayeed with this task.

It's time to put on your super skills of observation. What is their body language? Do they look at each other when they think the other person isn't looking? Are they laughing more at things that normally aren't *that* funny? What are they talking about? Can you manage to bump into her and make her drop her purse or bag or whatever? You know Tracksuit Guy will totally help pick things up.

Find out from Lanh how long he was tracking you before he "accidentally" dropped his book right by you and what made him decide to do it when he did.

Also, who in their right mind *leaves the house when she doesn't have to* in January in Minnesota?

@@@@@@@@@

Sent January 16
To: Jessamine Lewis <steamyenergy@gmail.com>
From: Naomi Wellington <myownperson02@gmail.com>
Subject: I am minuscule

Have you ever read *The Girl Who Drank the Moon*? I mean, I'm sure you haven't because it's a middle grade book and your kiddos are still too little, but there's this character, Fyrian, who is this tiny little dragon who thinks he's enormous, and everyone goes along with it because they love him. (I do, too. He's a fantastic character in the story.) I am Fyrian. I like to think I'm this Important and Amazing Teacher Doing All the Great Things not just for students, but also for my colleagues. Except there's a big difference between Fyrian and me.

Nobody thinks I'm a Simply Enormous Dragon. They don't pretend for me like the characters do for Fyrian. I'm not talking about the teaching part—everyone knows that is a thankless job, and I see different kinds of rewards in my students. I'm talking about trying to get somewhere in this organization so I can help write and change the curriculum. I volunteer for *everything* to show I am a "team player" (Don't you just HATE that phrase? Please, please tell me you don't use it with your employees.), and it feels like it goes completely unnoticed.

I know you think I'm a total doormat. Before you tell me again, I want you to know when the call went out for the new Steering Committee for our school, I responded with my interest and listed all I have been doing for our organization to prove my dedication. They're hoping to have the committee all set within the next couple of weeks. I'm also still waiting on the department curriculum review team, which I super want to be a part of because I've been learning so much through my tons of research.

Do you remember the YMCA camps we went to those couple of summers before we got to high school? I used to be so scared during those first few days. You know how terrible I used to be about making new friends. I was so shy (clearly, I've way outgrown that trait) and quiet. Like always, you led the way, so full of confidence and so *good* at everything! I am so grateful you helped me out, and as I've faced down Nick the Dick this year, I've channeled you. I've visualized my goal and assumed confidence, even when I haven't always *felt* confident. I think it might be working.

-N

@@@@@@@@@

Sent January 19
TO: JESSAMINE LEWIS <STEAMYENERGY@GMAIL.COM>
FROM: NAOMI WELLINGTON <MYOWNPERSON02@GMAIL.COM>
SUBJECT: THEY MEET

Leyanna and Lanh, of course. LnL. The Elles. Wait, not quite. Whatever. We all met at first at the Minneapolis Institute of Art, mainly because they currently have a jewelry exhibit. Leyanna's already seen it with Jackson and Whitney since Whitney has been her jewelry crafting hook-up, but she begged to go again. It's a pretty cool exhibit. Amazing beadwork and gold-plated sandals! I would totally rock those sandals or any metal shoes tbh. I don't know if Lanh was totally into the jewelry itself. He did, however, have a lot of interest in the histories of the various pieces and asked Leyanna a lot of awesome questions about how she makes her jewelry and her thought process behind it all.

Then we imagined famous people and others we know wearing various pieces. I took a few photos of what I could see on Tracy and Sayeed at the café. There was a crown Sayeed would absolutely rock. I kinda want Leyanna to make a replica of it for him. The point is, though, LnL were totally on the same wavelength and got all *Project Runway* with it all. Well, how I imagine *Project Runway* to be since I've never seen the show. Leyanna loves it (she watches it with Jax and Whitney)—and apparently, Lanh does, too!

We ate pizza for dinner because at least part of the meet had to be cliché, and now I'm freaking out because Leyanna loves Lanh, and this is why it's so nerve-wracking to have Potential Partners meet Permanent Children. She's all in love with him, and yeah, I really like this guy, but I'm not at love yet, and what if this doesn't work out after all?? What if I mess it up? What if I mess it up AND Leyanna hates me for it?

-N

Sent January 19
To: Naomi Wellington <myownperson02@gmail.com>
From: Jessamine Lewis <steamyenergy@gmail.com>
Subject: Re: They Meet

Mimi,

Stop overthinking it all! Enjoy this moment of maybe getting serious and also, *talk* to Leyanna about it. She's old enough. She can handle it and will understand your feelings.

He's hot. Leyanna likes him. You like him. ALL GOOD THINGS.

-Jess

@@@@@@@@@

Sent January 21
To: Jessamine Lewis <steamyenergy@gmail.com>
From: Naomi Wellington <myownperson02@gmail.com>
Subject: 12 is the new 16

Seriously. I didn't expect such problems until high school. Her grades aren't great, and she's been lying to me about school and her social life, and she keeps getting on me about wanting to do online school, but how is that supposed to work when I can't trust her to take responsibility for basic respect? And if she doesn't have any friends, how will that change when she stops going to school altogether?

She's not turning in work. What is that about? I guess I can't trust her "yes" answer to "did you finish all your homework" anymore. I tried to, but maybe now I have to be one of those parents who constantly checks the website and grade book. I never thought I'd have to micromanage my kid.

And I don't understand what's going on with her friends. She talks about a couple of people, but when I check her phone, there's almost nothing. Hardly any texts. Nothing in her Instagram. I even looked in her Google Drive stuff because I know some kids get around some of the age restriction filters and other parent stuff by communicating in a Google Doc or Slide. Nothing. What isn't she telling me about these kids? I'm worried she's already learned how to scrub her phone before I get to it.

She says she doesn't like to do the presentations, especially the ones as part of group projects.

"Honey, *nobody* likes to do group projects," I told her. "And yet, it's a unique social skill. You'll have jobs in the future working with people you like and don't like. With people who will share the work and those who will do hardly any of the work. It's how it is."

"It's more than not liking it," she replied. "I don't know how to do it."

"You all figure out who will do what and then do your part. Don't worry about the grade. If you are at least doing what you are supposed to be doing, I'm good with that."

I don't care if Leyanna doesn't get the best grades; I truly don't. I do care if she's not actually *doing* the work, though. I offered to have us do homework parties like we used to call it in the past when she had to miss so much school. She'd have her worksheets her teacher sent home every Friday, and I'd have my computer, and we'd work together at the dining room table. It was fun to have company, and I'd be able to easily pause in my grading to help her out with stuff.

"A homework party won't help anymore, Mom. It's not the same problem."

"Then what, exactly, *is* the problem?"

"I told you, I don't know how to do the group thing."

And there we are, full circle.

Lanh thinks she's trying to tell me something, but what? He doesn't know her well enough, yet, to have much idea, and I can't see it. Sometimes pre-teen is just pre-teen.

How is Isaac doing? Any more bedwetting incidents?

-N

Sent January 21
To: Naomi Wellington <myownperson02@gmail.com>
From: Jessamine Lewis <steamyenergy@gmail.com>
Subject: Re: 12 is the new 16

Mimi,

I don't understand why you are so against Leyanna doing online school. It seems like she matches up to many of the kinds of students you've been telling me about. The group dynamic. The non-existent social side. Maybe Lanh's right, and she IS trying to tell you something.

Isaac is telling ME loud and clear that what is happening with Mommy Faith is more stress than his little body can handle. We've reverted to pull-ups, which Faith is annoyed about, but I told her she wasn't the one having to wash the clothes and the sheets every day and therefore had no say. "I'm only worried about how this is affecting Isaac," she told me like I'm not freaking out about it, too. Supposedly, she's going to consult with her psychology professor colleagues, so THAT answer and solution will be fun. TBH, I think Isaac is relieved. He usually still wakes up because he's aware he's peeing, but can't seem to control it. We saw the pediatrician and ruled out infection. We've tried not having him drink anything for three hours before he goes to bed, but damn, if he's thirsty, who am I to deny him a few sips of water? Which is worse, having him cry for water or cry because he couldn't make it to the bathroom. Fuck if I know. With the bed at least staying dry, I've found Olivia snuggled up next to him some nights, and most of the time, Isaac has stayed dry when she does that. My heart grows five sizes knowing that girl is taking care of her brother while making me want to cry that she feels she has to.

We saw doctor number five today for Faith. We've ruled out a whole bunch more crazy, scientific-sounding bone and nerve things. I never knew there were so many diseases out there. The world around me got so much bigger in terms of people who have to manage pain every day. It really hit me. How many people do I see every day that might be suffering like Faith? She hardly ever wears anything with sleeves these days, btw. Tank tops in January because the fabric hurts.

Mina's father-in-law has Alzheimer's. One of her kids has a severe peanut allergy. Your mom's an addict. Your students have all kinds of shit going on. And here I am whining like a white girl in a YA novel.

Momma says God doesn't give us more than we can handle. I say that might be true, but it sure would be nice if He told us *how* to handle it all instead of just piling it all on.

-Jess

@@@@@@@@@

Sent January 26
To: Jessamine Lewis <steamyenergy@gmail.com>
From: Naomi Wellington <myownperson02@gmail.com>
Subject: Tết and my One-Word Resolution

So, I've got it, finally. My One-Word-Resolution for the year.

OPPORTUNITY

I'm going to seize the OPPORTUNITY to be more involved with the changes at work. All of the other stupid stuff going on at work? It's an OPPORTUNITY to be flexible. Too many classes? An OPPORTUNITY to learn more of the curriculum! Leyanna and I not always getting along? An OPPORTUNITY for me to get a preview of what's to come in her teen years and learn new ways to communicate. My mom calling or showing up at terrible times? Well, IDK. I guess that's an opportunity for... forgiveness? I'll have to work on that one.

I was going to skip the whole resolution thing because here it is almost the end of January, and everyone knows if you can't even get your act together to come up with something before the end of the first month of the year, then what's the point? Except, Lanh and I celebrated Tết yesterday, which is the Vietnamese New Year. Resolutions aren't really a thing, but I figured it was a good excuse to do it anyway. Lanh said our current relationship was an opportunity for something more. <3

Lanh and his mom did some prep work ahead of time because Tết is usually a multi-day celebration, and btw did I mention I MET HIS MOM? How did we already get to this point? She is awesome, exactly like how Lanh described her. Kind, but also? I wouldn't mess with her. It's easy to see how she was able to go to bat successfully for him in school and wherever. We finished putting together these sticky rice, pork, and mashed mung bean cakes called bánh tết, and then we prepared various puddings and candied coconut. Watching him and his mom work together was amazing. They had me working on the mung bean pudding, which involved simply standing next to the stove and stirring constantly. (I wouldn't have trusted me with anything else, either.) But Lanh and his mom? They were a well-oiled team. She'd spread out three different banana leaves, Lanh would spread on some rice, then his mom would place a chilled bean and pork log (kind of looked like little pre-cooked bread loaves) on the rice, lift up the leaves on both sides, allowing Lanh to put more rice on top and around the log. Then Lanh would have a string ready, and I got to help with this part. He'd cross the string, and I'd hold down one end while he looped the other one and tied it all up like a shoestring.

"Oh, that was so fast!" I told him. "I've been trying super hard to tie my shoes with only one hand, and I still really suck at it."

He kissed me right then, which wasn't embarrassing at all in front of his mom (sarcasm font), and then said, "That is one of the best things anyone has ever done for me. Thank you for trying to live in my shoes." I told him he shouldn't think too much of me for it because I've been trying different things, but I give up on it pretty quickly.

"Well, I don't know if you've noticed," he laughed, "but I don't often wear shoes that have laces."

His mom pointed a big spoon at me and said, "You would learn pretty fast if you had impatient friends and teachers waiting on you at daycares and schools, though." Lanh's smile kind of faltered as he looked away, giving me a glimpse into how hard his life was and can sometimes be, in spite of him making it look easy.

Anyway. Cooking for our dinner was an all-day event. The second best thing next to the food was I heard a lot of different stories about Lanh's grandparents, who live in Vietnam, and about Lanh as a kid, and hearing childhood boyfriend or girl-friend stories are one of my favorite things. Unfortunately, Lanh's dad and dad's side of the family have essentially disowned him and his mother. It was already tricky when Lanh was born with the genetic anomaly affecting his arm ("Lanh's father was not of the Buddhist faith," his mom said. "Instead, he thought it indicated bad luck. But look at this boy! He is nothing but good luck and joy."), but when Lanh came out as trans? His dad definitely couldn't accept that. "Good riddance," I accidentally said out loud, but Lanh's mom didn't take offense. She shooed the thought of her ex-husband away and agreed.

I suppose now I've met his mom, this means I should be ready to bring him to Sunday dinner soon, right? Maybe next weekend. I'm a little scared of what stories the Lewis family will share about me.

Chúc mừng năm mới! (That's "happy new year" in Vietnamese. Yes, copy/pasted from the web. I can *almost* say it kind of correctly.)(Not really.)

-N

@@@@@@@@

Sent January 27
To: naomi.wellington@aesamn.edu
From: mark.sumner@aesamn.edu
Subject: Steering Committee

Dear Ms. Wellington,

Thank you for your interest in serving on the Alternative Education Solutions Program Steering Committee. We took into account several factors to help us create a manageable and balanced unit and, unfortunately, could not accept all volunteers at this time.

Thank you for your dedication to our learning organization.

Best,

Mark Sumner
Interim Director
Alternative Education Solutions Academy

@@@@@@@@

Sent January 27
To: MARY.SLAUSON@AESAMN.EDU
FROM: NAOMI.WELLINGTON@AESAMN.EDU
SUBJECT: INTERIM **STEERING** COMMITTEE?

Hi Mary,

I hope things are going okay with your mom. I really do. I am sorry to bother you with this message, but I don't know what else to do since things seem to keep marching forward at work with no oversight. I mean, what is Karen doing as an assistant director if not helping keep things in check?

Mark the Shark is leading a Steering Committee. I don't understand how he thinks he can do this. Unless...are you not coming back? I truly hope this is not the case, as you created this school on such a solid foundation. I know you believe in continuous improvement, which I suppose a steering committee IS for continuous improvement, but how useful is it, really, for an interim leader to entertain issues he won't be able to implement or follow through on?

Again, I am so sorry to bother you with this as I know you'd rather not have to deal with work during this time with your mother, but I also know how much this school means to you.

-Naomi

Naomi Wellington
Society and History Studies
Alternative Education Solutions
"We realize the importance of our voices only when we are silenced." -
Malala Yousafzai

Sent January 27
To: MARY.SLAUSON@AESAMN.EDU
FROM: NAOMI.WELLINGTON@AESAMN.EDU
SUBJECT: RE: INTERIM STEERING COMMITTEE?

Oh no! I re-read my message to you after I had already sent it and realized I put in my not-so-professional-but-feels-accurate nickname for Mark.

I am sorry for this slip. I'm rather upset by all the issues arising at work.

-Naomi

@@@@@@@@@

Sent January 28
To: JESSAMINE LEWIS <STEAMYENERGY@GMAIL.COM>
FROM: NAOMI WELLINGTON <MYOWNPERSON02@GMAIL.COM>
SUBJECT: REESE

Do you remember the student I told you about who is pregnant? Who was forced into online school?

Her name is Reese, and she showed up at my door yesterday, bag in hand. And yes, I took her in. I'm sure it is only temporary. She wasn't kicked out of her house at all; she needed a break. Her father barely speaks to her, her sister is lapping up all the "good kid" attention, and her mother is pressuring her heavily about adoption.

Honestly, you know I wouldn't have turned her away, but I promise you I did pause to think. It was Leyanna who spoke up right away and said there was plenty of space in her bedroom for Reese to stay, and that was that.

Reese reminds me a little bit of you. I mean, except for the whole getting pregnant way too early thing since that was me. She's passionate and speaks her mind without worrying about consequences, and yet, there's a vulnerability about her. She's scared, and I remember some of that from the early days with finding out I was pregnant with Leyanna. I understand what she's going through, and I think I can help. Maybe I can even get her to write real essay exam answers that are 100% on-topic and not drifting into journal entries about her life!

She was kind of raw yesterday, so we haven't talked much about what her living with Leyanna and me will look like or all the things she's feeling. All I know is she doesn't want to give up her baby for adoption, and everything about living at home was making her feel squeezed in, trapped. When I think of myself at age sixteen and my mother...wait, she actually tried a stint in rehab that year. I got to stay with you and your family for a couple of weeks.

I can be her family for a while, can't I?

Leyanna wanted to cook dinner last night, and Reese jumped right in to help her, and then Reese offered to do Leyanna's puffs before school tomorrow (with a promise to do twists over the weekend) which then spurred Leyanna to offer a manicure to Reese.

I think it's all going to work out, and maybe Reese will help Leyanna through some of these rough spots.

I made Reese call home to ensure her parents knew she was safe, and then I talked to her mom (not comfortable), but in the end, she said she guessed maybe this was all for the best and that kind of near broke my heart, because it isn't, not really, but I'll do my best to be what Reese needs right now. I can be all the things my mom was not when I was pregnant. Driver for doctor appointments. Nutritionist. Cheerleader. Caretaker. Sober.

It's kind of the whole point behind being part of an alternative education program to help the whole student, right? I had teachers who helped me out of some tight spots, and it's time to pay it forward.

-N

@@@@@@@@@

LOVING FAMILY ADOPTION SERVICES

ADOPTIVE FAMILY PROFILE

Michael and Jessica

We are deeply moved by God's call for us to become adoptive parents. We will love and care for our child as God loves and cares for all of His children.

Basic Profile

Basic Profile

	Michael	Jessica
Age	28	27
Ethnicity	White/Caucasian	White/Caucasian
Education	Undergraduate Degree	Undergraduate Degree
Religion	Christian	Christian
Occupation	Youth Minister	Parish Program Secretary
Health	Excellent	Excellent
Smoking/Alcohol Use	None	None

Our Story

Michael and Jessica met each other four years ago on a mission trip to Guatemala. God opened their eyes to see all who are so less fortunate than them, and while ministering with God's Word to impoverished children, Michael and Jessica connected and discovered their shared passion for spreading the Word. They married six months later, and after three more mission trips to third world countries, God spoke to them and blessed them to take in a less fortunate child to be their own.

Age Preference (Y-yes, N-no, WTC-willing to consider)

_Y_ Newborn

_N_ 1-12 months

_N_ 2-4 years

_N_ 5-12 years

_N_ 13+ years

Race/Ethnicity (Y-yes, N-no, WTC-willing to consider)

_N_ White/Caucasian

_Y_ Black or African-American

_Y_ American Indian or Alaskan Native

_N_ Native Hawaiian or Pacific Islander

_N_ Asian

Post-Adoption Cooperative Communication Plan

Michael and Jessica look forward to including their adopted child's parent(s) in the child's life, such as celebrations and general visits and hope the relationship will remain strong and loving. They prefer full control over decisions involving faith, education, and contact with the child's biological extended family to help eliminate any confusion about his/her place in the adoptive parents' family. Social media photos must include adoptive parents with the child. Planned visits and phone calls are welcome!

@@@@@@@@@

ForumsForAll-Personal Message Center

Thread members: Susette, Maxine, Naomi, Lisa

Susette: Naomi, Lisa? You two were so helpful with Maxine; I wondered if you could help me out with something?

Naomi: What's up?

Susette: It's my mother-in-law.

Lisa: Oh, hell, no, Susette. We're not touching that one.

Maxine: Lisa! Let's hear her out. We don't know what she means, yet.

Naomi: Agreed, Maxine. Tell us more, Susette.

Susette: It's not what you think. I'm worried about her still living on her own. I want her to move in with me.

Lisa: Just you? What about your husband?

Susette: Oh, he and I divorced several years ago.

Lisa: And she can't live with him?

Susette: Well. He's not exactly...warm and caring. There's not much of a relationship between them. And by not much, I mean not at all.

Naomi: Oh Susette. I'm so sorry.

Lisa: So your husband is an asshat on many levels. Will you both be safe if she moves in with you?

Susette: Yes. He's not dangerous, just not a very nice man. His mother isn't doing well, and I take her out on errands—you know, shopping and the like. She fell recently and luckily didn't break any bones, but is moving more slowly than ever. I'm so worried about her, and she thinks it will be such an inconvenience to me to move in. I don't know how to convince her.

Maxine: Bless your heart, Susette. I think it's wonderful you want to take care of your mother-in-law like this.

Lisa: Okay, Susette. Let's put our heads together and toss around some ideas.

Naomi: Yes! We've got this.

Susette: Thank you. I knew you'd be the right ones to go to.

@@@@@@@@@

BOARD: 1984 by George Orwell

>**TOPIC:** Discussion Question 1: Fake News - does it exist?

>**TOPIC:** Discussion Question 2: What makes the interrogation of Winston successful or not successful?

>**TOPIC:** Discussion Question 3: What do we think about Orwell's idea of the future?

▽**TOPIC:** Our next book: *Things Fall Apart* by Chinua Achebe

Chester: Finally! A book written by a Black person about Black people. This 100 Books List is the whitest damn list I've ever seen.

Naomi: Right? I mean, who are people even asking when they create these lists?

Chester: Their white-ass college English teachers, that's who.

Lisa: Still a fucking male author, though.

Chester: Word.

Maxine: Well, I mean, we started this based upon a "100 Books to Read Before You Die" list from BookNook, but maybe... we create our own list? We could still use some of the books from the BookNook list, but change out for some of our own suggestions, too?

Susette: I wouldn't even know where to go with that. I started this club because I didn't have any idea what's good to read.

Grant: Anything you enjoy reading is good to read, Susette.

Tyrell: I nominate *Debt of Honor*, by Tom Clancy.

Lisa: Seriously, T?

Tyrell: YESSSS. This is Clancy's most underrated book of the Jack Ryan series. Everyone talks about *The Hunt for Red October*, but that's like saying "Piano Man" is Billy Joel's best song. Just because *October* got made into a movie first, doesn't mean it was the best book.

Lisa: "Most underrated." Really? *Really?*

Tyrell: Yes, REALLY, Lisa. Moby Dick was lame, and most of us agreed it was overrated—why can't this one be underrated?

Grant: If Tyrell likes it this much, I think it should go on the list. Just like I told Susette above, a book he likes is a good book.

Lisa: You like everything, Grant.

Grant: ¯_(ツ)_/¯

Naomi: How about we start a new board with all of our suggestions? Or the suggestions we've gotten from other people? We could alternate between our own list and the BookNook one. If we read one of our own, then the person who nominated it can lead the discussion.

Grant: I vote yes for Naomi's suggestion.

Chester: +1

Lisa: +1

Tyrell: +1

Susette: I'll get it set up!

DRAFT
To: Jessamine Lewis <steamyenergy@gmail.com>
From: Naomi Wellington <myownperson02@gmail.com>
Subject: rehab again, as if that will do her any good

...especially because it's court-ordered. She missed two of her drug checks, and I took her to this third one, but of course, she didn't come away clean, and now she's checked back into Do the Work. Sev waived the paperwork and registration fees for me like they usually do, and I don't know how I'll pay for her actual stay there, but Sev told me they'd work out a payment plan with me and not to worry about it. I don't know why they're so nice to me because I feel like all I've done in the past few years is lean on them for a mother who isn't worth it, but nowhere else will be as flexible and affordable as Sev and stupidly, I keep thinking one day it will all actually *work*.

Same shit. Always.

You don't need to hear it all over and over again, so I'm not sending this, but sometimes it makes me feel a little better pretending I'm talking it out with you. Under different circumstances, I know you'd understand.

-Mimi

@@@@@@@@

Sent February 08
To: Jessamine Lewis <steamyenergy@gmail.com>
From: Naomi Wellington <myownperson02@gmail.com>
Subject: Naomi's Place: the Salon Story

Homework? Grading? What of it? Does it matter when your home has been converted into a full-service salon and spa? Does it?

Because my nails have never looked so good, my skin has never felt this great (you can ask Lanh for verification), and my hands and feet are zen central, sending all kinds of "oh yes" vibes to the rest of my body. It's what happens when you go full-on SPA at home. We've been doing mani-pedis (complete with hand and foot massages), facials, and hairstyling. I currently have a wicked zigzag shaved along the sides of my head, and I love it (though Lanh does not like this particular thing as much as the smooth skin).

We've been gabbing away, and it reminds me of when Grams, you, and I would have our spa days. We'd gossip and listen to the best of Gram's stories of secret parties in parks that no longer exist because of "economic growth." Wouldn't a secret party be about perfect right now? Leyanna and Reese could stay home, of course; it would be only for you and me to attend. We'd dance and dance. Maybe have a drink or two. And laugh about anything and everything.

Reese talks about everything except home. She's not ready to face what may or may not change there once the baby comes, and she doesn't talk about adoption as any sort of available choice. What is my role here? IDK. Safe place to land, sure, but what else does that mean? I need to get her to open up again, if only a little bit, then I can persuade her to talk with a social worker.

What I have been doing is finding ways to talk about her class-work. While we do our nails or get dinner ready or fold laundry, we talk about different school topics, and I encourage her to then simply transfer what she said out loud to me to the page. Regurgitate.

She laughed at me. "Ms. W, you don't gotta worry about none of that. I promise I'm doing just fine in my classes, but I appreciate what you're doing."

And it's true. She left her computer open one night after going to bed, and she was still logged into her classes. She's getting all As and Bs! It's only my class where she's scraping by with a C- because she uses it as a journal.

I'm taking it slow with getting into the nitty-gritty of her plans for when the baby comes. I was older than Reese in many ways when I got pregnant and I had so much help. Reese is smart, but she's still *so* young and without the home support? I don't know what chance she has of raising a baby on her own. She has paper-work from an agency her mom made her go to, so she is, at least, considering it.

This might seem kind of...out there, but do you think Jackson and Whitney would be open to adoption? Is it too soon to bring it up? And if interested, do you think it would help Reese make a decision? She could get to know them, and considering how well things have gone with Jax and I raising Leyanna together, yet separate, having some sort of open adoption with Reese would probably be successful, don't you think?

-N

Sent February 09
To: Naomi Wellington <myownperson02@gmail.com>
From: Jessamine Lewis <steamyenergy@gmail.com>
Subject: Re: Naomi's Place: The Salon Story

HOLD UP. Do not get Jackson wound up in your student's messed-up situation. Or yours.

Just. Don't.

@@@@@@@@@

[Submitted by Reese Vaskin on February 10 at 01:16 AM]

Modern World History

Part 3: Short Essay

Compare and contrast Japan's isolation period with its modernization period.

Japan was all about keeping to themselves until they were forced not to, and then suddenly, they opened their eyes, got some power, and then used it against everyone else. Isolation wasn't so great, but keeping up with the times turned out to be worse for countries like Korea.

If my daddy wanted his isolation from me, then he sure got it. Part of his war with me is that the baby's father is white, and he said my boyfriend, well, ex-boyfriend, did what white boys and men do best: released himself of all responsibility. Ms. W, he ain't wrong about my ex, except then my daddy turned right around and blamed me for not knowing any better. He said I was a fool for letting my ex sweet-talk me into not using protection every time we had sex, and why wasn't I on the pill? And when I told my daddy that by putting it all on me, he was no better than my ex when it came to not taking responsibility. Let me tell you, my daddy about exploded when I said that. I know he thought about kicking me out right about then, for sure. I kicked myself out for him, if only for the night. I walked right on out of there and stayed with my friend, Yesenia, and by the time I came home the next day, he had stopped talking to me.

Sometimes I wonder if it would have made any difference if I hadn't walked out on him in the middle of our argument. Maybe if I had waited through all the yelling, he would have yelled himself out and been willing just to talk. And maybe he would have listened to me tell him how when I told my ex about being pregnant, he literally said, "Whoa, Reese, don't lay that on me. I'm out." And then he walked away. And maybe my daddy would have come around back to my side and hugged me as I cried about how sorry I was. I didn't mean for it to happen.

And maybe he'd understand when I talk about keeping the baby, I'm not saying I want to get back with my ex, because I don't, and I'm not saying I think it's easy to raise a kid, because I know it isn't, but what about it still being a part of me? What about it still being his grandbaby? It's like I'm Russia and he's Japan, and he doesn't like me keeping Korea, as if he ever should have had a right to it.

I'm doing the online classes to get my diploma. I'm working. I can take care of my baby girl. I can be a good mom.

@@@@@@@@@

Sent February 11

To: Jessamine Lewis <steamyenergy@gmail.com>
From: Naomi Wellington <myownperson02@gmail.com>
Subject: PLAN IS IN MOTION

I can't believe Lanh and I never talked about how we finally started talking. YOU WERE RIGHT. A MONTH. Lanh had his eye on me for a month. For as long as I'd been eying him.

And OMG, I never considered him dropping his book was *planned*.

😍😍😍

He totally-on-purpose dropped his book to spur on conversation. He said he'd been working up the courage to do something more. When he found out through Tracy and Sayeed (who are, I now realize, experienced matchmakers) I would probably be interested in him, he moved forward with Plan Dropsy (which 100% worked, and I can't believe I never suspected given how *not* clumsy he is).

Anyway, this is what we did. This morning, while Pencil Skirt Woman (PSW) and Sloppy Jock Guy (SJG) waited for their coffees (Sayeed purposely took his time making them), I went up with my own cup to, you know, add more whipped cream to it and when I bumped into Pencil Skirt Woman, OOPS! My coffee went flying out of my hands just far enough away so as not to splash on PSW's skirt, but also close enough so she and SJG didn't feel comfortable standing there anymore. (Let me tell you, what a RISK! I kid you not, Lanh, Reese, Leyanna, and I practiced it a few times at home, first.) I apologized profusely, then ushered them to a nearby table to sit at and wait together while I helped Tracy clean my spill, and then Sayeed called out to say he would bring their coffees to them.

"Are they still sitting at the same table?" I whispered to Tracy, who had the better vantage point.

"Mm-hmm."

Then Sayeed came around with their coffees, and I followed him as he set them at their table.

"I'm so sorry," I said as sincerely as possible.

"Oh, no harm done!" PSW waved me off. I don't think she was a bit mad!

"I'm glad it didn't spill on you!" SJG said. "It wouldn't have been a big deal on me since I'm not dressed so nicely."

"But you are dressed nicely!" PSW rushed in, maybe louder than she wanted. "I mean, for going to the gym or, well, not that you only have to wear those clothes for working out, maybe you—"

SJG laughed and put her out of her adorable, flustered misery. "Thank you. I do at least try to look presentable when going out for a run. Or to work. Or to a coffee shop in case I see a really nice woman there."

I swear, my heart fluttered right then and there as though I were reading the meet-cute of a rom-com novel. I didn't verbally excuse myself, worried I might ruin the moment. Instead, I backed away without a word. As I turned back to rejoin Lanh, I gave Sayeed a mini thumbs up.

I think we did it!!

-N

BTW, Sayeed is taking credit for hooking Lanh and me up. He's the one who told Lanh to drop his book. 😶

@@@@@@@@

Sent February 12
To: nick.jones@aesamn.edu
From: naomi.wellington@aesamn.edu
Subject: Re: spot check of exams

Hi Nick,

Thanks for checking in with me about some of the issues arising with my students and how they are interacting with the curriculum!

For one of the questions, you referred to a student who answered, "No Native American nation benefitted from any of our so-called 'peace' treaties or agreements." Did you take note of my comments? I did not score her exam right away because I wanted to clarify that she understood the content. I indicated later that our phone discussion did indeed show she understood the issues surrounding the contentious relationship European Americans continuously developed with Indigenous communities, and as such, I awarded her full credit.

You can see how the exam question was confusing? (To refresh your memory, the question reads: *"Describe how the Dakota* [btw, shouldn't this be Lakota, not Dakota? Or something else? And isn't it a problem that we don't know this for sure?] *and Ojibwe tribes benefitted from the fur trade agreements with the French."*) I believe the question's purpose is to find out what students learned about the fur trade and the conflicts surrounding it, but I don't think the question is very clear about that, do you?

This is yet another area of our curriculum that would benefit (<- a more accurate use of the word, right?) from a thorough review. Our students come from all walks of life and already possess deep critical thinking skills with regard to their worldview. They are wowing me with their ability to open my eyes to this broader perspective. Our current curriculum is outdated, Eurocentric, and doing a great disservice to them in its unaltered state.

I have expanded my research quite a bit to help me shift my lens through which I examine the world, and it would be fantastic to join with others to discuss how to put this into action as we update our curriculum, lesson materials, and assessments. (How did you like that extra self-promotion for the Curriculum Review Committee? :D)

Do let me know of additional questions!

Best!

Naomi Wellington
she/her
Society and History Studies
Alternative Education Solutions
"We realize the importance of our voices only when we are silenced." -
Malala Yousafzai

@@@@@@@@

Sent February 12
To: Jessamine Lewis <steamyenergy@gmail.com>
From: Naomi Wellington <myownperson02@gmail.com>
Subject: children's books

Tonight, Lanh and I thought it would be fun to share our favorite children's books.

Although, to be honest, I wasn't really thinking of "favorite children's book from when I was a kid" because, well, I didn't read a whole lot when I was young. It's not like my mom was ever going to take me to a library, let alone a bookstore, and I never brought books home from the school library since the time my mom ripped pages out to make a funnel because she suddenly had a mad, manic urge to make funnel cakes (which turned out as horribly as you might guess, btw).

So I went with one I loved reading to Leyanna—*A Mother for Choco*, by Keiko Kasza. It's so sweet, and I love how the mother makes it so clear about it not mattering if you look like your mom (or parent in general). Appearance isn't what makes a family. And if I'm 100% truthful, I don't think Leyanna cared much about the book, but the idea was Lanh and my favorite children's book, not Leyanna's. HA!

Lanh agreed on it being a solid choice for favorite.

Lanh's turn.

He didn't have an actual book. Instead, he pulled out his phone and showed me a photo of *The Five Chinese Brothers*. And on the cover alone, I couldn't keep my expression in check. The illustrations are those terrible ones that give all Asian characters squinty eyes and yellow skin. And they all looked alike.

"Yeah," he said.

"Yeah, this is your favorite book?"

"No. I meant, 'yeah, I totally get your reaction.'"

He said he didn't have a favorite children's book because this was the sort of thing his teachers kept suggesting for him. "My first grade teacher gave this book to me and said, 'Here's a story about you and your country!' and how do you respond to something like that when you're six? My mom threw it in the trash and sent me back with an envelope and told me to say we lost it."

Defeat dripped out of him as he told the story. He said it was only recently he discovered young adult books are growing in authentic characters, although he still hasn't found as many, yet, with characters with Vietnamese heritage.

"Let's go to the bookstore," I suggested. "Let's see what we can find."

So we did. At first, we got sidetracked by non-white books in general. We fell in love with Matt de la Peña's *Love* and Jaqueline Woodson's *The Day You Begin* and Yangsook Choi's *The Name Jar*. Oh, that one really made him happy. Do you have that one yet?

Lanh told me he chose his name with his mom. He had his own names in mind, but when his mom ended up being so supportive, he wanted her to share in his re-birth. "Lanh" wasn't his first choice, but his mom loved it, and he loves her, and it was an almost perfect moment between us, right there, sitting next to a giant stuffed Piggie and a child screaming about how SHE WANTED THE TOYS, NOT THE BOOKS!

Lololol.

(Not so funny were the "Looks" we kept getting. You know the ones. The ones where people think they have "almost" figured you out. Imagine if Leyanna were there, too. Queer(?) white woman with queer (?) man (?) from the "country" of Asia with bi-racial teen who they clearly kidnapped!)

He taught me a Vietnamese proverb. I'm copy/pasting it from a website because I have no idea how to type all the special marks —or wait, our language teachers taught us this, so I guess I do, but this is way faster: Ăn quả nhớ kẻ trồng cây. It means something like, when you eat the fruit, remember the one who planted the tree. "Lanh" might not have been his first choice for a name, but the process behind it, the seed growing into the tree it was meant to be is what mattered most. He doesn't speak much Vietnamese, really, but he said his mom is full of proverbs.

Anyway, the actual perfect moment came a few minutes later when we found a book written by a Vietnamese author featuring Vietnamese characters. We both nearly cried. *A Different Pond*, by Bao Phi and Thi Bui.

And now, you know what I'm going to do, yes?

I'M GOING ON A MISSION.

I will find All. The. Picture. Books.

-N

P.S. BTW, look for a package coming your way for Livvy and Isaac in a few days...

@@@@@@@@@

Sent February 16
TO: NAOMI WELLINGTON <MYOWNPERSON02@GMAIL.COM>
FROM: JESSAMINE LEWIS <STEAMYENERGY@GMAIL.COM>
SUBJECT: DIAGNOSIS

I thought about calling you. I thought about texting you. I thought about emailing you sooner, but I needed to sit with everything for a few days. Because, finally, we think we have a diagnosis for Faith.

It's not good.

After a billion tests and what feels like the same number of doctors, a rheumatologist called Faith up sort of out of the blue and said, "Can you come in? I think I know what might be going on." The way he said it sounded so convincing, so *hopeful*, and the doctor made sure we could get an appointment right away.

I was still a little skeptical because male doctors had been the least compassionate or helpful of the whole bunch, but at least he wasn't white. Indian, I think, and he apologized for how much Faith had to go through up to this point. Another doctor, the orthopedist we saw last week, had brought up Faith's case and her bone scans. The rheumatologist asked for more details. He then said there weren't many medical specialists out there who were familiar with what he was pretty sure Faith had.

CRPS. Complex Regional Pain Syndrome. It's also been known as RSDS, or Reflex Sympathetic Dystrophy Syndrome. Something happened to Faith's nervous system response. It's sending constant signals to her arm, basically telling the nerves to react— to *everything*. And since it's the nerves reacting hyperactively, a lot of the most painful things are light touches. It explains why wearing long sleeves has given her agony and why ice was always the absolute wrong thing, in spite of her arm looking swollen.

He referred us to a neurologist he knows who is the closest thing to an expert in CRPS in our area. Except "our area" means Seattle. That's over four hours away. How are we going to manage that? He said the neurologist might try a nerve block, which sometimes stops those constant signals from going out. However, he said the success rate with those nerve blocks isn't high, and it's not like it's a permanent cure. There are specific meds that might help somewhat with the pain, and regular physical therapy will be a must.

So far, it sounds hopeful and manageable, right?

God, Mimi, it's not. He says Faith will likely never be pain-free, and frequently the symptoms spread. It's usually progressive. It could move to her other arm, to both of her legs, her whole body, and because the nervous system is constantly on overdrive, all parts of the body react to compensate. There is no cure—only management.

She will always have pain, and it will almost certainly get worse.

He gave us a shitload of resources to help us learn more, and I have never felt so relieved and scared out of my mind at the same time.

Faith is in denial. She wants to see more doctors. She keeps insisting surgery is the answer. Dr. Patel finally showed her diagrams, and we both learned all about the sympathetic nervous system. He was incredibly patient and answered every single question Faith fired at him. He figured out how to appeal to her academic side, which finally worked. She cried, which made me cry, too.

I'm not sure how we're going to do this.

Sent February 16
To: Jessamine Lewis <steamyenergy@gmail.com>
From: Naomi Wellington <myownperson02@gmail.com>
Subject: Re: diagnosis

Shit.

Shit, shit, shit.

@@@@@@@@@

Sent February 20
To: Naomi Wellington <myownperson02@gmail.com>
From: Jessamine Lewis <steamyenergy@gmail.com>
Subject: Re: band concert

JFC, Mimi, he was a little late to Leyanna's band concert, and you're laying all that "I know he's your brother" shit on him and me. He didn't miss the GD concert, did he? He IS my brother, and he isn't perfect, but maybe sometimes cut him a little slack. He would do anything for that girl, and God knows why, but for you, too.

I'm sick and tired of you thinking I can be your go-to for all things you hate about Jackson. It's not all on him that you got pregnant, and he stepped up, didn't he? He provides child support, gives you primary custody, and lets you make all the decisions. He's not one of those mythical Absent Black Fathers all you white people say he is. He is Present and Engaged.

FFS, get a grip.

Sent February 20
To: Jessamine Lewis <steamyenergy@gmail.com>
From: Naomi Wellington <myownperson02@gmail.com>
Subject: Re: band concert

Jess.

Oh my God, I'm sorry.

To be totally clear: I adore your brother. Even if I'm mad at him, I still love him to pieces. He's fabulous with Leyanna—always has been, always will be. I know with all my heart this is true.

Of course he is present and engaged. I've never thought otherwise. *Never.*

I mean.

Okay. So.

I never told you the full story about the night he and I hooked up, and I never told you the whole story about when I got pregnant and later told him about it.

So yeah, we were at that one house party on campus and yeah, obviously we had been drinking, but I wasn't drunk, and neither was he. There are no fuzzy parts to that night, even though we both play it off that way. You and I were fighting, remember? You gave me a hard time for dating Alyssa. You thought I was stringing her along—using her because there's no such thing as being pansexual, right? I'm not trying to start another argument; instead, I'm bringing it up because Jax? He got it—especially that night. Over the course of our friendship, every time you and I fought, he'd listen to me. He'd defend you, just so you know, but he also saw my side and didn't judge me. He was funny and never treated me like a kid—and not even really like a younger sister.

That night at the party, he listened again. And he asked me about pansexuality, bisexuality, and heteromanticism. He heard me, Jess, like you never did. He didn't flinch. He didn't act all confused and ask a bazillion questions like so many straight people do. He simply nodded and went with it. He told me about how once he wasn't sure about his own sexuality because there was this one boy—and, well, I won't tell you the story because it's not my story to tell. But Jax realized probably most people kind of question themselves at some point.

We connected in a way we hadn't before. In a way I always thought we might.

We walked. Headed toward his place. He asked if I wanted to come up for a while.

It wasn't a drunken fall into each other. It was deliberate. Beautiful. I have never ever regretted that night with him.

When I found out I was pregnant, I told him first, not you. I'm sorry I lied to you about that part. I felt like pretending you were the first person I told was a way back to our friendship, which has always meant so much to me, but I had to tell Jackson first. It was the fair thing to do.

He was so great, Jess. I cry every time I think about it. He smiled when I told him. *Smiled*. No panic. No anger.

"I know we're too young to be parents," he told me, "and if you think we shouldn't go through with it, I'd understand. But I sure hope you decide to keep it."

It was crazy. Before I found out, we'd already figured what we felt for each other wasn't, I don't know, *relationship* emotion. I don't know if we were both wrong about that, and sometimes I've wondered...but I also know I've never truly felt like a single parent.

Jax is more than a friend and even more than family to me. When I say, "I know he's your brother, but..." what I'm really saying is, "I know he's your brother, but he is so much more than that to me, and I only ever truly want the best for him." So yeah, sometimes I get mad at him, but it's the "Obviously I know you are more than this, but sometimes you exasperate me" mad, okay? He and I are like Laurie and Jo in *Little Women*. I will always love him no matter what, and not just because he IS your brother. It's because he's Laurie. He's *Jax*.

I didn't mean to come off being so hard on him about being late to the concert because you're right, he is always Present and Engaged.

And...for what it's worth—I talk to Jackson all the time about decisions about Leyanna. There is no such thing as "primary custody" with us. We decide things together. It's never just me.

<3

-Mimi

Sent February 20
TO: NAOMI WELLINGTON <MYOWNPERSON02@GMAIL.COM>
FROM: JESSAMINE LEWIS <STEAMYENERGY@GMAIL.COM>
SUBJECT: RE: BAND CONCERT

Mimi, I just—wow.

First, I'm sorry, too. Faith had an awful night, the kids took forever to fall asleep, I've been working overtime for the past two weeks, and your email kind of tipped me over the edge.

Second, I know you love my brother. I know you think he's a good dad. Sometimes it's hard living so far away from you all and when it's been a bad night... I explode all over the people I love. I can't be there to protect my brother, so I pretend to do it virtually. If you're Jo, and Jax is Laurie, then I'm Aunt March. I want to say I'm Meg, but I'm not all that gentle. Obviously.

Third. You and Jackson. I don't even know what to say. I need some time on that one. Not "mad at you, ho" time, though, okay? To get all white on you to make sure you get me, I'm "processing." Plus, there's so much more—you don't even know.

-Jess

[11:38 Feb 20]

NAOMI

JESSAMINE

Sent February 21
To: Naomi Wellington <myownperson02@gmail.com>
From: Jessamine Lewis <steamyenergy@gmail.com>
Subject: Re: band concert

Okay, fourth. There's stuff going on with Jax. For one, I'm not supposed to tell you this, but he didn't swear me to it... Jax and Whitney broke up. It all went down just before the concert. That's why he was late. And there's more. So much more.

@@@@@@@@

[8:02 Feb 21]

NAOMI

Since when did you become such a good actor?

JACKSON

Yeah, IDK where you're going with this.

NAOMI

I'm sorry about Whitney.

JACKSON

...

NAOMI

...

NAOMI

Don't be mad at Jess. We kind of had a ...
thing. She thought I should know.

JACKSON

I'm not mad at Jess.

NAOMI

raises eyebrows

JACKSON

Maybe a little.

JACKSON

Actually, nah. I'm not.

NAOMI

Why didn't you tell me?

JACKSON

It was Leyanna's night. I didn't want to ruin it
for anyone.

NAOMI

You're too damn noble.

JACKSON

I don't think Whitney would think so. I wasn't
very nice to her before I left.

NAOMI

What happened?

JACKSON

Lots of shit. Too much to get into over texts.

NAOMI

Sounds like I need to kick her ass.

JACKSON

I'd love to see that.

NAOMI

Pervert.

JACKSON

That's where you went with that? Sounds like you're the horny one instead.

NAOMI

Maybe.

JACKSON

Thought you had it goin' on with that dude from the coffee shop?

NAOMI

I did. I do. IDK.

JACKSON

Do I need to step in and kick HIS ass?

NAOMI

NO!

JACKSON

Sounds like I do.

NAOMI

I think he's moving to D.C.

JACKSON

Damn. I'm sorry.

NAOMI

Yeah.

JACKSON

You wanna meet up at Chocolate Glacier? Bring along our girl.

Naomi

We'll be there in 10.

@@@@@@@@@

Sent February 21
To: Jessamine Lewis <steamyenergy@gmail.com>
From: Naomi Wellington <myownperson02@gmail.com>
Subject: first fight

Okay, so there was more to the whole irritable side of me a couple of days ago, too.

The first fight is a sign of a real relationship, right? It means you're solid enough to handle it?

Except, I don't know how solid we are right now.

Last week Lanh said he would be out of town Monday and Tuesday for a business trip, only it wasn't a business trip; it was an interview. He flew to New York for an interview with Teach for America.

When we met at the Cafe this morning for our (mostly) daily coffee and book chat, he was super excited, which got me all excited, too, in spite of not knowing why.

"I just had a super exciting interview yesterday!" was how he started our conversation.

Um, what? Interview? I was only a little confused because maybe he meant he and his team interviewed someone, or maybe they were doing some sort of pitch. Honestly, I still don't understand all the ins and outs of his job. He doesn't talk about it much. Probably because he doesn't super enjoy it; hence the career change. This excitement was good, though! Maybe the job was getting better, which would help him hang on to it while he finished his M.Ed and got licensed.

"Wow!" I told him. "Sounds great. What kind of interview?"

"Teach for America. I think it went really well!"

"Teach for America? I don't get it. Are you guys taking them on as a client?"

He laughed, which in hindsight SUPER PISSED ME OFF. "No, of course not. We don't do non-profs. *They* were interviewing *me*. I'm hoping to join the TFA corps."

Where was this all coming from? I swear he never talked about it, ever, until now.

It turns out he worked on his application materials all last month and knew about this interview for over two weeks now. And never told me about any of it.

And if they offer him a spot, he will accept it. And move, probably, to Washington D.C. In a month.

A month. WTAF?

"Why didn't you tell me about all of this?" I super hard wanted to yell or curse at him, but didn't.

He slid his chair around to be right next to me and took my hand. His eyes calmed me down. I've always kind of melted when he'd look at me so intensely like that with his beautiful brown eyes. "I was nervous. I didn't realize how much I wanted this until I got the interview request. What if they wouldn't accept me? I mean, look at me. In this country, I've got a billion strikes against me. I'm not white. I'm not technically able-bodied. I'm not cisgender. My whole life has been the world giving me a big fat 'NO.'"

"But all those things seem like they'd be in the 'pro' column for an org like Teach for America."

Wouldn't they? I'm not saying I couldn't get into the TFA corps as a white woman, but I think it's a *good* thing for them to be more attracted to people of color. I mean, it's not like our schools in lots of areas in this country are doing so great at this kind of recruitment.

"Wow. That is super white, able-bodied, and cis of you to say. Do you honestly believe it?"

Fuck. He was right. Just like you are always right when you tell me that kind of thing. There are a lot of ways I won't fully get it. I apologized and told him all of that.

And then I moved on. "So, the interview went great? They love you and see all the great things I see about you, too?" I tried to smile while saying it, I really did, but I couldn't. I know TFA will offer him a spot, and he's going to leave.

He smiled, though, and kissed me, and I almost forgave him.

And then he suggested me and Leyanna move down to D.C. with him. He said Leyanna wanted to do online school and I taught online; it seemed like an easy transition. Plus, we could meet some of his family from his mom's side.

You know. *Snap*. No problem.

"But Jackson is here."

He nodded, "I know. But you have primary custody, right? I know it might be difficult at first. I know it's not easy having—"

I stopped him right there, holding my hand up like a stop sign. "No, I don't have primary custody. Jackson and I are 100% co-parenting. She splits her time pretty evenly between us. It's how we've always done it. We've always agreed about living no more than a couple of hours drive from one another."

"Wow, really? That's an amazingly civil custody agreement."

Huh. Had we never talked about my situation with Jax? I guess not. Since it's always worked so well between Jax and me all these years, I forget it's not common.

So I told him we didn't have any official custody agreement and how back before Leyanna was born, we talked through how we wanted to work together to raise her.

"Hold up," he waved his arms at me and then moved his chair back to its original spot across the table from me. Jess, my heart sank right there. We have *not* broken up, but this maneuver? Not a good sign. Not that him moving to D.C. was a good sign, either...you know what I mean.

"You guys broke up *before* Leyanna was born? The way you talk about Jackson, I didn't think he was that sort of guy."

That sort of guy? What did that even mean? Did it mean what I think it did?

"That sort of guy? What are you saying?" I asked.

"I'm saying I figured something happened later on, after Leyanna was born, to make you break up. Age and maturity or something. I don't know. Instead, it sounds like he bailed on you early. The typical male, dick-move."

Wow, it's like he didn't even notice his own male, dick move of *not listening*.

"First," I told him, "what an asshole assumption you just made, in spite of everything I've ever told you now and in the past about Jax. Second, we were never 'together.' It was this one-time thing. Plus, we have Leyanna. He's family, so that's why we never had to do any sort of formal custody arrangement. When I said we 100% co-parent, I wasn't being euphemistic. So no, I am not uprooting and taking Leyanna away from him, nor am I leaving her and going on my own. We don't live together, but Jackson, Leyanna, and I are a family nonetheless."

And then my phone reminded me I had a department meeting in five minutes, and I could *not* handle another drag-Naomi-over-the-nailbed reprimand from Nick the Dick, so I stood to go.

"C'mon, Naomi. Don't leave like that."

I didn't want to leave "like that," and yet I was kind of glad I had to because I wasn't sure if his tone was calling me an over-reactor or if it was apologetic.

Leyanna's band concert was in the evening, and Lanh's stupid comments were in my head about Jax, which were unfair, yet contributed to my mood. It was never about Jackson, and then Leyanna got on my case AGAIN about doing online school at the end of the night. That girl is relentless, and OMG, it's almost March. Can't she just set it aside at this point and get through the year?

Lanh texted an apology. Later we talked, and he asked if he didn't get the TFA spot, could he try to be a part of my family, too?

Maybe he and I will be all right.

-N

Sent February 21
To: Naomi Wellington <myownperson02@gmail.com>
From: Jessamine Lewis <steamyenergy@gmail.com>
Subject: Re: first fight (50 billionth fight for us, tho)

That sucks about Lanh. I feel like he's been good for you.

Thank you for standing up for Jackson to him. I'm sure you've heard a little more about the story with him and Whitney by now, although he said he didn't tell you all the details yet, and could I do it because he isn't ready to face your wrath you're sure to feel about it.

And because it's late, I'm emailing it all to you instead of calling because I can't have you yelling through the phone right now. Plus, I don't have the energy for it. The whole thing is like it's from a goddamn Tyler Perry movie. We've now learned that Whitney is an ice-cold, granite-faced, top-of-the-line bitch.

First, you know about Whitney's affair. She's been seeing this guy on the side for several *months* now. Some slick sales guy from the dealership. I looked him up online with Connect-Me, and he's not even a *good* salesman. Been job hopping all year from dealership to dealership. How's Whitney supposed to be attracted to that over our Jackson, whose brains are spilling out of his head and owns his own successful business? I don't get it.

Second. OMFG, here's where it gets really bad. The first miscarriage? It wasn't a miscarriage. Whitney took the abortion pill because she didn't know whose baby she was carrying, and she didn't want to "confuse" things.

For real, Mimi, I had to close my computer just now and pace the living room floor for a good ten minutes to calm the fuck down after writing that part.

Third. The second miscarriage? Didn't happen. Whitney totally lied because she knew this one wasn't Jackson's. She was already pregnant before she and Jackson had started trying again after the first (non)miscarriage. Who the fuck fakes a miscarriage? The whole thing went down when Jackson found a bag with a new onesie in it. He saw the date on the receipt, and because his brain processes all those stupid details in two seconds, he realized it was from only a week ago.

Take care of my brother for me, k? And don't tell Momma about the abortion pill part. I think that would kill her.

@@@@@@@@@

[5:10 Feb 22]

NAOMI

I WILL KILL HER

JACKSON

You talked to my sister, I see

NAOMI

SHE IS THE SINGLE WORST PERSON I HAVE
EVER KNOWN

JACKSON

Right now I can't say I disagree

NAOMI

I WANT TO THROW THINGS

JACKSON

So throw 'em. I did

NAOMI

Can't. The girls are studying. Well, they're
acting like they are, at least

NAOMI

God, Jax. I'm so sorry about Whitney the Witch

JACKSON

Don't go pretending that nickname is new

NAOMI

It is! I swear! So many more…Whitney the
Worst. Whitney the Werewolf. What the Fuck
Whitney

NAOMI

I liked her

JACKSON

Yeah, well

NAOMI

OMG, what a stupid thing for me to say to you
right now. I'm sorry

JACKSON

It's nothing I haven't already been thinking or
yelling out loud over here

NAOMI

Wanna get some ice cream? Just you and me,
then you don't have to filter yourself

JACKSON

You know what? Yeah, that sounds good

NAOMI

See you soon!

@@@@@@@@@

Sent February 27
TO: NAOMI WELLINGTON <MYOWNPERSON02@GMAIL.COM>
FROM: JESSAMINE LEWIS <STEAMYENERGY@GMAIL.COM>
SUBJECT: USELESS

Remember that scene in *American Road Trip* where Teodoro
walks into the house and immediately knows something is
wrong? He knows his brother is messed up and feels the weight
of all the responsibility, and he leaves, knowing it's not fair for
him to get sucked into it all when he's trying to get his own shit
together.

I came home today to find Faith's car in the garage—early. I had
the kids, and I knew it was bad as soon as we came in through
the garage. The chairs were tipped over in all positions across
the kitchen floor. Broken glass in the sink. I got Olivia on my
back and picked up Isaac and trod carefully, not knowing how
much glass might be on the floor, too. I swear my ribs were
about to crack for how hard my heart was pounding.

I got the kids a snack and planted them in front of the TV and searched for Faith. She was in our bedroom, pounding her head against the wall, sobbing. I wanted to hug her so badly, Mimi, and I can't stand not being able to when she's like this. Technically the pain is only in that one arm, but when she goes through a flare-up—when it's this bad, she won't let me near her. It was all I could do to get padding between her head and the wall. I shut down all the lights and curtains and pulled up one of her meditation recordings.

All I'm ever doing is circling around how to help her. You know most days are not this awful, but it's still so new that we can't anticipate the sudden change—the triggers. I read every fucking thing I can get my hands on to figure out how to make things better, how to help her, and then each day I fall asleep, and the word that haunts me is "progressive."

It's going to get worse. We don't know how or when, but it will get worse.

And sometimes, I feel just like Teodoro and want to find every excuse not to come home.

I can hardly bear to see her in this much pain now. How will I be strong enough for her later?

-Jess

Sent February 27
TO: JESSAMINE LEWIS <STEAMYENERGY@GMAIL.COM>
FROM: NAOMI WELLINGTON <MYOWNPERSONO2@GMAIL.COM>
SUBJECT: RE: USELESS

Babe, I am so sorry. I'll avoid all the unhelpful platitudes save for one: You are one of the strongest people I know. I don't know how you will manage to support Faith as things get worse; I just know you will because I know how much you love her.

On the other hand, remember how frustrated we were about Teodoro's sister and parents in *American Road Trip*? About how his sister kept laying guilt on Teodoro for trying to make a way out for himself? I was so angry at her for putting so much on him. For almost destroying his future. So I don't know if you want to hear this, but...if you can't do it? It's okay. I know that sounds horrible and selfish and not at all what you're supposed to do when you marry and say those vows, but if it will destroy you, then do what you need to do. I support YOU.

-Mimi

@@@@@@@@@

Sent February 28
To: naomi.wellington@aesamn.edu
From: hope.jensen@student.aesamn.edu
Subject: I need help

Dear Ms. W,

My grade in your class (geography) is not good and i need 2 pass this class so i can graduate this year. i promised my mom i would get my diploma and i'm trying super hard but its been really hard 2 remember so many different facts and stuff for all my classes and super hard 2 focus because my mom is really sick and i spend most of my time taking care of her even though she says 2 leave her be so i can get some rest and put my energy into studying. i can't ever make the online sessions you or anyone else has and the recordings never seem 2 help me with the stuff i can't get my brain 2 remember. ive never been good at school and i thought this would be easier and in some ways it is because at least i dont have 2 be in class all day but its still alot of work and I dont know what 2 do can you plz help

Hope

@@@@@@@@@

Dear Naomi,

The new counselor here says letter-writing to our loved ones is a good first step to "recovery of relationships." I know your a big reader (remember our trips to the libary?), so I hope you'll read this hole letter.

I know I haven't always been the best mom. I didn't give hugs all the time and bake cookies, but I tried to be there for you. I chose jobs so I could stay home for you and never gave up when those jobs didn't always work out. I wish I didn't miss some of them school events, and I wish you didn't feel like you had to go and find a new mom. She'll never love you like your own mom—me. I promise.

Cause I'm gonna make it all up to you when I get out. Did you know I heard from your daddy a little bit ago? He's been writing me while I'm here (maybe you didn't know I could get letters and that's why I haven't heard from you?) and he has a great new business opportunity for us! He's real sorry about leaving. He's been having a hard time of it for a long time like us and didn't want to burden me like he used to until he got his life all turned around. But now he's ready and I'm gonna meet him in Chicago right when I get outta here, which should be in a couple a weeks cause things are going real good.

Maybe you and that girl of yours will come with me. We could have a fun girls road trip to a new life.

Write back to me, okay?

Mom

@@@@@@@@

BOARD: WE WERE HERE by Matt de la Peña

▽ **TOPIC:** Check-in question/poll: Red Hots, Hot Tamales, or Fireballs?

Naomi: Hot Tamales. They don't break my teeth.

Tyrell: Fireballs. If you're going in, go ALL IN.

Susette: They're all too spicy for me. *ducks*

Grant: I'm with Tyrell, Fireballs, except I drive my wife crazy when I have one because I complain about how hot it is the whole time.

Maxine: Red Hots! They're great for baking, too!

Chester: Hot Tamales. I got my reasons.

Lisa: Fireballs. Duh. Why bother with the other two?

▽ **TOPIC:** This book has Miguel using a lot of offensive language in his stereotyping of others around him. How does this reflect how he is processing his world and emotions? How does this change by the end of the novel?

Naomi: I confess, as much as I loved these characters (and I super loved them—they remind me so much of my students), I straight up did *not* like Miguel's use of certain terms to describe Mong, Rondell, and some other people he sometimes ran into. It was real, though, and I really like how you framed this question, Susette, because yeah, this makes sense. I sort of thought at first this was simply the author's characterization of Miguel. And his defensive behavior felt natural and expected to me, but I didn't think about how his stereotyping might have stemmed from defensive mechanisms, too.

Lisa: Well, I don't know if we can attribute all his prejudicial crap to trauma. Some of it might be how he grew up. I know plenty of kids who have gone through some awful shit and still remember people are real. I appreciated, though, how Miguel making sense out of his world around him helped him learn better along the way.

Chester: That sounded downright professional, Lisa.

Lisa: Fuck off, Chester.

Chester: 😂😂😂

Chester: For real, tho. You sound like you totally know what you're talking about. How do you know this stuff?

Lisa: Part of my job.

Chester: Which is?

Lisa: Are we being real? Or "realz?"

Chester: I'm being straight up, here.

Lisa: I'm a social worker. I work with adoptive families.

Chester: Cool.

Susette: Now I kinda want to know what everyone here does. We've been getting to know each other through our book discussions. I don't think we *really* know each other, though.

Naomi: Well, I know Lisa doesn't smoke.

Lisa: And Naomi has an awesome daughter!

Naomi: :) Thank you. She is pretty great.

Naomi: I teach online.

Maxine: I do product reviews. Mostly with cleaning tools.

Tyrell: Music mixing for TV show soundtracks and some small-scale films.

Chester: That is tight.

Susette: That sounds fun! More fun than payroll.

Grant: I'm mostly a stay-at-home dad, but I bartend part-time at night.

Susette: This is so fun! I love how we have come together like this. Thank you for sharing so much of yourselves. I love this group.

Naomi:

Lisa:

Sent March 06
TO: NAOMI.WELLINGTON@AESAMN.EDU
FROM: NICK.JONES@AESAMN.EDU
SUBJECT: SS CURRICULUM REVIEW

Hi Naomi,

Thank you for your enthusiasm in applying for the curriculum review committee. Unfortunately, in the interests of balance, we have reached our maximum number of members and cannot take any more at this time.

Thank you for your dedication to our department and learning organization.

Best,

Nick Jones
Department Chair
Society and History Studies
Alternative Education Solutions
"Never mistake activity for achievement." - John Wooden

@@@@@@@@@

Sent March 07
To: Jessamine Lewis <steamyenergy@gmail.com>
From: Naomi Wellington <myownperson02@gmail.com>
Subject: limbo

Lanh and I had been sort of dancing around each other for the past couple of weeks until yesterday, when we talked things out. I think we were both surprised by our feelings for one another and how we both saw so much potential for our relationship. It shocked the hell out of him when he realized he wanted me and Leyanna to come with him to D.C. if the job panned out. The realization blinded him, and he didn't think about how it could affect me personally. Didn't I feel the same way about him? Couldn't I see this as an OPPORTUNITY?

Talk about a hit to the solar plexus.

I thought I felt the same way about him. Or maybe I think I do. Except I can't take Leyanna away from Jackson. And I can't leave her. He gets it. I know he does. And so we've kind of...set it all aside for now because maybe TFA won't accept him. I don't especially want to consider him leaving when we've just gotten started.

And yes, we've definitely restarted, in a way. We're back to spending a lot more time together again and now, not only do we talk books over coffee/breakfast, we talk teaching, too. Regardless of what happens with TFA, Lanh will make a great teacher. He's funny, smart, and compassionate. We talk about his P.E. teacher in middle school who helped Lanh find safe spaces for changing (his GYM teacher—this has restored some of my faith in middle school gym classes and locker rooms) and encouraged him to research HRT during their health unit. We talked about my ninth grade social studies teacher who let me eat my breakfast in her room while we debated politics and she taught me how to look at history through different lenses and how it affects dominant and marginalized populations not only here in the US, but in so many other countries in the world.

Lanh wants to change lives. I can't fault him for choosing a path to help him do it. OTOH, can't he do it here in Minneapolis, too?

-N

@@@@@@@@@

Sent March 08
TO: JESSAMINE LEWIS <STEAMYENERGY@GMAIL.COM>
FROM: NAOMI WELLINGTON <MYOWNPERSON02@GMAIL.COM>
SUBJECT: IT'S ALL A SUBJECTIVE MAZE

I would never admit it to him, but sometimes, I understand Nick the Dick's point about grading. It would be kind of nice if all grading could be objective and straightforward. If there were perfect questions and 100% right or 100% wrong answers. Instead, it's all gray area.

These students of mine have answers to discussion and exam questions that are right and yet not right, and sometimes I don't know if I'm doing them a disservice by giving them full credit for stuff my history teachers wouldn't have when I was in school.

When a student points out that only white people like to think there are other causes for the Civil War other than slavery, I can't really fault them on that, especially when it's well-argued. Or that Trump is the same as Hitler when they show their research and analysis. Sure, not all of these students are the most eloquent in how they write it all out, but they are doing what any historian does—interpreting based on facts.

But, you know, the textbooks are looking for different answers—based on the same facts. Nick the Dick is constantly on my back about these answers that are *right,* but they're not the ones white history teachers have anticipated since a billion years ago. They're not the neat, tidy, prep school answers he seems to be expecting. Has he forgotten what kinds of students we have at an alternative learning school? That some are there only by the skin of their teeth? That we should be thrilled they are truly doing the work, the *thinking,* and interacting?

I love the "tell it like it is" responses from some of these students who might typically have turned in a blank exam paper in a traditional F2F classroom. I have others who give the rote, book facts, and I don't know, Jess. Tell me, which one is going to do better? I want my kids to think and push me, but am I supposed to show them how to assimilate instead?

Or is that stupid, "well-meaninged" whiteness talking? Or just plain ignorance?

-N

Sent March 08
To: Naomi Wellington <myownperson02@gmail.com>
From: Jessamine Lewis <steamyenergy@gmail.com>
Subject: Re: it's all a subjective maze

"Especially when it's well-argued"? Yeah, I guess you mean well, but I'm too tired to teach you stuff I thought you already knew.

You figure it out. I got my own kids to raise.

It's been a shit weekend, Mimi. I'm out for 24.

Sent March 08
TO: JESSAMINE LEWIS <STEAMYENERGY@GMAIL.COM>
FROM: NAOMI WELLINGTON <MYOWNPERSON02@GMAIL.COM>
SUBJECT: RE: IT'S ALL A SUBJECTIVE MAZE

Thank you, Jess. I guess I deserved that.

I'm sorry about your weekend.

@@@@@@@@@

Sent March 09
TO: NICK.JONES@AESAMN.EDU
FROM: NAOMI.WELLINGTON@AESAMN.EDU
SUBJECT: AT-PROMISE

Hi Nick!

I just watched this fantastic TED talk from a few years ago, and I can't believe we haven't embraced this guy's ideas here at AESA. He talks about changing the idea of "at-risk" students to "at-promise." I think he meant how our kids have a lot of potential—they have promise for going far when given the right opportunity and support. I like the idea of turning it around, too —we see them at-promise from *us* to provide them with that support, to provide them with the necessary resources.

This is what our program is meant to be about, right?

What do you think? I'd love to address this in our next staff meeting. Before then, I plan on speaking a bit about it in next week's department blog.

Cheers,

Naomi

@@@@@@@@@

Sent March 10

TO: JESSAMINE LEWIS <STEAMYENERGY@GMAIL.COM>

FROM: NAOMI WELLINGTON <MYOWNPERSON02@GMAIL.COM>

SUBJECT: I WANT TO THROW NICK INTO THE FIERY PIT OF HELL

OH MY GOD, I HATE NICK JONES SO MUCH.

And myself, because I am SO STUPID.

Why, why, why did I share with him before writing about it for our department? Why, why, why did I "ask" him his thoughts?

He took full credit for one of my ideas, and I want to squash him.

I want to yell, "That's *my* idea!" but it's not like it's even really my original idea. It was just a concept I thought we should run with, and to bring it up to anyone sounds... petty.

I've been emailing our actual director, who is on leave, and even though I get why she hasn't answered me, this school has always meant so much to her, and I wish she'd at least acknowledge the problems. Her silence is like an endorsement.

It's kids like Reese who are at risk so screw it. I'm gathering forces to stop this school's destruction.

-N

@@@@@@@@@

Sent March 10

TO: NAOMI WELLINGTON <NAOMI.WELLINGTON@MAIL.COM>

FROM: VOICE MESSAGING <VOICEMESSAGING@CLEAR-VOICE.COM>

SUBJECT: NEW VOICE MESSAGE FROM 612-555-3655

I see you're back to not answering my calls no more. I did rehab instead a jail for you and I bet you didn't even tell your girl about our opportunity waiting for us with her grandpa in Chicago, did you? I'm going and maybe I won't come back and we'll see if you don't start taking my calls again when you need something.

@@@@@@@@

Sent March 11
To: Jessamine Lewis <STEAMYENERGY@GMAIL.COM>
From: Naomi Wellington <MYOWNPERSON02@GMAIL.COM>
Subject: lunches

Do you remember the day we met, and you made fun of my lunch? My mom made me bring a bag lunch because she wasn't going to "fill out no damn poor form so people would think we were white trash" and then proved we were by packing a bologna and cheese whiz sandwich and a stalk of celery. I don't know if you remember what you said exactly, but I do because it made all the difference between making me feel bad and just cracking a joke and inviting me in on it. You said, "Girl, that lunch is whack, but your nails are outta sight, so I'm gonna sit with you 'cuz you all right." (Please do not take this as validation that you would "slay" at a rap battle. I think the time you used "I'm a wickitty wise lady / Who won't ever be your bibbity boo baby" proves that.)

I hated so much to have had that lunch. I would have thrown it out, except I was so hungry. My mom was so strung out that morning; there was no arguing with her about making my lunch instead of doing it myself like I usually did. Those random moments of "oh, I wanna be a MOM today, for like, five minutes" sometimes felt more painful than all the times she just up and ignored me or hit me up for cash.

Leyanna asked if she could stay with Jackson for longer than her normal week. Like for maybe a month. Or more.

And all I can think of is stopping and making a bologna and cheez whiz sandwich for her because maybe she'll remember that I am her mom.

Those five-minute moments from my mom? I hated them because I craved them.

I know he's your brother, but how can I say yes to Leyanna?

But am I only a celery stick if I say no?

-N

P.S. To be clear, I know he's your brother, and that is why I will obviously say yes. It still hurts, though.

P.P.S. Reese said it'll be okay because Leyanna is young and will figure herself out. There's like, five years difference between Leyanna and Reese. "She's young." *snort*

@@@@@@@@@

Course [U.S. History] Announcements

Announcement:

This Day in History - March 12

1884

First U.S. state college for women opens in Mississippi.

1894

Coca-Cola sold in bottles for the first time.

1933

President Roosevelt starts his fireside chats.

1945

Anne Frank dies in German concentration camp.

Today

~~Leyanna leaves me.~~

Josh and Nico model an awesome debate about the 22nd Amendment! Good work! You gave us all a lot to think about!

Announcement:

Study guides are due next Monday in order to review at the Study Session on Tuesday!

@@@@@@@@@

LOVING FAMILY ADOPTION SERVICES
ADOPTIVE FAMILY PROFILE

Sage and Willow

Basic Profile

Basic Profile

	Sage	Willow
Age	27	26
Ethnicity/Race	White/Caucasian	White/Caucasian
Education	Undergraduate Degree seeking an MFA	Undergraduate Degree seeking an MFA
Religion	Open	Open
Occupation	Teaching Assistant/Barista	Teaching Assistant/Daycare Assistant
Health	Excellent	Excellent
Smoking/Alcohol Use	Some recreational use	Some recreational use

Our Story

Sage and Willow met at a coffee shop during an open mic session three years ago and clicked immediately after listening to each other's poetry. They are both actively pursuing their MFA and love using each other as critique partners. They feel this accurately portrays how well they will parent together for a couple that can accept constructive criticism from the person they trust most, surely can work through any parenting challenges. Sage and Willow will welcome your child into their home and encourage their creative soul right from the start by offering choices as their child grows. They intend to unschool for a healthy and natural learning experience which will fully nurture the free, unfettered spirit.

Age Preference (Y-yes, N-no, WTC-willing to consider)

_Y_ Newborn

_Y_ 1-12 months

_Y_ 2-4 years

_N_ 5-12 years

_N_ 13+ years

Race/Ethnicity (Y-yes, N-no, WTC-willing to consider)

_Y_ White/Caucasian

_Y_ Black or African-American

_Y_ American Indian or Alaskan Native

_Y_ Native Hawaiian or Pacific Islander

_Y_ Asian

Post-Adoption Cooperative Communication Plan

Sage and Willow are, and always will be, a proponent of a fully open adoption, including a live-in situation for the birth mother before and after the baby's birth. "We will always be the child's constant and understand not all involved parties are able to bond with traditional commitment, so we must accommodate everyone's spirit."

@@@@@@@@@

Sent March 15
To: Jessamine Lewis <steamyenergy@gmail.com>
From: Naomi Wellington <myownperson02@gmail.com>
Subject: I might be in a teensy bit over my head

So, Reese is utterly and completely not ready to have a baby.

I mean, whoever is, really. I had no idea until reality hit me hard with Leyanna. Momma Junie flooded me with advice and photocopied magazine articles and books, though. I've been trying to do a little bit of the same for Reese, but she has yet to touch any of the reading material. Maybe an app would be better?

She has a job, which is good. She works at the front desk of her school district's activity center, which at times allows her to work on schoolwork when it's not busy. She spends all her money on baby shoes. As in, so far, she has sixteen pairs of mini ballet slippers, hiking boots (?? Where is this infant going to be HIKING?), snow boots, sandals, tennis shoes, patent leather shoes, crocs, and flip flops. FLIP FLOPS. (Although, they have a little strap for the back of the foot, and they ARE cute.)

I know. Obviously, she is working through some issues. I'm trying to reach her through essay comments because she's still "talking" to me through those. It's taking more time than I expected to get her to bridge over to talking to me IRL instead of through C- grading comments. So far, Nick the Dick has not completely squashed our grade book conversations since he can't usually remember who he's been spot-checking when spying on, I mean, "observing" our classes. I'm pretty sure he'd work a case for me to fail Reese if he tracked our relationship via Modern World History. (Although it would make for an interesting new textbook: "How to Put World Conflict in Family Conflict Context." Maybe I'll write a paper.)

Anyway. Baby shoes. "They're so cute!" She's not wrong. Maybe we could make a mobile out of them.

Jax picked up Leyanna today. She had so much stuff packed, and it's hard not to believe she's never coming back. She said goodbye to me, but didn't hug me. As she walked to the car, Jax stayed behind and did his best to reassure me. "It won't be so long. She needs you too much, you know."

I don't know, though. We've had so few good moments in the past several months; it's not enough to fool me into thinking she needs me. And when Reese showed up, I was replaced pretty quickly. Part of me didn't mind because a friend is what Leyanna's been needing, right? And I've listened to some of their conversations. Reese has been good for Leyanna. Like an older sister.

Here comes another round of tears.

-N

@@@@@@@@@

Sent March 16

To: Jessamine Lewis <steamyenergy@gmail.com>
From: Naomi Wellington <myownperson02@gmail.com>
Subject: it's official

Lanh got the offer for Teach for America and leaves in two weeks, and I'm obviously not going with him, and now we are officially broken up.

Why is everyone leaving me?

@@@@@@@@

ORDER [589] *07:57 AM*
-Naomi-
[1] 20 oz
Breve
x-tra Whip
[1] blbry muffin -TO GO -
[1] bagel - TO GO -
mple fr toast
[1] scone - TO GO -
cran-orange

@@@@@@@@

Sent March 17
To: Naomi Wellington <myownperson02@gmail.com>
From: Jessamine Lewis <steamyenergy@gmail.com>
Subject: Re: breakup

I'm sorry about Lanh. He seemed good for you, which means he'll undoubtedly be good for his future students.

I know you're hurting about Leyanna, too, and I appreciate you realizing she'll be in good hands with Jackson. He needs this. The whole Whitney thing is still beating him down.

For real, though? She needs it, too. Shit's falling apart around you, and you're just wading around in it instead of shoveling it all out. I get it, you care about your students (enough to house one,

I guess, too—what are you gon' do when that baby comes?), and I'm not saying they're not important, but wake the fuck up. You got family who needs you, too.

I'm tired of trying to be all understanding about stuff. I'm so fucking tired. All Of The Time.

@@@@@@@@@

Sent March 18
TO: JESSAMINE LEWIS <STEAMYENERGY@GMAIL.COM>
FROM: NAOMI WELLINGTON <MYOWNPERSON02@GMAIL.COM>
SUBJECT: HAIR

Reason #13 why it wouldn't have worked out with Lanh anyway. He didn't much like my short hair.

What is it with guys and long hair? I remember Jax's disappointment when I chopped all my hair off, and we weren't even dating (I mean, kind of not back when I was pregnant). I dated a guy a few years ago who kept making comments about other women's long hair. "Look how shimmery it is." or "Does your hair grow out curly or straight?"

It shouldn't seem weird that a trans guy would be disappointed in my short hair, but it kind of is. Wouldn't he have empathized a little?

It's trivial, and yet not. Why must we be judged by our hair? Why do people think it's funny (or worse, "cool," like they think they're "in the know") to call my hair a "butch" cut? It's short. Period.

Reese says Lanh was crazy for not liking it all spiked because she thinks it looks "wicked sexy," and I didn't tell her how Lanh did enjoy running his fingers through the spikes because I do have *some* boundaries, after all. Anyway, she's going to bleach and dye purple highlights in my hair tonight, and I'm going to put twists into hers. A regular girls' night in.

Partly.

I miss Leyanna.

-N

@@@@@@@@@

Sent March 20
TO: JESSAMINE LEWIS <STEAMYENERGY@GMAIL.COM>
FROM: NAOMI WELLINGTON <MYOWNPERSONO2@GMAIL.COM>
SUBJECT: REASON #29

Lanh was going to be a new teacher, and new teachers are either super idealistic or super whiny. What if he ended up being whiny? It would never have worked.

I mean, sure, super idealistic might have been okay. Best not to risk it, though.

Twenty-nine students showed up for my help session today. An all-time high! And they asked questions! And we talked about other stuff, too. I considered stopping the recording because I know what Nick the Dick will say: "Off-topic! Don't waste time on non-instructional material!" How else are these kids supposed to blow off steam? This way, they know they're not alone. If I were in a F2F classroom, colleagues and administration would cheer at the idea of such an engaged group, and yet here, I'll get reprimanded.

As difficult as this year has been with our stupid leadership, it's been my best year with students. We've really connected, and their assignments and participation show how this alternative form of learning truly is successful for kids who need something different.

I feel like I'm actually making a difference.

-N

@@@@@@@@@

Sent March 24
TO: JESSAMINE LEWIS <STEAMYENERGY@GMAIL.COM>
FROM: NAOMI WELLINGTON <MYOWNPERSON02@GMAIL.COM>
SUBJECT: DIGGING A HOLE TO SHOVE NICK THE DICK INTO

Five feet by five feet. Isn't that how deep and how wide each hole had to be for the kids in *Holes* to dig every day? I want to dump Nick the Dick into one that has one of those lizard nests. So get this, he steals my "At-Promise" idea (well, not *my* idea, but my idea to implement it) and tries to look all great, but then he turns around and tells us we have to fail any kid who still doesn't have 50% of the course completed.

He's doubling down on the late work thing by saying students can't make up any work that was due before February first. And Interim Idiot Director Mark is backing him up. I keep thinking of the counselor from *Holes*, too, the one who seems like he's all for helping the kids, but then he totally talks shit about the kid who doesn't know how to read as though he's dumb. Interim Idiot and Nick the Dick talk of how we need to maintain high expectations and then simultaneously act as though our students who work full-time jobs and take care of their younger siblings are simply lazy. Where the hell did our REAL director find these yahoos?

I think finally, we might be getting somewhere in blocking some of these changes. Some of us have been private messaging about what's going on, and I'm thinking of starting up a private group chat so we can at least vent to each other without fear of reper-cussions. We have a staff forum in the Academy LMS, and it's great for sharing ideas in general. We can't express our honest opinions about things, though. Every time we hint at frustration about a policy change, Mark the Shark swoops in and reminds us the forum is for professional, academic discussion. Like, what about our talk of policies is not professional or academic? We need a teacher's lounge. A place away from administrative ears to be real with one another. It's one of the challenges of working online only—we don't have happy hours or lunch hours where we chill out and complain—not for negativity, but to siphon off the negativity, you know?

In other words, I'm looking for the OPPORTUNITY to create this safe space for me and my colleagues. (See what I did there? I'm making my one-word resolution work!)

-N

@@@@@@@@@

Sent March 25
To: Naomi Wellington <myownperson02@gmail.com>
From: Jessamine Lewis <steamyenergy@gmail.com>
Subject: Re: rebellion

Naomi, you are seriously going to lose your job. Why do you have to fight everything so hard? Yeah, Nick-the-Dick has a stick up his ass, but that doesn't mean you have to have a bigger one up yours. Do you remember how hard it was to get this work-from-home-job with benefits? Look, I feel you and your passion for helping these kids, but you have your own kid to think about, and it's not a bad thing to step back and hold on to what's good about your job, you know?

Do they know one of your students is living with you now? What do you think will happen when they find out?

And what about everything else you've been doing? Leyanna told me about how you're always gone—giving rides to students to the doctor or the library or doing what all else. Jackson has the biggest blind spot ever when it comes to you, but even he's talked about how you're so wrapped up in your students' lives and your book club group that he's been doing more than simply having Leyanna live with him full time. He's been taking care of all her stuff—conferences, violin lessons, orthodontist appointments. Everything.

Do you know what's happening with Faith and me and the kids anymore?

And, tbh, you're kinda doing the White Savior act. You know what? We got enough movies about that already. Nobody needs yours.

Sent March 25
To: Jessamine Lewis <steamyenergy@gmail.com>
From: Naomi Wellington <myownperson02@gmail.com>
Subject: Re: rebellion

White Savior?

Fuck you.

@@@@@@@@@

Sent March 26
To: naomi.wellington@aesamn.edu
From: lauren.givens@aesamn.edu
Subject: Bingo

I'd say we should make this a drinking game, but I have too much grading to do yet tonight after the meeting...

DEPARTMENT MEETING BINGO

DEPARTMENT MEETING BINGO			
"For the good of our students"	"Effective immediately"	"Back to the topic-at-hand"	Stacy can't find the file downloads tab
Scott gets booted out more than once	Nick scolds Naomi	"Let me be clear"	Nick scolds Adán
Stacy asks a question that Nick JUST ANSWERED	"Well, it won't come to that"	"Please direct all questions to me"	"Adherence to this policy is of the utmost importance"
"Make it a priority"	"Can you hear me okay?"	Nick jumps ahead 2 slides	"To reiterate"

@@@@@@@@

Sent March 27
TO: NAOMI WELLINGTON <NAOMI.WELLINGTON@MAIL.COM>
FROM: VOICE MESSAGING <VOICEMESSAGING@CLEAR-VOICE.COM>
SUBJECT: NEW VOICE MESSAGE FROM 612-555-3224

Hi Naomi, this is Jules from Westside High. Your mom stopped in, and well, she was kind of off, if you know what I mean. I don't think she knows you've not worked here in a few years. I didn't tell her anything, so don't worry about that. I just thought you should know. I hope you and Leyanna are doing well. Bye.

@@@@@@@@

BOARD: LITTLE FIRES EVERYWHERE by Celeste Ng

▽ **TOPIC:** This book has a lot to look at! Let's start with the prevailing question: Who should raise May Ling/Mirabelle?

Lisa: What? No, no, no, we are NOT going there, are we? Everything about how May Ling was adopted was completely fucked up, which means there should have been no question about May Ling going back to Bebe. So maybe we could discuss THAT or all the other issues in this book about class, depiction of race, and misogyny.

Chester: I'm with Lisa on this. There were a lot of bigger issues in this story than the obvious one surrounding May Ling.

Tyrell: Word. How about how the only Black character ends up dropping his girlfriend without even trying to talk to her?

Grant: +1. Mrs. Richardson and how she treated Mia? Or why Trip and Pearl kept their relationship on the DL?

Maxine: Or how about how Moody talked about Pearl at the end? Thank you to Lisa and Naomi for reminding me that no one deserves to be treated so poorly.

Susette: Oh, y'all, I'm so sorry about the wrong question! I got it from a website, but I guess I should have thought it through a little more. Quick, check out my next post!

▽ **TOPIC:** One review I read talked about how Ng has a powerful understanding of human nature. How does this come through in the characters in Shaker Heights?

Lisa: Bless you, Susette. And no hard feelings about the original question. Obviously, it pushed one of my buttons because of my occupation. This question about human nature is fabulous. Even though some characters drove me insane, I recognized every character in the story.

Naomi: Recognize them? Hell, I think I've *been* some of these characters. I don't want to admit which ones.

Maxine: Me too, Naomi.

Chester: I guess I'd bet we all could relate to each of the characters at different times in the book. Regardless of how we felt about them. This is the whole point of the author capturing human nature.

Lisa: This is the second time in this discussion where Chester and I are on the same page. I need a drink.

Chester: Fuck off, Lisa. (<— Did that make you feel better?)

Lisa: (Yes, thank you. I was kind of lost there for a moment.)

Naomi: Maybe you're right about relating to them all, but based upon some other things going on in my life, some of the characters and their behaviors kind of hit close to home.

Chester: You okay, Nay?

Grant: Sometimes, the right book hits at the right time.

Naomi: I'm okay. Grant's right, though. I think I needed this book right now.

APRIL

***Naomi Wellington has started a new group,* AltEd Alternative Water Cooler**

Naomi:

Hey everyone! Happy Monday! (I know, right? I like to *try* positivity for Mondays...) Thanks for being part of our little "blow off some steam without fear of Big Brother" chat group. Or, BOSSWFOBB, as I like to call it. Lololol. What are you hoping to see this week? I'm hoping one of my kiddos will meet with me during office hours this week because every time he does, he turns in some work later that day.

Lauren:

Hey all! I've been busting my butt to get more than just a couple of students to show up for my office hours. This week I'm offering to reveal one of the actual questions on the next unit exam if a student drops by. I'm sure this is totally against some sort of rules, but honestly, if it helps them to know what they are supposed to be learning, I don't care.

Rochelle:

That's a great idea, Lauren! I tried the extra credit thing before, but no one seems to care about that. If you're not doing the work, a few bit points aren't going to matter. Do you tell them the answer to the question, too?

Lauren:

Oh, no. I figure if they have one direct question, they should pretty well be able to nail it because they'll for sure study directly for that question (I hope?).

Scott has left the group.

Tammy has left the group.

Naomi:

Well, that was fast.

Lauren:

They're going to go rat on me, aren't they?

Naomi:

:(I hope not.

Lauren:

It's okay. I don't care. I'm sick of being scolded for trying to help our students.

Corynn:

Right? I get that they don't want us to mess with the curriculum a bunch, to be consistent or whatever, but aren't we teachers? Aren't we supposed to help our students work through it?

Lauren:

It's nice that you say "they" when we all really know it's Nick.

Naomi:

So it's not just me? He's been giving all of you a hard time, too?

Lauren:

Yes. "It has come to our attention..."

Bobbi:

Nick? You don't think he's just, IDK, following orders? Passing along what our directors are telling him?

Adán:

Some of it is that Bobbi, but most of it is Nick. He's on a power trip.

Corynn:

He does know that we're a school and not some major corporation, right?

Naomi:

There are some big online vendors out there now that are for-profit. Maybe he *is* gunning for a corporate position.

Adán:

So basically, he's a metaphor for our society. Step on the hard-luck cases in order to get ahead. Great. Just great.

@@@@@@@@

Sent April 06
To: Jessamine Lewis <steamyenergy@gmail.com>
From: Naomi Wellington <myownperson02@gmail.com>
Subject: re-decorating

Do you remember Susette? The woman who started up the online book club I'm doing? Lisa and I met her today. She's trying to get her mother-in-law to move in with her and couldn't figure out how to convince her to do it. Lisa, Maxine, and I suggested getting a room ready and made-up for her MIL to see how much Susette wants her there. To make her feel welcomed. We spent the day painting, moving furniture around, and finding bits of pieces of things her MIL enjoys. Yarn for crocheting. An easy chair with a small table and lamp. A T.V. A rolling T.V. tray for eating while watching. Wordsearch puzzle books. An iPad.

The next time Susette takes her MIL to lunch, she's going to bring her back to her place to show her the new room. How can she not want to live there? It sounds like her own son doesn't care about her even though her daughter-in-law—who isn't really related to her anymore since Susette divorced the idiot son—went the extra mile to make her feel welcome. To still be part of her family.

Isn't that all anyone wants? To feel wanted and part of a family?

@@@@@@@@@

Sent April 09
To: AltEdAllStaff@aesamn.edu
From: mark.sumner@aesamn.edu
Subject: Evaluations

Dear Staff,

This message is a friendly reminder to complete your self-evaluation forms by close of business, Friday. Together with your department chairs, I will be reviewing your self-assessments, your chair's observation reports, and any other documents and contributions.

Final evaluation reports for the year will be complete and available to you in two-three weeks' time.

I look forward to your input on your self-evaluation forms.

Best,

Mark Sumner
Interim Director
Alternative Education Solutions Academy

@@@@@@@@@

Alternative Education Solutions Academy
Self-Assessment and Reflection

Please rate your performance from this past year openly and honestly. Your supervisor will use this information to complete your performance evaluation and will also lead to goal development for the upcoming year. If you feel there are significant discrepancies after receiving your performance evaluation, you may request an appeal. Appeals will be granted on a case-by-case basis.

SECTION ONE: TEAM EFFORT

__x_Top Performer ___ Core Performer ___ Low Performer

Guiding questions:

Have I consistently attended all meetings and professional development sessions?

Have I been on time for events?

Have I cooperated with colleagues and supervisors in a team effort?

Have I considered the good of all vs. the good of one in my efforts?

Have I given my team 110%?

Have I contributed to the Academy in meaningful and productive ways?

Comments:

Wow, these "guiding" questions are more like loaded, leading questions. Where did this new evaluation come from?

I rated myself a Top Performer because I have put in herculean efforts to meet expectations this year. I have certainly given MY team 100% (Note I didn't put 110% because really, it's a bit unfair to put an impossible percentage in there, don't you think?) In all areas, I have toed the line and played nice as often as my conscience allowed. (I'm being "open and honest" as requested. Go team!)

SECTION TWO: SERVICE

__ Top Performer _x_ Core Performer __ Low Performer

List the ways you have contributed to the Academy in service beyond standard teaching duties.

Comments:

Blogged.

Spoke my mind.

Got rejected for two committees.

SECTION THREE: STUDENT ACHIEVEMENT

_X_ Top Performer __ Core Performer __ Low Performer

Provide evidence of student success and achievement in your courses. Under the umbrella of the Academy's guidelines, describe how you contributed towards your students' academic achievement.

Comments:

Well, I'm glad there was SOME kind of connection to students in this evaluation.

Check my "reprimands" file for evidence on how I contributed towards student achievement.

@@@@@@@@@

why am I nervous for presentations?

what does anxiety feel like?

what is the difference between anxiety and being nervous?

why am I scared around big groups of people?

@@@@@@@@@

[7:45 Apr 10]

NAOMI

Hey J.

JAX

Hey Nay.

NAOMI

Have you checked Leyanna's grades recently?

JAX

Yeah. I thought we made sure things were clear with her back at conference time.

NAOMI

Me too. What's going on with her?

JAX

She keeps talking about being nervous about giving presentations. I have her practicing them with me, but she won't do them for the grade. I don't get it.

NAOMI

Think we should talk to the school counselor?

JAX

Can't hurt, can it?

NAOMI

I'll email him tonight.

JAX

She misses you.

NAOMI

Are you sure? She hardly ever returns my texts.

JAX

Because she's 13.

NAOMI

I have to get all my intel from Reese.

JAX

She and Reese do text and video chat a lot, for sure.

JAX

You can get info from me, too. You know I'm not keeping her from you.

NAOMI

No, I know. It's just

NAOMI

…

JAX

I know. She'll come around.

NAOMI

When?

JAX

When she's 30.

NAOMI

JAX

JAX

🕊 sorry, Nay.

NAOMI

Liar.

JAX

🕊 for real, though, I bet it won't be much
longer. Maybe a few more weeks.

NAOMI

That's a lot of days.

JAX

I'll work on it, but you gotta work on things,
too. Get your priorities straight. You know what
I'm saying?

NAOMI

I hear you, Jax.

JAX

Do you tho?

NAOMI

I do. I promise.

JAX

Okay

NAOMI

Okay

@@@@@@@@@

LOVING FAMILY ADOPTION SERVICES
ADOPTIVE FAMILY PROFILE

Lamont and Nathaniel

Basic Profile

	Lamont	Nathaniel
Age	33	35
Ethnicity/Race	African-American	African-American
Education	Master's Level	Undergraduate Degree
Religion	N/A	Christian
Occupation	School Counselor	Small-Business Owner
Health	Excellent	Excellent
Smoking/Alcohol Use	Non-smoker, occasional social drinking	Non-smoker, occasional social drinking

Our Story

Lamont and Nathaniel are proud to share how they met at a Pride parade ten years ago. They watched it from the skyway above, both admitting neither of them had intended to come, yet were drawn to it when walking through the skyway. They share this story to remember how they opened to each other as they risked something new, and this is what they hope to teach their child. They dated for a year before Lamont proposed (not marriage—it wasn't legal yet, in Minnesota), and Nathaniel immediately accepted for a commitment ceremony. Since then, they have worked together to create safe spaces for LGBTQ youth, homeless youth, and any other youth who are at-risk in their home environment. They are excited and ready to grow their family in their own safe space for a child who needs a safe place to land.

Age Preference (Y-yes, N-no, WTC-willing to consider)

_Y_ Newborn

_Y_ 1-12 months

_Y_ 2-4 years

_Y_ 5-12 years

WTC 13+ years

Race/Ethnicity (Y-yes, N-no, WTC-willing to consider)

_Y_ White/Caucasian

_Y_ Black or African-American

_Y_ American Indian or Alaskan Native

_Y_ Native Hawaiian or Pacific Islander

_Y_ Asian

Post-Adoption Cooperative Communication Plan

Lamont and Nathaniel understand how incredibly difficult it must be for someone to choose adoption. They also know, despite the strides our society is making, how challenging it might be for someone to choose them as a forever family for their child. Lamont and Nathaniel encourage a broadly open relationship. And while they prefer always to be the primary caregivers of your child, they will not shut you out if or when you decide you want to be more or less involved.

@@@@@@@@@

Sent April 11
To: Jessamine Lewis <steamyenergy@gmail.com>
From: Naomi Wellington <myownperson02@gmail.com>
Subject: adoption matchmaking

How has Faith been feeling? Still a lot of pain? Have you figured out some effective ways of managing it?

Any more stories about attention-seeking sales associate?

I really miss hearing from you.

Reese has been reluctantly meeting potential adoptive parents. Some of them have been obviously not anyone she would choose. My guess is she's going through the motions so she can say she at least looked into it. Her coup de grâce question at the end is always, "What if two years later, I decide I want to raise her all on my own because I'll be ready, then?"

It's the most uncomfortable room at that moment (because yes, she's been having me come along with her to these meetings). One couple looked shell-shocked, and I don't know if it's because they hadn't fathomed this possibility or if they had and it was their worst fear (it would be mine, for sure). Two other couples laughed awkwardly and said something like, "well, I guess we'd figure something out if that situation came up." Another couple said flat out, "Then we'd get our lawyers to fight like hell and remind you we are *not* placeholder parents."

Reese had merely nodded. "Respect."

As we drove home after that meeting, I commented on her reaction and if that meant she would consider them.

"Hell no. I got mad respect for them holding their ground and fighting for their baby, but in the end, she'd still be MY baby, you know what I'm saying?"

Today we met a couple who was, well, almost perfect. Interracial marriage and one of the potential parents was in education. They were funny, supportive, and had a million questions for Reese. Favorite food? Drink? Movie to watch when the world sucks? Comfiest clothes? Most interesting class? (She answered

World History. What? "For real, though, Ms. W. It's about more than the exams.")

When Reese asked them the magic question, they paused to think. To really think. "We know, going into an open adoption situation, that this could happen. We know it could happen at any time. This is why we welcome the broadest amount of involvement generally accepted in these situations. We *want* you to be a part of your child's life. Our child is yours, too. We also don't want you to think we'd be complacent if you suddenly wanted to take the child out of our lives. We have to think about what is best for our child at all times, and when we say 'our,' we mean *our* child." They circled a finger around to include themselves and Reese. "We'd fight to work it out for all of us. But mostly for our child."

On the drive home, Reese was mostly quiet. Eventually, she opened up a little. "I'm not saying I'm interested, but if I were, I think I'd choose those guys."

I nodded. I would, too, if any choice were given to me. They were balanced, realistic, super ready to raise children, and 100% genuine.

And then, finally, came the question I'd been waiting for. Reese asked me if I'd be willing to adopt her baby.

No lie, I've obviously thought about it. I've thought about it since the day she showed up at my door. I can't believe *you* never asked me about it. Probably you were worried I'd say yes. I can't argue with you about this worry except I said "no." I like the idea of having more kids, but I keep holding out hope I'll be with someone one day, and we'll decide together to have kids. Maybe by birth. Maybe by adoption. I don't want to do it on my own, and I don't want to guilt Jax or the rest of your family into raising the child with me when they had no say in the matter because I know Jax. He'd take on the responsibility, and I'd let him, and it would add on to more debt I owe all of you. I owe all of you so much already—so much I don't know how I'll ever repay it all.

I didn't tell Reese all of this. I didn't tell her it made me feel nineteen years old again, and I didn't tell her how her asking me didn't make me feel mature and responsible. Instead, I felt as foolish and selfish as I did when I told my mother about Leyanna.

I didn't like saying "no" to Reese. Wasn't I acting in loco parentis for her? If it were Leyanna asking, I wouldn't hesitate. Obviously. What does it say about me to say no to Reese? It's different, isn't it?

Or is it?

I wish you'd tell me like it is on this one.

I hope you're okay.

-Mimi

@@@@@@@@@

Sent April 13
To: Jessamine Lewis <steamyenergy@gmail.com>
From: Naomi Wellington <myownperson02@gmail.com>
Subject: matchmaking updates

Jess,

It occurred to me I never updated you on the matchmaking progress at my coffee shop. Honestly, I haven't been spending as much time there as I used to. I'm sure you can imagine why. Lanh, I assume, has moved to D.C. by now, so it's not as though I'm worried about running into him. Instead, the café reminds me too much of him. When I told Sayeed and Tracy about our break-up, Tracy immediately disappeared, and soon after, Elton John's "Sad Songs" came on through the speakers. I kind of saw the appeal of it when in the right sad situation. Tracy was disappointed because she said we looked good together. Sayeed, on the other hand, went full-on Sayeed and claimed Lanh had no idea what he was doing in leaving someone like me behind. How could he not see what a gift he'd had in his grasp?

I cried and ordered all my stuff to go and didn't return for a week.

It got easier, especially after I found a new table with a completely different view of the café. Some of it was enlightening, and some of it depressing. Gorgeous Hair Babe has a super trash mouth! I don't know how I feel about it because, *gorgeous* hair! Except, her trash mouth gets kind of mean. I don't know who, exactly, it is she talks to on the phone, but I don't think I'd like to be on the receiving end of her insults and cursing. Dark Haired Indian Man and Older Black Guy have been chatting it up a bit lately. Not romantically or anything. They sit at separate tables next to each other. It's kind of funny to think how they're not sure if they are friends yet, or not.

The best news is Pencil Skirt Woman and Sloppy Jock Guy are together! They appear to take turns buying each other their coffees, depending on who gets there, first. Their conversations are all about what they've got going on at work for the day, and should they go out in the evening or wait until the weekend? The weird result of this new pairing is how Super Suit hasn't shown up in a long time. I wonder, did Super Suit get set aside by SJG and this new relationship? Did Super Suit only meet his brother at the café because one of them was going through a phase? Is Super Suit okay with not meeting his brother at the café anymore?

I wish you were here with me to contemplate these questions. You've always had such great stories, which is probably why you are so good at managing people. You understand their behaviors and can figure out what they're thinking or wanting. I DO know your job is about more than folding clothes the right way.

And my job is about more than teaching kids the convoluted facts of history. History is all about perspective, and as both teacher AND historian, I have a duty to understand my students' perspectives as best as I can. My kids' lives are messy, which means sometimes my job gets messy. It's not about saving them. It's about shaping their perspective so they can get ahead and about shaping others' perspectives about them. People judge these kids. I know because I was one of them, and I didn't get ahead all on my own. I had Momma Junie not only feeding me and welcoming me into your home, but I learned about family by her making me help out with dishes and cooking. Because I was spending so much time there, I should pull my weight, shouldn't I? And Daddy Joe taught me to drive. And Jax tutored me through Calculus and Chemistry.

And you, Jessamine, for everything else—for keeping my spirit alive.

I wish you'd write back. Answer my calls. Return my texts. Bring back my spirit.

-Mimi

@@@@@@@@@

DRAFT
April 15
To: Jessamine Lewis <steamyenergy@gmail.com>
From: Naomi Wellington <myownperson02@gmail.com>
Subject: pool

Do you remember back when Leyanna was little, and you were still living in Minnesota, and you, me, and Jax bought that kiddie pool from a garage sale? We were coming back from the grocery store for your mom, and Leyanna—she must have been about two years old—yelled out, "FWOG!"

Jackson said, "Where, baby?" And you pointed to the garage sale as we passed it, "There. It's a kiddie pool. Jackson, stop. We MUST get it."

"Yaaasss." Jackson made a u-turn so fast, I thought Leyanna and I were both going to fly out of the back seat window.

Then came the problem of how to transport it. We thought we could transfer all the groceries into the front and back seat (you know, because who cares where we would all sit) and jam it into the trunk, only to find out it didn't fit in spite of the trunk being totally empty. (It was Jax's tiny Mazda Protege. Why did we ever think it possibly could have fit?) Then we transferred all the bags back into the trunk and decided to put the pool on top of the car and hold it in place with our hands. It's not like we were going to get on the highway, right? Piece of cake.

Except it wasn't. Jax held it down on one side, and you and I had it on the other, and then Jax would suddenly have to let go, and the wind would lift it up, and I can't believe it only flew right off the top of the car once. It took us thirty minutes to drive the two miles home! It didn't help, I suppose, to be laughing our asses off at the craziness of it all. Probably we should have had one of us sit with it while the others drove home to get some rope or something. We kept laughing and yelling, "C'mon, we got this! It's only another few blocks!" with Leyanna shouting, "Yay! Fwog!"

Why can't our lives still be like back then? When did it all get so serious?

-N

@@@@@@@@@

[9:52 Apr 17]

JACKSON

Hey Nay

NAOMI

Hey J

JACKSON

Minnesota's Largest Candy Store just re-opened for the season. I need me some Pop Rocks and Sno-Caps.

NAOMI

And I need me some cherry jellies and 95 different flavors of taffy.

JACKSON

Road trip?

NAOMI

Def. Leyanna, too?

JACKSON

☹ no. Moms has got her working in the greenhouse all weekend.

NAOMI

Oh.

JACKSON

C'mon, Nay. Just us two. Like old times. I'll catch you up on what's been happening with the cousins since you missed last week's Sunday dinner.

NAOMI

Ok

JACKSON

That's what I'm talking about. Pick you up at ten tomorrow.

@@@@@@@@@

DRAFT
April 20
TO: JESSAMINE LEWIS <STEAMYENERGY@GMAIL.COM>
FROM: NAOMI WELLINGTON <MYOWNPERSON02@GMAIL.COM>
SUBJECT: HOW I KNEW

Every day, Reese opens up more and more about her feelings about having a baby. It brings back so many emotions about when I found out I was pregnant with Leyanna. So much is different, of course, because while I was still young, I wasn't near as young as Reese. Support from my parents was non-existent, although the overwhelming support from Jax and your family more than made up for it.

A part of me still wishes I could have shared it all with my mom, the mom who was real to me for maybe five days my entire life. I kind of hate how much my heart still feels about those five days. I wish I didn't remember the day we went to an amusement park and giggled together on spinning rides and over-shared cotton candy. I wish I didn't remember the time she was sober enough to listen to me cry about a bully at school and how she took my side and taught me ways to fight back.

I also wish I didn't have her look of disappointment stuck in my head, accompanied by the words she used when she found out I was pregnant. "Hope your bastard child ends up as ungrateful to you as my bastard child is to me."

I remember crying on your shoulder. Do you remember what you told me?

"You get five minutes for me to hug you and for you to be sad. After that, you are done feeling sorry for yourself, you hear me? DONE. Blood ain't the only way you get family, and you got family in spades with me, Jax, and all the rest of us."

I am so sad about Reese's parents. I don't know how this happens.

And if she doesn't have the same kind of family support like I had with you, what chance does she have?

She's starting to realize this. She told me it was time to get real. She'd fallen in love with the idea of being a mom, but she was at Wal-Mart the other day and saw a classmate of hers with her own baby. "Ms. W, she was yelling at her baby who can't even walk yet. I want to say I would never do the same thing, but how do I know? I go crazy when I break a nail. What will I do if the baby drops my phone and breaks it?"

The adoptive parent profiles keep coming. She shows them to me so I know she's no longer completely disregarding the whole idea. To be honest, a lot of the potential parents have not been promising. You think I'm acting the white savior? I've got nothing on some of these white, bible-thumping, cis, het couples. A few have potential. There's still the gay couple we met a couple of weeks ago.

I never considered adoption. Well, I suppose I did for a hot second when I thought about my childhood and how it could have been different. I knew it wouldn't be the same for Leyanna, though. For one thing, Jax had already graduated by the time she was born and had his first real job. He always had it all together. Can I admit something to you? He was my escape hatch. If I discovered I couldn't handle it—the whole mom thing? I knew Leyanna would be in good hands with Jax. And I don't mean for a week or whatever. I mean forever.

Once. Once I had thought about it for real. There was a day when Leyanna was about four months old...I had two major exams coming up the next day, and I had bombed a presentation in one of my history courses earlier in the day. *History*. My best and favorite subject! How could I have messed up the one thing

I was super good at? Leyanna started crying and wouldn't stop. I tried everything, and soon I was crying, too. I was so tired, Jess. I wanted to be better than my mother, and I didn't feel like I was at all. You were in France for one of your study-abroad programs (longest months of my life—until you and Faith left—longest years of my life). I called Jax, who, of course, came over right away, and as soon as our baby girl was in his arms, she quieted right down.

The next day, I texted Jax. "I can't do this. She was meant to be with you." Then I turned off my phone because I didn't want to see any of his supportive comments. If he'd been smart, he would have told you about it, and you would have come my way and totally kicked my ass. And yet, maybe he figured this was something we had to work out on our own. He showed up at our door three days later, Leyanna in his arms, and said every time she heard a woman singing—on the radio or otherwise—Leyanna would look around, searching for me. And then she'd cry. I sing all the time, as you know (probably why you kept leaving the country), and she'd attached herself to me through my singing. "She's meant to be with you, too," Jax said.

He told me we would always have days where it would all seem impossible, and maybe it would be if we were each on our own, but we had each other. Together we could handle raising a child. "It doesn't have to be even between us to be fair," he reminded me. "Sometimes you need more help, and sometimes I do. We'll keep working it out."

Here's a question that has always nagged at the back of my brain. Why didn't Jax want us to be a couple? To be truly together? I know I told you we both agreed we weren't truly in love with each other or wanting to be in a relationship, but it's not true. I wanted to. I would have. Jax didn't give me a chance, though. After that one night, we sort of tried to see each other in secret because we were worried about how you'd react. Except, life got so crazy with Grams going into the hospital for pneumonia, we put things on hold. When I found out I was pregnant, he took it great, just like I told you, but he also neutralized our relationship. "Our curiosity got the better of us, Nay. We're better as friends, though, don't you think?"

I didn't know how to react. Part of me wanted to argue; the rest of me didn't want to ruin the good relationship we already had—had always had. So I agreed. All these years later... I still don't understand. Our one-night stand had been more than curiosity. Or maybe it's faulty memory. The same way I can't seem to let go of certain memories of my mother.

And maybe I'm stuck on it all now because Reese's experience keeps bringing it all back to me.

I wish I had you to talk to right now.

-Mimi

@@@@@@@@@

DRAFT
April 23
To: Jessamine Lewis <steamyenergy@gmail.com>
From: Naomi Wellington <myownperson02@gmail.com>
Subject: crossing lines

I almost kicked Reese out of my home today. Today she got Leyanna to skip school (SKIP SCHOOL! She's only in sixth grade!). I was so angry with her for thinking she had any right to influence my daughter to make such a poor choice.

Our shouting match was a doozy.

Until she screamed about how much she hated her parents, and it sort of popped some kind of bubble inside of me. My anger seeped away in the air around us. And then she decided she wanted to confront her ex-boyfriend's parents, of all things, in case they didn't know they were technically going to be grandparents and wanted Leyanna with her for moral support. I don't know why she thought a twelve-year-old would be some kind of support for it. I guess I haven't considered, though, how Reese has lost most of her friends because of this pregnancy. It's like she's a pariah. Or as if they think it's contagious.

The confrontation didn't go well.

OBVIOUSLY. And let's not even talk about how many things could have gone wrong and might still go wrong getting those white parents involved. They called her a foolish whore that their son would never have been involved with and asked her to leave. Which she did, but did so while screaming back at the couple, according to Jax, who got the story from Leyanna. It was Leyanna who got Reese away from the house before the couple could call the police.

Reese is a mess right now. Leyanna probably is, too, and my heart aches for not being able to take care of her right now. I know Jax has her, but it's not the same. It just isn't.

As for Reese, I'm not sure how to guide her—or if I should. She clearly doesn't have much coming from her parents right now, and she hardly ever keeps her appointments with the social worker. I'm all she has. Looking at my track record... well, God help her, right? Reese for sure likes the *idea* of raising her child. I'm not sure she truly *wants* to. IDK. Is it expecting too much for a sixteen-year-old to want to have a baby?

I have at least one other student online who does. She emails me photos. I know it's not roses and rainbows all the time for her, and yet her photos with her son are full of smiles, and she shares stories. Reese talks like....well, like she's a character in a book. She says all the right things. Does (mostly) all the right things. I don't hear the emotion behind it all, though. She has more emotion about her current family than her future one. She has more emotion about the TV show, *Pose*, than the baby. (Although, let's face it, *Pose* causes ALL the feels. I haven't *not* cried during an episode yet.)

I remember when Leyanna used to get hiccups when I was pregnant with her. It made me giggle, knowing a single hiccup was enough to make her whole body move inside me—and so much I could feel it right along with her. I wanted her to be sitting in front of me, old enough for us to try all the ridiculous tricks for getting rid of hiccups. I saw the future with her.

I'm not sure Reese sees her baby at all.

-N

@@@@@@@@@

DRAFT
April 24
TO: JESSAMINE LEWIS <STEAMYENERGY@GMAIL.COM>
FROM: NAOMI WELLINGTON <MYOWNPERSON02@GMAIL.COM>
SUBJECT: WHY DO I LIVE IN MN

It snowed a foot today. A FOOT. FFS, it's April, and it's supposed to be all tulips and daffodils right now. I tore down all my little sparkly lights and threw out all my candles because fuck "hygge" or "lagom" or whatever. I'm done with this stupid cold and snow. Leyanna still won't move back in with me, you think you have the market on "life is hard," and Reese is in full-on denial about her whole situation when she should be nesting or something.

Nick the Dick is making my life miserable, but who cares, right? I only want to save all my kids and be The Hero. It's not like I want what's best for my students or anything. Right now, he's "spot" checking all of my courses daily. I now have three formal "reprimands" (who even calls it that, anymore?) in "my file," which means evaluation time will suck, unless Mary comes back before the end of the school year. Honestly, evaluations from an interim director can't possibly be fair, can they?

Today was a snow day for all of our local schools, and normally I'd take advantage of my flexible work schedule and snuggle in with Leyanna in front of a sappy movie—or maybe a scary one because we both can only handle scary in the middle of the day. We'd make popcorn and hot chocolate with lots of marshmallows, and then we'd read our own thing, together. I don't even know what she's reading right now. How did we get here? And why am I the bad guy? Why isn't Jackson the mean parent? Why is it always the mom?

Half of her grades are terrible, and she doesn't have any excuse for them. She refuses to do presentations, and I understand how nerve-wracking they can be, but she wouldn't even practice them with me to help her out. I told the teachers I'd work on them with her, and now it seems like I'm not supportive. And no, her teachers aren't actually *saying* I'm not doing my job...and yet clearly, somehow, I'm not. You wondered why I've put all my time into my students? It's because I couldn't figure out what else to do with Leyanna.

Jackson hasn't had the magic bullet, either, so what good is it doing to have her be with him 100% of the time. I know he's your brother, but...well, nothing. I'm not angry or upset with him. He's been really open with everything and running into the same roadblocks I have. Teachers love him, though. Everyone thinks a single dad is awesome, you know. With the exception of the Language Arts teacher, I am now only cc'd on messages instead of sharing the "To" line. I'm sure it only took one email from him for me to be relegated to the equivalent of BTW.

Snow in April is evil.

"That is all."

-N

@@@@@@@@

[4:28 Apr 27]

JACKSON

Hey Nay

NAOMI

Hey Jay

JACKSON

How come you've been missing the past two Sunday dinners?

NAOMI

...

JACKSON

C'mon. Momma got mad at me when she found out you been skipping.

NAOMI

Found out? Why wouldn't she know?

JACKSON

Uh, she's out in Washington with Jess?

NAOMI

Wait, what?

JACKSON

You didn't know?

NAOMI

No. Jessamine and I... well, we're kinda on the outs right now.

JACKSON

Yeah, that tracks. Momma mentioned
something, but you'll get past it. Is that why
you haven't been coming by?

NAOMI

I guess.

JACKSON

That's crazy.

NAOMI

Why? Wouldn't it be weird if the person your
sister is mad at shows up at her family's
Sunday dinner?

JACKSON

The "person"? You're acting like you're some
random friend. You're family.

NAOMI

But

JACKSON

But what? You think you're the first person to
be on non-speaking terms with someone else
in the family? Hell, I'd hardly ever be able to
show my face in that house if that were the
rule.

NAOMI

JACKSON

It's not sending a good message to Leyanna,
either. You not showing up to see her.

NAOMI

It's not like she talks to me. She doesn't
respond to my texts or answer my calls.

JACKSON

Really, Nay? You being the child, here?

NAOMI

It's painful getting the cold shoulder from my daughter at Sunday dinner. I don't know what to do.

JACKSON

Show up is what you do.

NAOMI

Why is Momma Junie in Washington?

JACKSON

Damn, you don't know that, either?

NAOMI

Know what????

JACKSON

Jess left Faith. Took the kids. They're staying in some long-term hotel place. Momma went to help her out.

NAOMI

Fuck. Why didn't you tell me?

JACKSON

Nope. You know I don't do that. No stepping my foot between sisters. Besides, I thought you knew that. I figured that's why you both stopped talking to each other.

NAOMI

God, Jax. I'm a shit. I told her if she had to leave, I'd support her. And where am I?

JACKSON

So call her.

NAOMI

She's the one that stopped replying to me.

JACKSON

Do you support her?

NAOMI

JAX.

JACKSON

...

NAOMI

You know I do.

NAOMI

I DO.

JACKSON

Exactly. Call her and tell her that. Maybe that's what she's waiting for.

NAOMI

Thank you.

JACKSON

Family, Nay. It's what we do.

NAOMI

I haven't even asked about you. Are you okay?

JACKSON

Yeah, actually. I am. I feel like I can finally breathe, you know? Well, almost. There's one thing I still gotta work out.

NAOMI

How can I help?

JACKSON

You got enough going on. I got this.

NAOMI

And Leyanna? Is she okay?

JACKSON

Yeah, she's good. She misses you.

NAOMI

I miss her, too.

JACKSON

Yeah.

NAOMI

I've messed so many things up, Jax. I don't
know where to start with fixing it all.

JACKSON

You. Start with yourself. You're stoking too
many fires. You know what I'm saying?

NAOMI

Okay.

JACKSON

Okay.

JACKSON

Don't worry about Leyanna. She's good and
will be ready to come back when you're ready,
too. But, you gotta show up, you hear me?

NAOMI

IDK

JACKSON

Nay.

NAOMI

I'll try.

JACKSON

Okay.

NAOMI

What would I do without you?

JACKSON

I got you, okay?

NAOMI

Okay.

@@@@@@@@@

Sent April 28
To: Jessamine Lewis <steamyenergy@gmail.com>
From: Leyanna <leyannaagogo@mail.com>
Subject: stuff

Thank you for trying to help my mom and dad understand my anxiety problems. You'd think Mom would look at my grades and think, "Ohhhh, I get it," but she doesn't. She thinks I'm just not trying very hard. Dad just says, "But you do fine at Sunday dinners, and there's always lots of us there."

I can't figure out making them understand how my anxiety is FOR ME. Dad thinks I do fine during Sunday dinners and holidays around the family, and he's mostly right because I don't interact a lot. I listen and nod and answer, and that's it. And I'm GOOD with that, you know? But class discussions where I'm called on randomly, I freeze. A couple of times it's almost been like an asthma attack, and I've been able to get away with that excuse. I looked it up, and now I know it's called a panic attack. Giving presentations in front of the whole class? No way. And small groups where I don't get to choose the group are really bad, too.

I don't know why I'm suddenly this way. Mom says I'm not making friends. Well, that's not true. I DO have friends. Only, they're not the kinds of friends most people think of. We have a program in our school that has kids who have major developmental differences than most everybody else in the school. Some teachers say it's developmental delays and some kids say other not very nice things AT ALL. One of the teacher helpers says she calls it developmental difference because for each of these kids (who are all around the same age as me—a couple of them are in 8th grade, though), she says they are developing at exactly the rate they're supposed to for their situation. She says we can't say they're delayed if it's already at their own pace.

I think she's right, especially because lots of kids don't think the students in this room (the room they mostly stay in all day) can talk or anything, and they're wrong. They don't always use words out loud like the rest of us do, but Isabelle is my best friend, and she and I talk in all kinds of ways. Sometimes she uses a picture card, or a tablet, or taps my arm in different places or rhythms. She's funny, and she knows all about my anxiety, and she understands because every time Ms. Lancer (she's the teacher in the classroom) says Isabelle is going to visit her homeroom, Isabelle gets nervous, too. We tell each other jokes as we walk down the hall to homeroom, and I think it helps both of us.

Trevor had a birthday party last weekend, and both Isabelle and I were invited. I'm super relieved to be living with Dad right now because he took me to the party and didn't make a big thing about how both Trevor and Isabelle use wheelchairs. He's used to seeing all kinds of people when he makes his house calls for work, which I think some people would be surprised because no one thinks about how many different kinds of people want help setting up or fixing audio and video tech stuff. Dad's always got stories. Like one guy was blind and does video streaming online and wanted to set up an easier way for his camera to give feedback about how much light he was positioning on himself and his guests. Or the woman who wanted a keyboard to hook up to her computer for some kind of cool visual thing to show how the music looked for her deaf son while she played. And the loads of people needing help with normal things, but use wheelchairs or canes or walkers, or other stuff.

Anyway, after the party, he asked me why I hadn't told him and Mom more about my friends, and it's because she'd probably act all weird about it all and try to FIX them or something. Or blame them for why I'm not doing very well in school. Or think they're why I want to do online school. Or some other weird thing. I love my mom, but she Just Doesn't Get It with me. It's like she's hoping I'll be anything EXCEPT be like her students, and I don't understand why doing online school is a bad thing for me, but a good thing for them?

Reese says Mom's probably worried I'll get "ideas" from other kids online. What "ideas"? Ideas of getting pregnant? How would that even happen if I'm not hanging out with other kids in person? Reese and I sometimes meet up at Cane's, and she buys me a Texas Toast and a lemonade, and she helps me with my homework. She thinks I should ask about videoing myself for presentations and my Language Arts teacher is cool with the idea, but my Social Studies teacher won't accept it because it's not teaching me how to learn about public speaking.

Mom used to fight for me at school when I had all my asthma issues. Before I moved in with Dad permanently, she used to go on rants about how bad things were getting for her students online, and I wished I could have told her that another reason I wanted to do online learning was so she'd fight for me again like she does with her students.

I also wish you'd taught Dad better on how to do hair. He offers to help me sometimes, but both times I've said "yes," I ended up re-doing it in my room before going to bed. Now I tell him I've got it.

-Leyanna

@@@@@@@@

BOARD: ANIMAL FARM by George Orwell

>TOPIC: Discussion Question 1: Why does Orwell choose pigs to be the leaders? How do they get to be the top animals so quickly and easily?

▽ **TOPIC:** Discussion Question 2: During the debate about whether or not to start building a windmill, Orwell has this line: "...indeed, they always found themselves in agreement with the one who was speaking at the moment." How does this relate to politics or even to life in general?

Maxine: Uh, are we sure we want to talk politics in this forum?

Susette: The whole book is pretty political, so I think we should try it.

Maxine: If you look at social media, it's all just shouting... and then everyone piles on with one thing. Snowball got run off in that same way.

Tyrell: And you have to be the loud one; otherwise it's like what Pink Floyd says about us just being bricks in the wall.

Maxine: Tyrell's right. I've never had that loud voice. And loud always seems to equal "majority," even if it isn't.

Lisa: Maxine, you don't even leave your house. You'd have to be SUPER loud to even register.

Chester: And there's our loud voice of the group. ^^^

Lisa: Fuck off, Chester. I'm saying that you at least have to show up. How is anyone gonna hear you if you're not even in the room?

Maxine: Here. I'm here. And here, I actually have a voice.

Grant: Maxine is right. She's here, showing up. Sometimes we have to find different ways to be heard.

Naomi: Me too. I really like how we all listen to each other here. There isn't any shouting. Well, I mean, besides Chester and Lisa.

Tyrell:

—

MAY

—

WHAT UP, PEEPS?™

AltEd Alternative Water Cooler

Cameron joined the group.

Julia joined the group.

Cameron:

Am I in? Am I part of Dumbledore's Army?

Lauren:

If you mean Naomi's Army, then yes, welcome to our newest members from the electives department!

Naomi:

Well, it's really BOSSWFOBB, but welcome!

Corynn:

She's being modest. Naomi is our fearless leader!

Leslie joined the group.

Analise joined the group.

Cameron:

Does anyone know if Mary is coming back before the end of the school year?

Corynn:

I haven't heard. I'm honestly worried she might not come back at all.

Lauren:

And leave us stuck with Sumner? Noooooo.

Adán:

I've been trying to get info out of Karen because I think she's been talking with Mary on/off all year. At least, I hope so. I know I haven't been able to get a response.

Naomi:

I'm glad I'm not the only one who was trying to get in touch with Mary. I mean, I get it right now. I can't imagine how tough it was for her to lose her mother after so much time taking care of her.

Cameron:

Well, if she doesn't come back, we need to do something. We can't let Sumner ruin this school. I signed on with Mary when we started this academy because I believed in our mission to work with struggling students.

Lauren:

What do you propose we do?

Naomi:

Take our concerns to the Board of Directors.

Adán:

Yes, Naomi. Exactly what I was thinking. Maybe we can bring up Nick, too.

Corynn:

YES, PLEASE.

Cameron:

Yeah, I've heard some things. Is it all true?

Naomi:

Probably. He's the worst.

Julia:

Does he really force you to submit grading summaries with reflections every week?

Lauren:

YES. Because we all have time to wax poetic about grading the way we do in order to make HIM happy, of course.

Julia:

He sounds awful. I'm so glad we still have Belén in charge of our department. TBH, it's weird she's had to work so hard on our behalf. Usually, electives kind of slide under the radar.

Cameron:

Sumner's infecting all corners. Power corrupts.

Naomi:

Absolutely.

@@@@@@@@@

Sent May 04

To: Naomi Wellington <naomi.wellington@mail.com>,
Jackson Lewis <jlewis@audaciousaudio.com>
From: Tim Rivera <trivera@pvms.k12.mn.us>
Subject: resources for Leyanna

Hello Ms. Wellington and Mr. Lewis,

A couple of Leyanna's teachers have spoken with me about concerns they have had about your daughter this year. It seems she had a few issues with adapting in some areas with middle school academics (while at the same time thriving in other areas, including a fantastic partnership with a specific population in our school).

First, I apologize for being unaware of Leyanna's difficulties until now. I think one of our peer groups would have provided a lot of help early on and helped us identify some of her specific struggles more quickly.

Second, I want you to know Leyanna's teachers speak very highly of her. Her grades do not fully reflect her efforts and potential, but I think we can help turn that around. I'm attaching a couple of articles to help get us talking about how best to support Leyanna. I hope you will give me a call as soon as is convenient so we can set up a time to meet and share ideas for getting your daughter where she wants to be.

Thank you,

Tim Rivera
Counselor
Prince Valley Middle School

Attachment <WhatIsSocialAnxiety.pdf>
Attachment <12strategies.pdf>

@@@@@@@@@

[9:33 May 05]

NAOMI

L, why aren't you at school today? Sick again?

[10:00 May 05]

NAOMI

L, c'mon, baby, I'm not asking you to open up or have some kind of "hey, girlfriend" conversation. I just want to know if you're feeling okay.

[10:14 May 05]

NAOMI

Hey J

JACKSON

Hey Nay

NAOMI

What's up with Leyanna? Why isn't she in school?

JACKSON

We decided to do a "Take Your Daughter to Work" thing today

NAOMI

A what, now?

JACKSON

JACKSON

> She wasn't feeling super great this morning,
> but is doing better now and wanted to come
> with me on a repair/sales call. This guy lives
> out a ways, so I'll check in with you later, cool?

[5:03 May 05]

NAOMI

Hey J

NAOMI

Are you back yet? I think we should talk.

NAOMI

Do you think Leyanna was faking being sick
this morning? I think I've discovered a pattern.

NAOMI

I feel stupid for missing it.

NAOMI

I feel stupid for missing a lot with our girl.

NAOMI

J?

[5:36 May 05]

NAOMI

Have you heard from Leyanna today?

REESE

> Yep

NAOMI

Is she back home at Jackson's?

REESE
I think so

NAOMI

Do you think you could take your headphones
off and talk with me?

REESE

fine

@@@@@@@@

[Submitted by Reese Vaskin on May o8]

Essay Response

2. Describe how guerrilla warfare changed the power structure between underdeveloped nations and first world nations.

Ms. W, you know I got nothing but mad respect for you, but look, your daughter is a hot mess. I don't know why you didn't fight to keep her from moving outta your place completely, but at least she had her Daddy's place, unlike me. I don't know your ex—or whoever Leyanna's baby daddy is to you—very well, and it sounds like he's a good guy, but your girl? She needs her momma, too. She barely talks about anything except jewelry and beads and stuff, and it's not because she thinks she's going to become some sort of famous designer. It's because she doesn't want to talk about everything else going on in her life. School has been no picnic for her this year, do you know that? She hates it. She hates how you aren't listening to her, and she hates how you keep her out of the loop with who you are seeing or dating or whatever.

Score: _o_/15

Feedback from the instructor:

Reese, I have tolerated your communications with me through exams and quizzes all year, but this has crossed the line. You might be on the verge of becoming a mother but you are NOT a mother, yet, and I don't need a SIXTEEN-year-old giving me advice on how to parent my child. Just because you have your own problems does not mean you can start them between me and my daughter. If I knew taking you in would also mean you would attack my parenting skills, I might have thought twice. There was no need to "fight" for Leyanna to stay because she has a good home with her dad. I'm sorry this isn't the case for you, but don't go putting my daughter in the same category as your situation. And, as you know, school isn't always a cakewalk. Case in point: you and all of your classmates here at the Academy. Leyanna is only thirteen, and it is my responsibility to make decisions I think are best for my daughter. You don't have a mother who cares enough to help you make the best decisions on your behalf. My daughter does. And to be perfectly honest, YOU came to ME, not the other way around. You were looking for a mother. Here I am.

@@@@@@@@@

Sent May 11
To: naomi.wellington@aesamn.edu
From: mark.sumner@aesamn.edu
Subject: Notice of Suspension of Duties

Dear Ms. Wellington,

Attached is official documentation of your Suspension of Duties, which is effective immediately, to end upon formal review of contractual and ethical offenses, at which point a decision will be made in one of the following two directions: reinstatement or termination of employment.

Please sign the attached and return it within the next three days, else forfeit your right to a formal review.

Thank you,

Mark Sumner
Director (interim)
Alternative Education Solutions Academy
Attachment <NWellington_NoticeofSuspension.pdf>

@@@@@@@@@

WHAT UP, PEEPS?™

AltEd Alternative Water Cooler

Naomi:

Hi all. I've been suspended. So I think it's best if I don't hang out here for a bit.

Corynn:

Oh no! What happened?

Lauren:

What did Nick do? Or was it Mark? Are you fighting it?

Naomi:

It wasn't them. I messed up. You guys be sure to keep fighting the good fight.

Adán:

Naomi, are you okay?

Naomi has left the group.

@@@@@@@@@

[3:18 May 10]

NAOMI

I stopped by your place today to drop off
Leyanna's black shoes for her concert.

NAOMI

I saw a copy of The Alchemist sitting on your
living room table.

NAOMI

And then I said to Leyanna, "huh, I'm reading
this right now, too."

JACKSON

...

NAOMI

And then she said, "yeah, it's the one you guys
are reading for your weird candy store book
club, right?"

JACKSON

...

NAOMI

And the way she said, "you guys"

JACKSON

...

NAOMI

I said, "you guys, as in me and your dad?"

JACKSON

Nay. Hold up.

NAOMI

And then she got this guilty expression. She
said she didn't mean to say that.

NAOMI

Probably I shouldn't have done it, but I went into your room and saw ALL the books I've been reading for MY "weird candy store book club" on YOUR shelf

JACKSON

Just, wait. Let me explain.

NAOMI

And so I asked Leyanna if you'd simply been tracking what I've been reading (except why not just ask me) or if you were actually IN the book club?

NAOMI

Which one is he? I asked her. Not Grant, we met him at Maxine's. Not Maxine. Not Lisa. Tyrell?

NAOMI

No, she said. He's a different guy. We got to meet him when Dad took me with him to work that one day.

JACKSON

I know it's irrelevant, but you should ask her about that appointment.

NAOMI

SERIOUSLY, JAX?

NAOMI

Then I realized the only person left was Chester. I mean, I feel like someone close to me not long ago said, "you never know who people really are online." YOU GOT THAT RIGHT.

JACKSON

Chester. Chester is me. I'm him.

NAOMI

WTF, Jax? Or should I say, WTF, CHESTER?

JACKSON

...

NAOMI

WTAF. Why would you do that? Why would you
gaslight me?

NAOMI

No. I'm not answering your call. I don't want to
talk to you.

JACKSON

C'mon, Nay.

NAOMI

Wait. When you went with me and Leyanna up
to Maxine's, was it because you were trying to
protect your identity? Did everyone else know?

JACKSON

No. I promise. No one else knew. Knows. Well,
T'Rell knows now. Leyanna and I met him
during my work call.

NAOMI

Thanks for ruining the one thing that was still
going right in my life. The one thing *I* hadn't
ruined yet.

JACKSON

Nay. Babe. Answer the phone. Let me talk
to you.

JACKSON

Nay.

@@@@@@@@@

Sent May 14
To: Naomi Wellington <naomi.wellington@mail.com>
From: Voice Messaging <voicemessaging@clear-voice.com>
Subject: New Voice Message from 612-555-7100

Hello, this is Prince Valley Middle School calling to notify you that Leyanna was absent from one or more class periods on May 14. Please contact the office at 612-555-7107 to let us know the reason for your child's absence.

@@@@@@@@@

[9:16 May 14]

NAOMI

Seriously, Leyanna? Are you SKIPPING school? Where are you?

NAOMI

ANSWER YOUR PHONE

[11:11 May 14]

LEYANNA

Mom?

LEYANNA

Mom, r u there?

NAOMI

LEYANNA. WHERE ARE YOU AND WHY ARE YOU NOT AT SCHOOL?

LEYANNA

Plz stop yelling i need ur help

NAOMI

What's wrong? What happened?

LEYANNA

It's reese she says her water broke what do we do??????

NAOMI

Where are you?

LEYANNA

Canes

NAOMI

What? Why are you…nvm, I'll be there as soon as I can.

@@@@@@@@@

GENERAL OFFENSE POLICE REPORT
PUBLIC INFORMATION RECORD

Bkg date	Bkg time	Name of Suspect	Age	Address
05/15	10:04AM	KRISTINE WELLINGTON	48	Stanton Ave/28th St

Offense 1	Offense 2	Offense 3
DISORDERLY CONDUCT	POSSESSION OF DANGEROUS DRUGS	OBSTRUCTING THE POLICE

@@@@@@@@@

[11:16 May 14]

NAOMI

Jax

JACKSON

Hey Nay! You forgive me yet?

NAOMI

Where've you been? Nvm, I need your help.

JACKSON

You have it.

NAOMI

You're not going to like it.

JACKSON

You still have it.

NAOMI

My mom was arrested. Possession and some other shit.

JACKSON

I know you're not asking me to step foot inside that police station, right?

NAOMI

…

JACKSON

Nay?

NAOMI

Shit, no. I'm sorry, no. I would never.

JACKSON

K. What's going on with you?

NAOMI

Reese is in labor. She and Leyanna are at Cane's. I'm picking them up and bringing them to the hospital. Meet me there later to pick up Leyanna?

JACKSON

Damn. Ok. What do you want me to do about your mom? Call someone to bail her out?

NAOMI

NO. IDK why I brought her up. I'm done with her. She can rot in jail for the rest of her life.

JACKSON

Babe

NAOMI

DON'T 'BABE,' ME

JACKSON

...

NAOMI

...

JACKSON

A'ight. Meet you later at the hospital.

NAOMI

Ty

@@@@@@@@

DRAFT
May 27
TO: JESSAMINE LEWIS <STEAMYENERGY@GMAIL.COM>
FROM: NAOMI WELLINGTON <MYOWNPERSON02@GMAIL.COM>
SUBJECT: BABY FABIOLA

Jessamine,

The past several days have been overwhelming, and I miss you so much it hurts. I'm so sorry for how things have been. I have messed up everything.

And by everything, I don't mean only us. I mean everyone and everything around me.

Reese had her baby. She's beautiful. And she changed her mind at the last minute and decided to keep her after all, and I said, "of course you want to!" and then I was the one who broke the horrible news to the now heart-broken daddies, who took the news so incredibly graciously, and this broke my heart because what had I done? How much had I influenced Reese along the way when I didn't know her well enough to do it? All I ever wanted was to help and support her because she wasn't getting it from her own parents, and as I looked at those two understanding men and how they seemed as though they knew this would happen, all I could think was, what the fuck have I been doing?

I want to start at the beginning of this story, though, so maybe you can understand how I got here.

With no job and no Leyanna to hurry out the door, I've been waking up late. Super late. I didn't see any point. Reese did her own thing, so she didn't need me in her space all the time.

A phone call from Leyanna's school woke me up. Another robocall to say she was absent and to please let them know why. She was skipping school. AGAIN. I furiously texted her and then tried calling her. Naturally, she ignored me. I tried calling Jax, and I know he's your brother...

Look, am I ever allowed to be angry with him? I think it's fair for me to both love your brother AND be mad at him. The point is, I've been mad at him for something I haven't told you about, AND Leyanna's been skipping school under his watch. Whatever. You're not talking to me anyhow, so I don't care. He wasn't answering his phone, either. And since I was already mad at him, I became irrationally angrier at his being busy with his job. Maybe too successful to notice what was going on with Leyanna. I mean, wasn't that supposedly the problem you had with me?

Work emailed me to set up a meeting to discuss my suspension and decide whether or not I'd be reinstated or released from my contract. Without Mary there, I have about an ant's chance in the gutter during a rainstorm of keeping my job.

Then, I got a call from the police. About my mother. She was causing a disturbance on some residential street corner—propositioning people, of all things—plus she had all kinds of drugs on her (duh). Ten in the morning. Only my mother can get high and do moonlight dramatics in the middle of the day. I thought she was in Chicago, hooking up with my dad on some great business deal. Who knows what happened with that. I guess I can be grateful it wasn't two in the morning instead. When I got to the station, Leyanna texted me. And like the bitchy mother I am, I responded crabby and demanding, except it turned out Reese was in labor, and both were scared out of their minds.

I talked them through everything as I drove to get them. Had Leyanna time contractions. Had Reese match her breathing with mine. When I got there, they were outside because apparently they were disturbing the other customers inside. WTAF. (I had a few words with them a couple of days later, and you better believe they will not worry so much about inconveniencing other customers in the future should something like this happen again.) Reese was a mess. I mean, I guess I don't know how you deal with the immensity of labor when you're only sixteen, but she had always seemed so calm about everything else surrounding being pregnant. Anyway. I called her mom, but only got her voicemail. I left a detailed message and hoped maybe she'd at least show up.

Reese got an epidural, and I sent an argumentative Leyanna home with Jax. The whole labor and delivery thing might have been an interesting life lesson for Leyanna. OTOH, who knew how long it would be? Also, I wanted to have some real talk with Reese. No more essay exam confessionals. Did she agree to adoption because of her dad? Or because she believed it to be the best thing?

"I just don't want to be alone," was Reese's answer. It was like she spoke directly to my heart. I understood completely, and it's what changed my mind about helping her out with raising the baby.

I would not let her be alone. And so I broke the news to Lamont and Nathaniel, and it was as horrible as you might think, and then Reese's mom showed up.

Except, it wasn't her mom. It was her sister. WTAF?

OMG, Jess, I didn't know how badly I had messed up, but at that moment, I had an inkling of the magnitude of my screw-up.

Did I tell you I was suspended from my job?

You were right. I will probably lose my job.

This is why:

Reese's parents died in a car accident about a year and a half ago. Her sister has full custody. From what her sister, Mariah, and I can piece together, Reese created a story that was part their actual parents and part fictionalized parents from a book she had just read (*Red at the Bone* by Jaqueline Woodson, btw, which Mariah vouches for as one we need to read). Not surprisingly, Reese had taken the death of their parents hard, especially their dad, because the bit about her being a daddy's girl was true. Mariah didn't deny being especially upset upon finding out Reese was pregnant. Mariah is twenty-two and landed a pretty decent job with a marketing firm and is making enough money to support them, but not a baby and is definitely not on board with helping raise the baby. She travels a lot and recognizes how this contributed to not really knowing what was going on with Reese.

I'm an idiot, Jess. Back when I talked to who I thought was her mom when Reese showed up at my door, I was actually talking to her sister. I never looked up her file because I assumed I had all the information I needed. I was making sure Reese was at least communicating with the social worker, but I never talked to her because A) I'm not her legal guardian, and B) I wasn't sure what would happen if it was readily known Reese was staying with me.

And here I've been acting as teacher, parent, AND social worker when I had no business doing anything except teacher.

And now I'm being mother because Reese is all kinds of ways depressed. The only good that has come out of this all so far is that Mariah has been showing up on a regular basis to get Reese out of the house, once to the doctor to get a prescription for an anti-depressant, sometimes to see the social worker, and other times simply to have coffee together. I recommended Polar Café, knowing Tracy and Sayeed would fix them right up.

Meanwhile, Leyanna and I had an epic fight.

Grades. Skipping school. Lack of communication.

And ultimately, about her very real social anxiety.

She's right. I haven't been listening. To her—or to you.

I'm so sorry, Jess.

I have so much to fix.

-Naomi

@@@@@@@@@

[11:57 May 31]

JESSAMINE

Mimi?

NAOMI

JESS! Hey!

JESSAMINE

Faith attempted suicide

NAOMI

Fuck. If I call you right now, will you answer?

JESSAMINE

Yes

@@@@@@@@

BOARD: THE ALCHEMIST by Paolo Coehlo

>**TOPIC:** Discussion Question 1: Alchemy usually focuses on turning something into gold. What is something you felt you could turn into gold in your life?

▽ **TOPIC:** Discussion Question 2: What is your "Personal Legend"?

Maxine: Where's Naomi?

Tyrell: I was wondering the same thing. She's usually up and into the discussions early.

Lisa: Maybe she thinks this book is too stupid even to comment.

Grant: Hey now, I dug this one. It really spoke to me. Seems like something that Naomi could also relate to—so yeah, I hope everything's okay.

Chester: Y'all. I messed up.

Lisa: WHAT DID YOU DO, CHESTER?

Chester: She's pretty ticked off at me, and now I think I ruined this book club for her, which is the last thing I wanted because she loves this club.

Lisa: I repeat. WHAT. DID. YOU. DO.

Chester: My name's not Chester. It's Jackson. I joined this group without her knowing, and now she knows.

Lisa: Wait. Jackson, as in the Jackson we met up at Maxine's back in December? That's messed up. WTF?

Tyrell: Dude.

Maxine: Oh Jackson, you dear heart. Whyever did you pretend to be someone else here?

Jackson: Back in college, we were together. Kind of. For one night. Then we had a kid together, but *we* weren't together. But I always wish we had been. I just... wanted to be close to her without crowding, you know? We used to talk books all the time. And now, we suddenly had this chance, but I think I've blown it.

Maxine: Where are my tissues?

Lisa: Under all your damn Amazon boxes, Maxine.

Grant: C'mon, Lisa. Step back.

Lisa: Yeah. I'm sorry, Maxine. It's Chester I'm pissed at. I just fucking hate liars. Especially lying men.

Susette: I think what you did was romantic, Jackson. I think Naomi will see that.

Chester: No, Lisa's right. She's not the only one I lied to.

Lisa: Cheating, Chester? What a terrible ring to it. Adiós, Jackson. Time to lose you, not Naomi, that's for sure.

Chester: I hear you. I just wanted to clear the air before I logged out of the group. If it means anything, I really dug getting to know you all and talking books. The new list we created is on my fridge. I'm gonna keep reading from your recs. Peace out.

Maxine: Poor boy. I think you were a little too hard on him, Lisa. We met him. He was so kind and helpful.

Lisa: Maybe we should let Naomi have the final say.

Grant: Fair.

Tyrell: Since we're all coming clean, here. My name's not really Tyrell. It's T'Rell. The forum wouldn't let me put in an apostrophe for my screen name, so I fudged it.

Lisa: Oh my god, T'Rell. IT'S LIKE I DON'T EVEN KNOW WHO YOU ARE ANYMORE.

Grant: Don't Stop Believin', Lisa.

Tyrell: Yasssss.

JUNE

Sent June 06
TO: NAOMI WELLINGTON <MYOWNPERSON02@GMAIL.COM>
FROM: JESSAMINE LEWIS <STEAMYENERGY@GMAIL.COM>
SUBJECT: WELL.

Mimi,

I have the biggest headache from all the crying I did these past few days. I don't mind, though, because I needed all those tears, and a lot of them towards the end were good ones. I miss you so much already.

I still can't believe you brought everyone out here. How do I start to tell you what it all meant to me?

I guess first, Reese is good people. I know I gave you a hard time about over-involving yourself with her and her situation, but I get it now. She needed more family, and if anyone understood that need, it was surely you. I know you always doubt your role in our family, but sometimes I forget your shitty past. Sometimes I forget how I need to remind you: You Are My Sister. End of. All of your students are lucky to have you, babe because you don't ever forget to tell them how important they are and how you are there for them.

Second, you and Jax? 100% behind you two. Always have been. When Jax told me years ago how he would have married you in a heartbeat, but worried it might mess everything up because you weren't ready for all that yet? I cried. It felt like the one true thing to come outta everything for you. And then he told me how relieved you seemed when he backed it all up, and I knew it was because you were scared. It was too easy with him, and everything you'd seen about love and family meant "doubt." He was right. You weren't ready. Waiting for you guys to find your way back to each other has been brutal, though. I didn't know if it would ever happen. I was happy for you and Lanh, but I'm ecstatic about you and Jax.

Third, your relationship with Leyanna? #Goals for me with my kids. I know you had on blinders for a while. We all get caught with them on sometimes. Leyanna texted me yesterday, "Mom SEES me. She's my best friend again. 🤍" < — yes, even the included heart.

Finally, Faith. I don't know what will happen for us. I wish I could say her suicide attempt was the thing reminding me how I never want to lose her. I still feel shitty about how it isn't. We were having some problems before she got hit with all these health issues, you know? I never wanted to admit it, but it's true. And now? Can I tell you the absolute truth? I don't know if I want to go through all the work to see if we still fit together. Faith has agreed to do all the therapy for herself—emotional and physical. We both agreed to do marriage counseling, although it will have to be virtual because Faith took a leave of absence from WSU and is going to live in Seattle for a few months with her mom while she works with the new specialist out there. I know we both need to be invested in it if we want success, except the question hangs over my head: what does success look like? I'm trying so hard to hold onto your words about doing what's best for me, even if it means leaving.

If it were only me...and maybe starting my argument with those words should tell me everything. Except they don't because the truth is, it isn't only me. It's the kids, and it's Faith, and it's me and Faith as an entity. We have our own selves, but we created an Us. It would be almost easy simply to walk away from it all. To leave Faith's pain behind. To pursue only what I want to do.

Except it wouldn't be easy at all. I'm scared to be separated from her while we figure things out because I don't want to know what that truly feels like. And yet, I think we need to be apart so we can face those emotions and work on ourselves and learn how to be better together once more.

I know tomorrow is a big day for you. Call me with the news, okay?

<3

-Jess

@@@@@@@@@

Alternative Education Solutions Academy
Disciplinary Summary for Naomi Wellington
June 07

Description of infraction(s):

1. *Social relationship with current students.*

Ms. Wellington has, on multiple occasions, driven students to work, doctor appointments, and other locations. Additionally, she has created study sessions in areas outside of the online shell. It is the administrative team's belief that Ms. Wellington has crossed professional lines and formed inappropriate relationships with her students, endangering their academic and emotional welfare.

2. Inappropriate communications.

On May 08, Ms. Wellington interacted with a student through exam feedback that crossed over into inappropriate, insulting, and damaging comments. Through this interaction, we learned not only of the student's new living situation with Ms. Wellington, but also a pattern of emotional conversations that may or may not have influenced the student's decisions to leave her home and/or her subsequent choices regarding the student's unborn child. This situation fractures the professional distance necessary for a student's cognitive and socio-emotional development.

Additional notes:

Ms. Wellington has, over the course of the school year, received several reprimands for insubordination in various areas related to policy meant to benefit student achievement.

Recommended Action:

Ms. Wellington's actions surrounding AltEd's students and her unwillingness to meet expectations indicate the clear course of action: termination of Ms. Wellington's contract.

Reporting Authority:

Mark Sumner, Director (interim)

Nick Jones, Society and History Studies Chair

DISCIPLINARY ACTION TAKEN:

After reviewing all documentation presented to me by reporting admins, collecting a full narrative response from Ms. Wellington, and reading overwhelmingly supportive statements by other members from our Academy faculty and staff, and after bringing my recommendation to the Academy Board, the following disciplinary action will be taken:

Ms. Wellington will be suspended, with no loss of pay, for the summer.

Additional Notes:

Ms. Wellington is a dedicated teacher who is 100% supportive of her students, a commendable trait when accessed with balance. When collecting the complete picture of this past school year, it is easy to understand both *why* Ms. Wellington tipped the balance (stretched thin in her teaching responsibilities, rapidly changing policies, lack of proper support from administrative staff, a student load in high need of assistance and support) and *how* she must still remain accountable for her actions. The board and I agree that while beyond the necessary scope of Academy faculty duties, most of Ms. Wellington's interactions with students were not harmful and indeed were conducted out of true compassion. The insubordination reprimands, while perhaps not always merited through some questionably placed policies, will remain in her file. Additionally, the relationship with Reese Vaskin crossed into uncertain territory regarding ethical practices, and therefore it was decided a three-month suspension an appropriate consequence.

It is with great hope that Ms. Wellington will take advantage of this suspension to rest and regain balance as she enters into the new school year this fall.

Mary Slauson, Director

Alternative Education Solutions Academy

@@@@@@@@

Leyanna Wellington
Language Arts 6
Hour 2
June 08
Defining Moment

Some people might wonder if a thirteen-year-old can possibly have experienced anything in life to have a defining moment. I wondered the same thing. Of course, this turns out to be not thinking very hard. Some kids my age have lost a parent, or a brother, or even a grandparent they were close to. Others faced illnesses or got pregnant and had to make really hard choices. How we react to those kinds of things is what determines a defining moment. But what if your life has been pretty "normal"?

That's my life. Pretty normal. I have asthma, and when I was younger, I had a lot more breathing issues and ended up missing school a lot. But none of that led to a defining moment; it was just how it was. Starting middle school was kind of a big deal, especially since a lot of my friends went to the other middle school and not mine. It was hard, but figuring that out was not my defining moment, either. Everyone adjusts to things eventually. Instead, my defining moment was something small, but it helped me find my voice and give me what my Language Arts teacher calls "agency."

I have a hard time making friends. Partly it's because when my asthma was really bad, I missed a lot of school and missed out on a lot of other parties, sports activities, and other things because either I'd get a major asthma attack, or it might make me have one, so it was better to avoid some activities altogether. Sometimes parents—especially moms—are the ones who encourage the avoidance because they get worried and want to protect their kid. Not my parents. They always encouraged me to keep trying things and figuring out ways to help me manage my asthma. If I'm honest, I'd say they were really great about that. The other truth, though, is that I hated them for it.

You see, my parents wanted to believe the reason I didn't have a lot of friends was because of being sick so often. They didn't know how nervous I got around groups of other kids. My heart would race, and I'd feel sick to my stomach. Sometimes it would trigger an asthma attack, too. My teachers just thought I was shy and quiet and let me be. They didn't know I wasn't contributing to group activities because louder kids always take over, and in elementary school, you aren't really graded on anything.

In elementary school, I could always use my asthma as an excuse to sit out of things. Team sports in Gym? I said I couldn't breathe and then spent extra time in the nurse's office after using my inhaler. For birthday party invitations, I told my parents there would be a big bounce house, or my classmates had pets that shed a lot, both triggers for an attack. "Are you sure you don't want to try it out for a little while?" they would ask me, sad and concerned I was missing out on all the fun. I assured them I was fine with not going and often said they weren't very close friends, anyway. This was true, but never the real reasons for not going. I was happy not to go! No worries about feeling sick.

Starting sixth grade was different. There's no hiding behind others in the classroom because it feels like everything is graded and so much relies on saying things out loud. Discussions. Presentations. "Cooperative" learning activities. Teachers randomly calling on you to give answers you haven't prepared. I didn't try to participate. It was too hard. I avoided coming to school on days I knew I might have to give a presentation or lead a discussion. I shrugged all of the time when I was called on, even if I knew the answer or had ideas. I couldn't share them because they all disappeared from my head as soon as my name was called. So I more actively used my asthma as an excuse.

The biggest challenge was finding a way to explain all of this to my parents. They have always been my most dedicated supporters and cheerleaders, and when I tried to advocate for myself, my explanations came out all wrong. They didn't understand, and I didn't know the right words to help them understand. I took it out on my mom, mostly. I don't know why I blamed her, except in my head, I kept thinking she blamed me for having to quit her job three years ago, and that was why she didn't want to hear it was for nothing. I was still a mess she couldn't fix.

Because I know she will read this, I want to include how I know all of that is messed up. Mr. Rivera says it's all a part of stories we tell ourselves to make sense of things we don't understand. I don't blame you, Mom. I promise. And I know you don't blame me.

One of my aunts recently tried to take her own life. She has a disease that causes her a lot of pain twenty-four hours a day, and it got to be too much for her, and she tried to find a way out.

My parents call this kind of thing a "wake-up call," something that makes you stop and realize something has to change. My mom said she got one of these a few weeks ago about me when something happened with her job.

For me, I looked at my aunt and how desperate she felt, and even though I've never thought about hurting myself, I know anxiety of any sort, like mine, can lead people to that sort of choice. I knew I had to make my parents truly listen to me. A friend of mine from school has physical and cognitive development obstacles, and she said when her parents found out about it when she was a baby, they didn't understand what it all would mean, so they researched it like crazy. Listening to my aunt, I heard her say the same thing about her wife (the aunt in the hospital) and how she had been learning everything about my aunt's condition.

I realized I had to do the same thing. I searched for all the things I felt when faced with a group activity or a presentation, and with each new search, I learned more terms and phrases to help me search some more. Fear. Dry throat. Immobilization. Trembling. And most important: Social Anxiety. These were all the words I learned how to put together to explain to my parents what I had been experiencing for so long.

This was my defining moment. Speaking to my parents clearly and with evidence to back me up got their attention. I wanted to throw up afterward because standing up to them like that ended up being a trigger, but I pushed through. Also, they could see my physical reactions, and maybe it wasn't a bad thing for it to be so impossibly hard to do.

I'm proud of myself for doing it. I know things will be different now. School will be easier. And most of all, I know my parents will support me like they always have. I don't know how everything will change, and yet I know I already have, which is how I know I've experienced a defining moment. I'm not sure when another one will come, but now I'm ready for it.

@@@@@@@@@

[Submitted by Reese Vaskin on June o8]

Essay Response

2. *Describe how the global economy reacts to government coups.*

Ms. W, I don't know if you'll ever see this because of whatever's going on with your job and all, but I want you to know I'm okay. Everything's okay. My sister and I talked for a long time after we got back from Washington and agreed that having Lamont and Nathaniel adopt Fabiola was the best thing. I wanted to *want* to be a good momma to my baby, but the only way to do that is to give her up to parents who already know all the right things to take care of her and love her. I don't even know if I'll ever want more kids of my own when I'm older, and that's probably the most obvious thing staring me in the face about why everything was wrong about me keeping Fab. Maybe it's because I'm only sixteen, and that's why being a mom sounds miserable, or maybe something's wrong with me and my maternal instinct is broken. I can almost hear your voice in my head saying, "Nothing about you is broken, Reese. Don't let anyone make you think otherwise," and I'm trying to believe you. My sister says the same thing. The social worker says I only held on to Fab as long as I did because I felt abandoned by my parents, even though it wasn't their fault. She says it's never wrong to do what's best for my baby. What would have been best for me is if my parents didn't die in a car accident. The best thing I can do for Fab is make sure she'll always have someone there for her, and I know those guys will be. They've been super good about letting me still see her sometimes, and I hope she won't hate me when she gets older for not really being her momma. Maybe when we're both older, I can learn to be a better momma, and she'll see how I needed to grow up some more.

Anyway. I'm thinking about going back to regular school next year, but if I don't, I hope I can have you again as my teacher, and I promise to try harder to answer the exam questions for real more often. Thank you for being someone I could trust, even though I wasn't always someone you could do the same.

@@@@@@@@@

Sent June 10
To: Jessamine Lewis <steamyenergy@gmail.com>
From: Naomi Wellington <myownpersono2@gmail.com>
Subject: Opportunity

Jess,

I know I've said this before and then failed at it, but I want to try again. I 150% support you and whatever decision you have about Faith. I love Faith, but YOU are my sister, and I will always be on your side. No matter what. I'll be thinking of you during your first couples counseling session. I'm so glad we got to talk more about it all last night. I know email and texting fits our schedules and the time difference so much better, but I miss talking with you "live." You're the only person worth talking on the phone for. For realz.

Re: my subject line. This past week has totally shoved my one-word-resolution into my face. Mostly in good ways. As in, shifting the ways I was using it for work. Using it for ways to find balance, like you and my boss, Mary, have suggested (thank the good lord she's back). Not gonna lie; I'm going to need you to throw "white savior" in my face to help me. I know you won't always mean it literally. It will also simply mean "wake up and step back, Naomi." It will remind me to rely on others to help be a support for my students. I have work family, too.

I've been chatting with one of the counselors at Leyanna's school, Tim Rivera. He's been really great and told me to forgive myself; being a single parent can be overwhelming sometimes. Except, I've never thought of myself as a single parent. It's weird, isn't it? Maybe Jackson's right and we wouldn't have made it if we had tried to be a couple way back when, and yet he's the one who held us together anyway.

Tim also suggested a compromise. What about Leyanna doing online courses part-time? She enjoyed working with her classmates in the DCD program; it didn't make sense to completely separate her from school if it meant isolating herself within the classroom. She should be integrated into other situations in the same way as her DCD classmates. We're looking into him helping create a schedule to allow her to do mornings in school and online courses in the afternoon at home. Or maybe she does the online work in school, under supervision. She had a good relationship with the media specialist, so she might be able to do her online studies in the library if she wanted to.

This all feels so much better than converting her to 100% online. I like this blended approach, and Tim said he could work with her on her social anxiety, too. He's had small groups in the past for just such a thing. And we also are shopping around for a therapist. Best thing yet is Leyanna spent her first full week back with me. I missed her so much!

I talked to Nathaniel, one of Fabiola's adoptive parents, a couple of days ago. Did you know he and Jax have met before? He's pretty sure they have met at some kind of small-business conference. I can't believe how small this world is sometimes. Fabiola is thriving—I heard her sweet gurgles in the background, and he says Reese has visited a couple of times. I asked if he was worried she would change her mind again. He said he and Lamont simply couldn't live in the worry about it, so they set it aside. Can you imagine the ability to do that? To just say, "NOPE." Obviously, I don't have this skill, haha. (Too soon to joke about this major shortcoming of mine??) Anyhow, he said he didn't think she would. There was a noticeable difference about her from their previous meetings. She was settled and at peace. I'm happy it's working out so far, but I also know she has a long way to go before she'll be truly settled with everything. It's a lot of change she's going through. I hope she'll let me keep in touch. I know I shouldn't get so attached (I KNOW!), but this is Reese. She's almost like another daughter to me at this point.

OH! I CAN'T BELIEVE I FORGOT TO TELL YOU ABOUT THIS NEXT PART! Remember Sayeed? And Tracy? Well, I mean, of course you remember them, but do you remember when I was appalled at Tracy's lack of interest in Percy Jackson? And how it's because of the tiring prophesies and kids who can't get real help because the adults withhold it? In an epically romantic gesture, Sayeed created a graphic novel entirely about a mother and her daughter who save the daughter's other mother from a mythical monster. No chosen ones. No prophecies and the mom and daughter figure out where and how to fight it from librarians, Google searches, and mapping. OMG, it is amazing. Tracy said he started working on it the very night we had the argument about it.

"Isn't he the best?" Tracy asked me, with the biggest cheese-eating grin I have ever seen her wear.

She's in love.

YESSSSS.

So. I have a whole summer staring at my face since I'm suspended until school starts again next year. I seriously don't know what I'm going to do with myself. Leyanna wants us to take up hiking, and it makes me exhausted and itchy already thinking about it. We'll do it, though, of course. Jax says it'll be the best and most exercise I will get in my entire life so far.

And, I know he's your brother, but...he's right, obviously, and btw, I'm totally in love with him. Stop gagging because I know this makes you happy. It makes me deliriously happy, too. We're taking it slowly because there's a lot at stake with the family and Leyanna. And yet, I know it's all going to work out. Everything feels right with him, as it always has.

You know what else feels right? His dinner rolls, which he's bringing to Sunday dinner today. I could live on those rolls. I'm also looking forward to no questions about my dating life, although I suppose those questions will be replaced with others about when we're going to get married and have more babies. (I don't mind.)

Love you, babe.

<3

Mimi

@@@@@@@@

Dearest Naomi,

Jessamine told me you love communicating best by email, but that still feels too impersonal. My mother taught me the social grace and courtesy of a handwritten letter, and you know your Grams; she knows best.

First, I want to tell you I'm sorry. I'm sorry if, somewhere along the way, you got the impression that you aren't truly a part of our family. I remember you once telling me your parents didn't love you. Like any adult, I reacted by saying, "I'm sure they do. They just don't know how to show it right now." You're older now, and even though I can't imagine a momma not loving her baby, I've never been comfortable with how I responded to you that day. You knew I was spouting platitudes. I tell you now, I honestly don't know if your momma loves you or not, but she has not done right by you. And if you doubted me, then I have not done right by you, either.

Baby, I love you as my own. Period.

Second, a part of you will still always wonder about your momma. And one day, she might genuinely get all cleaned up and get you to be a part of her life again. If that day comes, I'll still be here for you, no matter what kind of relationship you want or don't want with her. You need to trust and follow your heart.

Finally, maybe we can't get an official, government-stamped form that says you are a Lewis, but this letter? This piece of paper right here is <u>our</u>

official document that you are a Lewis and will always be a Lewis. Even if things between you and Jackson don't work out (although I know it will, you two have always been meant to be—I saw that a long time ago). Family members argue. They hurt each other's feelings. Then they forgive each other. And through it all, they're still family, and they still love each other.

I love you, baby girl.

Momma

@@@@@@@@@

BOARD: ANIMAL DREAMS by Barbara Kingsolver

▽ **TOPIC:** Discussion Question 1: Codi starts out feeling like she doesn't "fit" in the town of Grace, but by the end, Grace is home. What happens to help her become comfortable with her roots?

Grant: Family. It's a powerful thing. She came back for her dad, but found so much more than that. I know finding my own family saved me and gave me direction.

Naomi: I agree. Homero's lack of direct interest in Codi and Hallie when they were young reminded me of my own parents, but I found my real family through my best friend and her family, much like Codi does with Emmaline (and, of course, her blood relatives).

Maxine: I wasn't 100% sure about joining up with this book club. Now I think of all of you as family. You've given me a place to fit in.

Susette: Oh, Maxine. How nice! And I agree! You all are such lovely people. I'm so happy you agreed to do this with me.

Lisa: You guys are da bomb. Except for maybe Chester. He was an ass.

Jackson: There it is! Chester warned me about you, Lisa.

Lisa: Warned you not to be a douchebag, you mean?

Jackson: 😄 Thanks for letting me back in, guys.

Lisa: Well, it wasn't unanimous.

Naomi: 🤍🤍🤍

Lisa: Don't get all gooey-eyed gross on us, Naomi.

Naomi: Don't worry, T'Rell will re-route us with a song.

Tyrell: Y'all, I got nothing. Except I've got Zotz candy on my mind ever since Lisa tried to sound cool by saying "da bomb." I think Viola would love Zotz.

Maxine: And Nut Goodies.

Grant: Bottlecaps for Loyd, for sure.

Jackson: Yes! And Codi, I'm sorry to say, loves Crows.

Lisa: That's awful. But also true. Hallie's all about the candy cigarettes because it is so wrong, and it's her guilty pleasure purely because of nostalgia.

Naomi: "Keepin' It Real"

Tyrell: Are you taking my lines?

Lisa: Just "Roll With It," T'Rell. If you want, you can take my role and curse me out.

Tyrell: That's all I'm asking.

Naomi: What's our next book?

Complex Regional Pain Syndrome (CRPS) or Reflexive Sympathetic Dystrophy Syndrome (RSDS) is a syndrome that is "...characterized by a continuing (spontaneous and/or evoked) regional pain that is seemingly disproportionate in time or degree to the usual course of pain after trauma or other lesion." (rsds.org). Essentially, in the most basic of descriptions, it's the sympathetic system (part of the nervous system) gone haywire. The brain sends continuous "fight or flight" messages to nerve receptors, resulting in continuous pain.

CRPS is rare. It affects around 200,00 people in the U.S. and is three times as common in women vs. men. It usually presents itself after an injury, even if minor. Causes are still uncertain. Each case of CRPS is different and responds differently to treatment. The earlier it is diagnosed, the higher the chances are of effective treatment and potential curb of progression, although much is still unknown about these possibilities.

Because of the constant, intense pain, people with this syndrome often become addicted to narcotic painkillers and some die of suicide.

The following resources offer more complete information for both those diagnosed with CRPS and for their loved ones and caregivers. If you are someone with CRPS, I hope in some small way more people will have a glimpse into what you are living with and that you are getting as much love and support as possible. I see you.

Living with RSDS: Your Guide to Coping with Reflex Sympathetic Dystrophy Syndrome - Linda Lang and Pter Moskovitz, MD

https://rsds.org

https://burningnightscrps.org/crpsrsd

ACKNOWLEDGMENTS

No one publishes a book alone.

At least, I hope they don't because it is not an easy task!

So let's start with thanking a few specific people who have directly helped me with *All I'm Asking* (in no particular order, because there is no ranking...all contributions are necessary):

To my mother, Phyllis Book, who was super nervous about reading and critiquing my very first manuscript, but learned "I can take it" and has since then read all of my manuscripts and given me valuable feedback.

To Jen Escue, who has been with me from the beginning of my far-reaching plans to publish, read my words multiple times, always given me honest feedback, talked me off the metaphorical ledge, allowed me moments of pettiness, shared in the wild ups and downs of my publishing journey, and most of all for her wonderful friendship. Also, for being a perfect travel partner. The idea for this book was conceived in the hot springs just outside of Machu Picchu, which means we definitely have to keep up our traveling tradition.

To Niambi Jackson, who read an early version of this manuscript and also gave me so much valuable feedback, but really, for totally *getting* this story. May every author have a reader for each book who "gets" your story.

To Erin McDonald, my cousin and friend who helped especially with CRPS details, but also gave valuable feedback on various parts of the manuscript.

To Isabel Ngo, Sheila Athens, and Bradeigh Godfrey for reading portions of this manuscript to help with different aspects of the story, especially Vietnamese culture and limb differences.

To Tammy Harrow, Alison Hammer, Jennifer Klepper, and Cerrissa Kim for reading early portions of the manuscript and offering: you guessed it, valuable feedback.

To Suzanne Park—the only brave volunteer to join me for dinner at The County Line while at a writing retreat in New Mexico, for talking me through how to give levity to serious stories. Hopefully, I struck the right balance!

To Elena Mikalson, Elizabeth Parman, Mike Knudson, and Brian Hurley for their generosity of time and knowledge regarding various details including psychology, retail management, police reports, and adoption. As with CRPS details from Erin, any and all errors are completely mine.

To Sarah Hanson of Okay Creations for the beautiful cover design.

To the Women's Fiction Writers Association (WFWA) for opening the door to helping me understand what kind of fiction I write, for the friendships formed, and the collegiality.

To my fave fictionistas in the Ink Tank, an extraordinary group of authors who I love knowing, reading their works, commiserating with them, celebrating with them, and who humble me with their immense support.

To my husband and partner, Andy Rundquist for putting up with so many tears and general crabbiness when writing and publishing things don't go my way, but also for lifting me up and believing in me and reading all of my words. And not complaining when I say I need to get away to write. All my love.

To my kids, Ash, Charlie, and Leo who have not yet read any of my adult fiction, but maybe they are reading this now, and if so, I hope they liked it as much as Cloud (or, okay, at least liked it). Also, they are all my heart and I hope they see that through all the rejection, we all figure out what success means. As much as this book in the world is success, each and every one of them are my greatest successes. Always.

When I started writing again after a break that started just after finishing my undergraduate work and lasted about fifteen years, I shared my little secret with my sister. And then after I got going and thought, "maybe I can actually publish this" and shared excerpts with my sister and three others (okay, I'll share who: my husband, my mother, and my mother-in-law), none of them laughed at me. I am forever grateful to them for this.

That was several years ago, and this is an entirely different manuscript. I know a lot of writers and authors who don't have family and friends who either support them or much care about this writing "hobby," so I have eternal gratitude for my own friends and family who have always supported my writing and publishing goals. Not a single person has laughed at me or said with sarcasm, "oooh-kay." (Not even one of my brothers, when I told him about writing fan fiction!)

What I'm saying, is even if some of my friends and family are not listed in these acknowledgements, you are seen and appreciated. Thank you.

And to you, dear reader. Thank you. I am so happy you read my words. 🤍

Chapter One

When I got the call telling me my brother and sister-in-law died in a car accident, a tiny hope buried deep inside of me fractured and fell away. I didn't realize I harbored the dim expectation of one day forging a new bond with him until I discovered it could never happen now.

It hurt. Not an engulfing and keening hurt, more of a quick jolt of disappointment, and then it disappeared. I met the reaction with logic. We hadn't been close for ten years, and it didn't make sense to expect profound grief, did it?

And yet, with Brian, it felt like there should have been a chance. Once upon a time, he and my sister, Layla, and I were the LBJ society. Layla-Brian-Julie. Only, I never liked how this sibling nickname got the order wrong. I guess the presidential reference held greater sway than birth order, LJB.

My heart seized in relief when I heard the kids remained unhurt; they were not in the car with their parents. Brian and Elaine had two kids—four-year-old twins, Lucy and Mikey—and their safety overrode my conflicting feelings about my brother. Though my boss told me to go home, I stayed to make all the calls to answer my questions first. Where were the twins now? What would happen to them?

Three phone calls later gave me my answers, stunning as they were. The kids were in emergency foster care with a friend of Elaine's, who also ran a daycare the twins attended Tuesdays and Thursdays. In a little more than a week, they were coming home with me.

Me. Brian and Elaine named *me* guardian for their kids. Not my happily married sister, living in some house waiting to fill up with children, not some couple who were probably their best friends from church and had kids of their own. Instead, they were to live with the aunt who never wanted children and chose the single life more often than any long-lasting relationship.

I didn't go straight home. My apartment suddenly seemed empty and lacking. It reminded me how I remained decidedly alone. I headed to The Grey Shade, a men's gay bar in downtown Minneapolis my best friends Gemmi and Sean co-owned. They weren't open yet, but Gemmi would at least be in the office by now.

I found a parking spot on the street and when I walked to the back door, I almost smiled at the music floating through. "Soul Power" by James Brown, one of the few artists from the 70s Gemmi and Sean could agree on for the bar's playlists.

Gemmi and I used to rock out to 70s music when we were room-mates and we had so much fun trying to convince Sean to have a 70s night at the bar. Our interests ranged through the entire decade.

"Girl," Sean told us, "our boys are *fly*, they don't want any such drivel. The oldest we're going is 90s and even then we're not doing any Backstreet Boys or Vanilla Ice. Have some self-respect, will you?"

"Zeppelin, Queen, Stones," Gemmi started.

"Clapton, Boston," I chimed in.

"Nope. Not happening in our club, my charming, but woefully out-of-touch-with-the-queer-scene-friends."

"And you're calling it a 'club' instead of a bar, you walking stereotype," Gemmi scoffed. "There's another problem right there."

He put a fist to his heart. "Damn, girl, where's your head at? We are not just 'a bar'. We are the 'It' place in the Warehouse District."

Gemmi was the money and the brains, Sean was the heart. Despite our protestations, we were fully aware he knew what he was talking about. Gemmi always ceded to him in matters of style.

I pounded on the door now, to be heard over the music. When no answer came, I second guessed my decision to come here. I had to call my mom. Oh God, it was going to be awful. It was hard enough making the calls to find out information about everything; how did I share the news? How would I figure out how to tell my dad or my sister when I hardly ever spoke to them? I pulled out my phone and steadied my fingers in order to text Gemmi. I needed the moral support.

The music stopped, and the door opened a moment later.

"Mai," Gemmi exclaimed, using her Puerto Rican-influenced term of endearment for me. "What fun! What are you doing here?"

When I didn't answer, her cheerful expression changed as she pulled me inside and instead of leading me over to her office, she directed me to the bar, sat me on a stool, then rounded to the other side to pour me a drink.

"What'll it be?" she asked.

"A Coke."

She overturned a glass, filled it with ice and before picking up the soda gun, she reached for a bottle of Jim Beam. "And with a shot?"

I shrugged and let her decide for me. She mixed in the bourbon with the Coke, slid it over and leaned forward on the bar, the beads at the end of her electric green-highlighted box braids clattering on the surface like thrown dice. "What happened?"

I told her about my brother, and she asked all the right questions. How do you feel? Are you upset? Do you care? Do you feel bad about not being more upset? What can I do to help?

"You can help by telling me how in the world I am going to raise Brian's kids."

"His kids? Oh wow. Sure you don't want me to make this drink a double?"

I managed a brief smile and shook my head.

"When do you get them?"

"Next Tuesday, unless plans change with the memorial. They're staying with a woman named Lynette and her husband Dan up in Duluth. We agreed—well, she suggested, and I agreed—they should stay with them until after we got things squared away down here with the funeral and everything. Is it up to me to figure out all those arrangements? I haven't called anyone, yet, Gem. How am I supposed to talk to them? How I am I supposed to do any of it? I don't know how to raise kids. I've never wanted to learn how. Why would they leave them with me?"

Gemmi held my hand. "You've always told me how much you like filling in with the childcare room at the community center. And my nephews love when they get to see you."

My head dropped, and I dug my hands into my hair before they fell again to the bar. I reached for the stack of coasters nearby. In fact, when I filled in with the childcare room from time to time, I enjoyed myself. I considered this while mindlessly building a structure of sorts with the bar coasters. I liked to play Legos, blocks, and cars with the kids. Or reading stories. Little Grace sat in my lap last week as we read *Fox in Sox*. She giggled each time I took a deep breath to rattle out the tongue twisting verses.

I didn't dislike kids. They said funny things and loved it when you played *anything* with them. However, liking children and wanting to *have* them yourself are different things. Unfortunately, most people didn't get this concept. Surely I hated children if I didn't want any? What kind of woman didn't want kids? Oh, it's because she didn't like them. This often led to opinion number two: I must also be terrible with them. On the other hand, if a kid *did* like me, we'd close the conversation circle with how I was defective for not wanting one of my own.

I pushed my makeshift house down, scattering the coasters into a haphazard mess, my brain and emotions mimicking the chaos. Gemmi pulled my phone out of my purse and slid it towards me through the disarray.

"Call your mom, babe. We'll figure out the rest later, right?"

I nodded, and she slipped away, back to her office to give me some privacy.

***

"Julie? I can't talk right now; I'm in the middle of a showing."

Why answer the phone, then? I was glad she did, though, because I couldn't bear to wait for a call back. The queasiness almost overpowered me.

"It's about Brian, Mom."

"Oh honey, whatever he's done now to offend you can certainly wait to be shared with me later."

"No, it's not—"

"I can't talk. I'll call you —"

"*Mom.*"

Something in my tone pierced through. When she spoke again, her voice dropped. "What is it?"

"He's dead."

I wasn't sure what to do with her silence, and my gaze cast about for something to ground me. Stray scuff marks along the baseboards on the floor earned my filmy focus. I started to tell my mom what happened until background conversations on her end interrupted. In a brisk voice, she told me she'd call me back, and then hung up.

I thought the nausea would ease after breaking the news. Instead, the sudden disconnect jarred me and I sat as conflicting emotions flickered around me. The shock of losing my brother faded away, but the bits and pieces left behind about my future with the kids still stunned me.

My mother's callback sent those pieces scattering.

"Was it fast? Did he suffer?" Her words came out in pinched, shallow tones.

"They didn't say. It sounds like it was pretty quick."

"The kids?" Her pitch rose. "Were the kids in the car, too?"

Her fear stabbed me. I rapidly assured her they were fine, and then I told her the rest.

"Really? He left the twins with you?" Her voice remained thick with suppressed tears, so I couldn't tell if my mother expressed doubt or hope with her comment. Given her own lack of involvement in raising me and my sister and brother, maybe she was grateful Brian and Elaine didn't leave their four-year-old kids with her.

I closed my eyes and dug a knuckle into my forehead for letting that thought take over right now.

"All things considered, doesn't it make sense?" I asked, ignoring my own doubts.

"Oh Julie, yes. Yes, of course it makes sense. Despite everything, you were definitely the obvious choice for Brian to make. He isn't... wasn't very good at showing it..." She couldn't hold the tears back any longer. "He loved you very much."

Her grief overwhelmed me. I hated being the one to give her this news. And now, I hated Brian not only for dying, but for dying without warning, without any chance to figure out exactly where I stood with him. Without any chance of eventually being able to become a real aunt for Lucy and Mikey. Without any chance of pulling him away from the damn church that preyed upon him while he was still young and vulnerable.

"Where are you, Mom?"

"I'm in my car, outside of the house I was showing."

"Go home. I'll meet you there, okay?"

She murmured an assent, and as I left the bar and started driving, I considered my mother's words. *He left the twins with you?* I could question Brian's decision all I wanted, but when it came down to it, my mother was right since technically the kids were already mine.

1. Naomi has a blind spot when it comes to her daughter, Leyanna. Is she missing signs? Or simply disregarding them? Why might she do either? Does Jackson have the same blind spot? How/why might this be?

2. What do you see as the bond between Naomi and Jessamine? What keeps their friendship strong?

3. Teachers often face two conflicting ideologies from parents and communities: On one side, teachers are expected to be everything for a student while they are at school--to act *in loco parentis,* and on the other side, they face accusations of overstepping via curriculum, dress code, or in recent times, masking. Does Naomi cross the lines for either ideology? How does she approach her students and how their lives affect their learning?

4. Jessamine tells Naomi that sometimes facing overt racism is easier than all the micro-aggressions and "well-meaning" behaviors. Do you agree with Jessamine? What are the layers of prejudice and bias Jessamine faces? How do these layers impact her energy to adapt to the life changes she faces?

5. How does the book club forum play into Naomi's life?

6. It is often said that there is more than one kind of family. Who makes up Naomi's family?

7. What does it mean to act as a "white savior"? Is Naomi acting as "white savior"? What makes you think she is or isn't?

8. Do you think Naomi's director, Mary Slauson, offered a fair assessment and judgment of Naomi's job performance leading up to her suspension?

9. This story in this novel is told entirely in emails, texts, forum posts, and other forms of communications. Some novels use these structures, but also include "standard" narrative form with them. How does the lack of narrative prose affect this story? What is missing from the story? What is added to the story?

ABOUT THE AUTHOR

J. Marie Rundquist believes a day isn't complete without time spent reading. Stories she loves best—to read and to write—feature characters from all walks of life who learn from one another. When she isn't writing, you'll find J. Marie exploring all the K-12 public education world has to offer through teaching, learning, and supporting others in their educational roles.

In spite of trying to live in other parts of the U.S., J. Marie accepted her fate and now embraces six-month winters in Minnesota, showing off photos of hiking in sub-zero temperatures. She lives in the Twin Cities with her family, two cats, and a never-ending supply of Dr. Pepper.

Keep up with my latest news, book recs, and other fun tidbits via my newsletter: jmarierundquist.com/subscribe.php

Photo credit: Kate Ann Photography

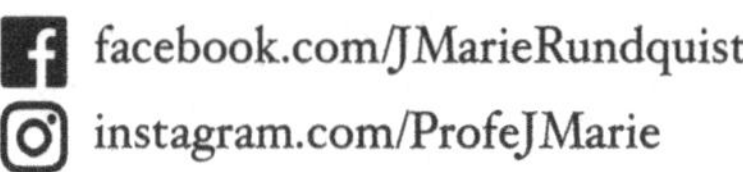